BELOW THE BELT

BAUM'S BOXING: BOOK ONE

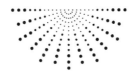

E.M. LINDSEY

Below the Belt
E.M. Lindsey
Copyright © 2022
2nd Edition

This book is a work of fiction. Any resemblance to persons, places, jobs, or events is purely coincidental.

Editing by Bailey Polanco
Cover by Golden Czermak with FuriousFotog

Content Warning: This book contains ableism and ableist language, intimidation, threats, blackmail, violence, and past permanent injuries.

I would like to dedicate this book to B- for being the first person who taught me how to love.

EM LINDSEY LINKS

EM's Discord
EM's Patreon
EM Lindsey's Website
Free Short Stories
EM Lindsey's Amazon Account
EM Lindsey on Instagram
EM Lindsey on Bookbub

CHAPTER ONE

"Okay n-nuh-no, this was a b-bad idea. This was…no, I c-can't." Noah's grip on his phone became a little shaky when his palms began to sweat. He pinched it between his ear and shoulder to swipe his palm over his too-stiff, too-new sweats- which he was pretty sure still had a tag still attached showing the price,right under his left ass cheek. He could feel his tongue getting tangled, his stutter worse than usual, and he took a deep breath to calm himself.

In his ear, a deep, gravelly voice sighed into the phone's speaker. "Yes, you *can* do this. First of all, it's not good for you to have this much pent-up frustration. You're going to explode and end up throwing a desk at some smart-mouthed freshman, and I don't really have the disposable income to bail your ass out of jail, or house you until you get a job teaching children how to write in cursive."

"I would never," Noah began, but as he had all through their relationship and now through their subsequent friendship, Ryan ignored him and went on, using his lawyer voice which, to Noah's dismay, always worked.

"Secondly, you're strong, and you're quick on your feet. I wouldn't have sent you there if I didn't think you could hold your own. Not to mention, it's a beginner's kickboxing class, man. You're going to jump rope until you want to puke and die, then punch a bag for fifteen minutes and be done. Trust me, okay? It's a great studio, and I've known the owners a long time. I spent good money on those passes, and they're worth every dime."

Noah pinched the bridge of his nose, biting back a retort about how the last time he trusted Ryan, he found him balls deep inside the dog-walker like some sort of cliché gay-ass rom-com minus the happy ending he would have deserved with some flustered, adorable barista at his favorite coffee shop. No, instead they parted ways and paid the four grand fee to break their lease, and Noah spent the next three years living in a cramped studio apartment until he found a decent sized apartment near campus, which was convenient now that he couldn't drive. Noah got the afghans they picked up in Sedona, Arizona and Ryan got the Keurig, and somehow five years later, they managed to retain a friendship—and apparently now a ten class pass to Baum Boxing.

All it ended up being was proof that you could forgive nearly anything and forget almost nothing.

"I'm going in," Noah said after a beat. In truth, he knew Ryan was right. He was fit, he worked out every day at the campus rec center, and he wasn't some stereotypical weedy Classics department nerd with his tweed suit and wire-rimmed glasses.

Well, okay, he *was* all of that, but those things sat on a six-foot frame with decent biceps and a six pack he'd carefully cultivated since he had time for exactly zero hobbies apart from a hundred crunches a night. And Ryan was also right that Noah was starting to feel a little wound up tight. He was presently single, lonely, and dealing with his mother who was not-so-subtly trying to sneak in that maybe his relationships with men hadn't been working out because he was just waiting to meet a nice Jewish girl, "…and sweetheart, they have a very nice Hillel on campus, I looked it up on the Google and they do a lot of events there. Surely you'll be able to meet someone. There have to be other Jewish teachers on that campus."

"I'm gay," he had said tiredly, though he knew she would never hear him. She loved him but that love wasn't enough to erase her life-long dream for her sweet boy to be all the things his father would have wanted. Some days he was glad his father never lived to see his disastrous coming out, though he was half-sure his father would have used his quiet, gentle way of shushing his mother and easing her into acceptance.

Either way, his mother plus his students reaching the all-time high of post-midterm burn-out was starting to wear on him. And beating the shit out of a heavy bag for forty-five minutes once a week might actually have some benefit.

Noah ended the call without a by-your-leave and slid the phone into his back pocket. He had the stamped pass in his hand, and his small gym bag hooked over his left shoulder. The first thing he noticed after opening the door was that it was hot and humid. The second thing was that in spite of those things—likely due to over-worked, sweaty bodies—it didn't smell like the inside of a gym bag and for that he was eternally grateful. He didn't think his barely-manageable curls were going to love the humidity, but it was only for a short while.

The man at the desk was tapping away at the computer but looked up when the door chimed, and his face stretched into a welcoming smile. He was attractive in the typical, I-work-at-a-gym way, with bulging muscles. His hair was short, thick and dark, clipped at the ears, eyes so brown they were almost black, skin a rich, deep tan, and his fingers were impossibly thick—the third one on his left adorned by a simple, elegant band.

"Can I help you?" he asked, his voice surprisingly higher than Noah was expecting.

"Yeah," Noah said, shifting his bag just to give himself something to occupy his hands with. "Yeah, I'm here for the b-beginner's kick-boxing class. I got this pass as a gift." He set it on the counter and the guy snatched it up. "Not sure what I need to do for that."

"Waiver," the guy said, and went back to the computer. The credit card port screen lit up with some instructions for Noah to initial and sign with the stylus. "And we can get you some wraps for your hands unless you have your own. We sell them here for fifteen bucks if you want to add that. The public ones aren't bad but uh…"

"A little gross?" Noah offered with a half grin.

The guy laughed. "We try to be accommodating, but I like to offer."

"A set is fine." He dug into his pocket and handed over his card. It only took a moment to pay the fee and sign the waiver. The guy initialed his first stamp, then pushed the card back to Noah. "S-so can I change or…"

"The class starts in twenty," the guy said and came around the counter. "Why don't I show you around first and see what you're comfortable with. I'm Wes by the way."

Noah noticed a plaque on the wall off to the side bearing some sort of award and the name Westley Baum in bold, italic cursive. "Is this your place?"

Wes puffed up his chest a little, looking proud. "It is. Opened it seven years ago last month. We had a big to-do for the anniversary and everything. Had some of my old Marine buddies come by, it was pretty sweet. Too bad you missed it, but we do one every year."

Noah was taken aback by just how open and friendly Wes was, like Noah was an old friend and not some stranger off the street. He followed the guy past a row of hanging bags, stopping in front of a long mirror with rack after rack of free weights.

"This is a great place to warm up if you want to come in early before class. You get a half hour before and after each class to yourself to warm up and wind down. Most of the beginner classes don't really use the time, but it's open to everyone." He clapped Noah on the shoulder, then steered him around the corner to a room which opened up to two boxing rings. One of them was occupied by one man and one woman.

Noah could see the woman's face plain as day. She was tall, muscles well defined, her long hair tied in a bun just under her helmet. Her lips were stretched around her mouthguard, and her bright brown eyes were wide and playful. She had her gloved fists raised as she danced a little in front of the guy.

Noah couldn't get a good look at him. He was in shorts only, his naked back and legs covered with severe, mottled scarring. It didn't detract from the rippling muscles of his shoulders, or the round curve of his ass. His right arm was covered in intricate, black swirling tattoos that cascaded with his movements. He had short, thick black hair in waves and from his profile, Noah could see a sharp jaw covered with a five o'clock shadow.

"Ah. This should be fun. Sibling rivalry," Wes said with a chuckle. He waggled his eyebrows at Noah. "My best friend and his sister like to duke it out from time to time. Safer than when they were teenagers wielding kitchen utensils."

Noah snorted and shook his head but watched as the guy took a swing at his sister. She dodged expertly, got him in the face with a couple of short pops. Noah knew next to nothing about boxing, knew there was probably some technical terms for what she was doing, and for how the guy was blocking her. But he didn't much care. Their movements were fluid and gorgeous, like a vicious, violent dance he would be too terrified to join.

It didn't last long. The woman was good, but the man had an advantage in spite of a limp Noah picked up on a few minutes in. He wasn't nearly as mobile, but he was strong and got her twice in the face before she held a hand up to surrender. Or give. Or...whatever. He'd learn the terms eventually.

The two of them touched gloves and then the guy pulled one off and gave her a pat on the back before using her as a support to get over to the side of the ring. Noah watched, feeling some type of way as the guy took off the helmet and spit out his mouthguard, and for the first time showed his face. He was stunning. Not in a usual way, not in a way that would grace magazine covers.

He was scarred across the left shoulder, up his neck, and along his temple near his left eye. It was like someone had taken a paint brush full of burning coals and flicked it at him. There were signs of reconstructive surgery which left places there pulled tight, the skin shiny. The rest of his skin was a rich tan, his nose almost Grecian in a way, sharp and thin, and his mouth full and set in a frown.

He didn't appear to notice them right away, and Noah reached up, rubbing at his blind eye as was a bad habit of his since he'd lost it three years back. He focused his sighted one on the guy who had lowered himself into a chair and was taking two orthotic braces from his sister. The last strap done, he finally looked up and his eyebrows shot up to his hairline when he realized he had observers.

"What the fuck, man?" he asked in a gruff, rich voice.

Wes laughed. "You know you love an audience. Anyway, this is our fresh meat—taking the beginner kickboxing class. That there's Anna, she's the head instructor for kickboxing and this asshole's sister."

The aforementioned asshole stood up by bracing himself on the side of the ring. His steps were slow, but they were steady as he walked over, mopping his sweat with a long, over-bleached towel.

"And this is Adrian. He doesn't actually do anything here except take up space and beat the shit out of people who have a little too much ego," Wes said, giving Adrian a punch to the shoulder. "He does hold a couple of titles, but he doesn't like to brag." Wes' tone was mocking, but in a playful way, and Noah was certain that even under the dim lights, he could see a faint blush rising on Adrian's cheeks.

He remained silent though and looked almost relieved when Anna walked up with two bottles of water and a huge grin on her face. "Don't listen to anything Wes tells you. He might have opened this place, but he hasn't been able to beat me in a match since we were twelve."

"Don't mind her. She's just the kind of woman who will pick on a paraplegic without remorse," Wes said, and when Noah looked a little stunned, he laughed and clapped his shoulder. "I'm talking about myself, I'm not actually being insensitive. I had an SCI during my last deployment when our truck crashed, and I can walk, but my legs are still pretty fucked up."

"*And* he knows I've been able to beat his ass since we were teenagers and he likes to make excuses," she said, winking.

"She's also my wife and the mother of my child," Wes said in a low tone, looking suddenly and absurdly fond as he grinned at her.

"If you kiss her in front of me, I am leaving and never coming back." They were the first words Adrian spoke, his voice very rich, very hoarse. If Noah didn't have iron control, they would have gone straight to his dick. He couldn't keep his eyes off the guy, which was probably dangerous. He suspected Adrian was ex-military just like Wes, and there was every chance in the world he was straight and probably not interested in some gay, nerdy professor mentally divesting him of what little he already wore.

The three of them bantered and Noah felt distinctly like an outsider, no matter how welcoming they were being. He also half expected Adrian to bolt. He kept looking over at Noah nervously, like he was seconds away from exploding, but he held fast in his silent way of socializing.

"So, Noah was it?" Anna asked, sizing him up for a moment. "What do you do?"

"Oh…I'm at the University," he started.

"Oh shit, Adrian too!" she said with a grin, glancing over at Adrian who seemed to be suddenly fascinated with the water cooler. "What school are you in?"

"Humanities," Noah said absently, then cleared his throat. "N-not a heavy load this term—University politics. Right now I've g-got Classical Greek and Ancient Greek texts which are all done in koine so…"

Before he could get the rest of what Ryan called his "nerd shit" out, a man wearing a Baum's Boxing tank top burst in. "Uh, hey man, we got a problem."

Adrian sighed. "Is it Mike?"

The guy looked chagrinned. "Yeah, sorry. I was refilling the paper towels and didn't see him come in. He's got Connie in the back and…"

"We've got it," Wes said. He offered an arm to Adrian which allowed the man to move a little faster, and then Noah saw him grab a cane from the wall before they hurried out.

After a beat, Anna sighed and shook her head. "I promise it's rarely drama around here. Normally it's just a gym with some classes and occasionally a set of twins beating the shit out of each other. Figuratively speaking."

Noah raised his brows. "You and Adrian?"

She shrugged. "Me and Adrian, though the moment we sprung

from the womb we decided it would be the last thing we would ever willingly share again." She winked, then clapped him on the shoulder. "Come on, let's get you situated before class. Have you boxed before?"

Noah shook his head as they walked out into the main room again and he saw a few people getting ready. To his surprise, he saw two guys with prosthetic legs, and one with a prosthetic arm. It occurred to him far too late the reason Ryan had sent him here and he faltered.

Anna noticed and her eyes took on a somewhat hard tone as she turned to him. "People with disabilities can fight just as well as anyone else, they're entitled to space here and if it's going to be a problem…"

Noah held up a hand and couldn't stop a slight laugh. "My ex—also m-my friend, long story and really complicated—bought me p-passes here and I'm starting to see why." When she looked confused, he raised a finger to his eye and tapped it. The weird, hollow sound of his prosthetic was heard even over the thrum of the gym music, and her eyes widened. "Three years ago. Bad car accident. The doctors tried to save it, but the eye was dying. It started shrinking a month after the wreck and eventually they had to t-take it out. I also have this st-s-stammer which acts up when I'm nervous, and vertigo from the head injury so I can't drive, and I think my ex must have realized this…uh. This could be a decent place for me."

Her face softened. "Sorry, we just get a lot of assholes up in here with bad opinions."

"I get it," he said. He recalled vividly the way the head of his department had questioned his ability to do his job with limited vision, with the new stutter, and with the way he'd get dizzy spells. He'd had to work twice as hard to get the guy off his back, and even after three years the guy still watched him for any sign of weakness. It was exhausting. "My ex just didn't tell me."

"Your ex. The long story but it's complicated ex?" she asked with a half-smile. She gestured toward a glass swinging door and nodded toward the massive floor mat where several jump ropes waited. "Is it like a friends with benefits kind of thing, or somehow you ended up weirdly friends in spite of your past thing?"

Noah couldn't help but laugh as he followed her to the small cupboard where brand new packs of hand-wraps were waiting. He took the offered one and gently pulled the plastic wrapping off. "It's more the second one. We lived together for a couple of years, then Ry cheated, and things went a little sideways. But after my car accident, Ry showed up when a lot of people didn't, and it changed things between us."

"Pining?" she asked. When he gave her a curious look, she held up her hands in defense. "I'm nosy, that's all. You'll get used to it."

Noah didn't want to point out this was a ten-day trial which was not a lot of time to get used to anything. Mostly because he was already feeling at home here, and as much as it annoyed him that Ryan had targeted a place specifically for disability—especially since Noah had been steadfastly trying to ignore his own to keep his job secured —he felt safe. He didn't feel like the weirdo whose eye moved differently than his other, who would have to make excuses for the accommodations he needed. And Ryan had his faults, but he *did* care.

"I'm not p-pining," Noah said. He gave a frustrated grunt as he dropped the end of the wrap and it rolled away, unraveling across the mat. He turned so his sighted side faced it and reached out to grab the end, but Anna stopped him with a gentle hand.

"Let me show you how to wrap it first. There's a trick that makes it easy and prevents micro-fractures in your fingers when you're at the bag. Then you can practice a few times before the rest of the class gets here. You'll like them, by the way, the rest of the class."

"Are they all disabled?" he asked quietly.

She shook her head. "Mostly stay-at-home moms."

"Oh. Well. I should fit *right* in, then," he said a little wryly.

She laughed as she rolled the wrap onto itself tight, then turned his hand over to start near his thumb. "Actually, I think you will. You're adorable as hell so if you're looking…"

"Gay," he blurted out of sheer panic and frustration at another person trying to play matchmaker. He knew it wasn't her fault, but his mother had created an emotional twitch that fired off without warning. Clearing his throat and trying to calm himself, he fixed his eye on her hand to watch what she was doing. "Sorry. S-sorry uh…if that's n-nuh-not welcome here. But I'm g-gay, and…yeah. My ex, uh—Ry is short for Ryan. He's a m-man."

"Jesus. You'd think having a gay twin would make me a little less constant at assuming everyone's hetero, but here I go." She squeezed his wrist gently. "I am *so* sorry."

Noah shook his head, feeling relief that last only a moment until he realized what she had said. Her twin was gay. Adrian. Gay. Probably taken though, considering he was hotter than hell and a fucking boxer and apparently a teacher at the university too. "It's no worries. I get it."

"I'm sure you do, but it was shitty of me. Adrian spent a lot of time dealing with the aftermath of don't-ask don't-tell bullshit and even though universities are more open with the LGBT community…" she trailed off.

"Yeah, trust me I get it. I've dealt with my fair share of the b-bullshit." He didn't really want to mention his boss right then, so he simply held out his other hand and tried to pay attention to what she was doing. "What uh…what department is your brother in?"

"Business school," she told him.

That was…unexpected. He definitely didn't look like any of the faculty there, though he probably did clean up well. Too well. His mouth went a little dry and he glanced away, clearing his throat. "It's no surprise we haven't run into each other, then. There's not a lot of Classics and Business crossover. Well, some gen-eds but you know."

Anna laughed. "I don't know. I got my BS in nutrition and got certified and I'm a part-time middle school PE teacher because apparently I hate myself."

Noah couldn't help his laugh. "Oh. Yeah…that's." He shook his head. "One of my best friends used to be a high school history teacher and I don't think there's enough salary in the world that would get her to go lower than college now."

Anna shrugged. "It's not that bad. I mean, okay it *is*. They're hormonal demons who could probably be classified as sociopaths for the three years they're in that little prison, but they're also really brilliant and most of them are trying, you know? I don't hate it, and I only have to deal with them for an hour a day, *and* I can make them run laps when they're being assholes." She gave his hand a pat just as the door swung open and a small group of women walked in. "You go practice that for a while. Class starts in ten. Oh, and there's water bottles by the cooler if you want to grab yourself one."

Noah nodded, carefully unwinding the wraps as Anna went to say hello to the rest of the class. He wrapped them up tight, then moved out of the room and took a seat on the bench near the water cooler to gather himself and practice a bit. He'd been distracted and with his depth perception issues, it wasn't easy to remember exactly what she'd done.

He got mostly through his right hand, but his left started shaking a little and it didn't feel right. "Fuck," he grunted to himself. "What the f-f-fuck am I even d-*doing*?"

"You've got it between the wrong fingers, and it's inside out," came the husky voice Noah had both wanted and not wanted to hear. He glanced up and saw half of Adrian who was mostly on his blind side. "Let me help. You're shaking."

"Happens sometimes, I c-can't help it," Noah said a little defensively. He gave a small start when all of Adrian appeared in his visual line, crouched down a little awkwardly because of the braces now hidden inside the legs of his sweats.

"It just takes practice," he said. His tone was still gruff, but his hand was tender. So tender it made Noah ache, made the loneliness in him blaze to life which was not what he needed right then. "You have to pinch here," Adrian said, then pushed the fabric between two of his fingers. "Give it a twist, then hold it and wrap it." He demonstrated, slower than Anna had done which Noah appreciated.

"Thanks," he murmured. "I uh...c-c-class...it..." For someone who spoke to a group of people for a living, he certainly sounded like a disaster right then. He wondered how badly Adrian was judging him, but when he dared a glance at the man's face, Adrian looked mostly amused.

"You should get in there. Anna is nice, but she's also brutal and she doesn't care how new you are, late people get punished."

Noah gulped, but couldn't help a half grin as he pushed up to his feet. He grabbed for a water bottle but missed and flushed deeply when his hand closed around air just an inch shy of what he was aiming for. Even after three years, his missing eye was still a pain in the ass sometimes.

Adrian didn't comment, grabbing the bottle and pressing it into Noah's hand. "See you around?"

Noah nodded a little dumbly, then hurried into the room before Anna could make him work for his misdeed.

"I SAW THAT," Wes said as Adrian collapsed on the leather couch in the back office.

Pinching his eyes shut with thumb and forefinger, Adrian refused to look up. "What?"

"Don't what me, asshole," Wes said. He hit Adrian in the face with a slightly damp towel, but Adrian refused to move his hand down. "I mean, I get it. He's cute as hell and kind of adorable in that nerdy librarian way. You think he's an undergrad?"

"You mean is he some twenty-year-old fetus?" Adrian asked, finally looking over at Wes who was lounging back in his chair with his feet up on a footrest. "He looks pretty young, but I'm kind of a shit judge. He said he was in classics, so maybe a grad student? I don't know why it matters."

"Because you want to get your dick all up in that," Wes said with a wicked grin.

Adrian flipped him off. "He's a total stranger who wandered into your gym. Plus, you have a policy about dating customers."

Wes rolled his eyes. "That's for my employees, and you're definitely not one of them, no matter what you want to think about your time here. It's an important policy to keep shit like Mike from happening again."

Adrian grimaced, trying not to think of the twenty minutes it had taken to calm the guy down and get him out. Connie had bailed the moment Wes and Adrian had come into the back room, and it was only the threat of calling the police that got Mike to see reason. The guy had the potential to be decent, but he had zero emotional control and it made Wes and Adrian uneasy. Connie had enough going on with her PTSD, the last thing she needed was some urchin trying to force her into a relationship she wasn't ready for.

Luckily, she had her boys at her back, but they couldn't be there all the time and it made Adrian uncomfortable knowing how many hours she was out there on her own. Mike seemed to get the message today, at least, and Connie would probably come back later in the evening when she was ready to blow off steam.

"Anna likes him," Wes said when it was clear Adrian had no plans to take the conversation further.

Adrian groaned. "And somehow you think that makes me want to ask him out more? Which I don't want to ask him out at all. He's not... he's not my type."

"Bullshit," Wes coughed. "And you're allowed to go after your type, man. No one is watching you, you don't have to make excuses, and you have room in your life for a little dating. He was cute, and he's a student which means you can probably go for cute-ass lunch dates on campus."

"God, what the fuck is wrong with you?" Adrian growled, mostly because the very idea of it made something warm flare to life in his belly and he didn't want that. Not now. Not ever. He'd just gotten himself to a place he was stable enough to finish his degree and get to working on his own life. He was in the School of Business, and he was currently working with the University on a project proposal to make campuses more accessible for students with mobility issues.

He had a lot of life plans, and an emotional upheaval could fuck him nine ways to Sunday—and not in a good way. He just didn't have the capacity. Even if the guy had gorgeous eyes, and curls he wanted to dig his fingers into while he was shoving his dick...

"I know that look," Wes told him.

"And I'm out," Adrian said. He pushed himself to standing and reached for his crutches, leaving his cane behind. On low impact days he didn't need a lot of assistance, but the nerves in his legs were fucked beyond repair, literally, and going a round with Anna in the ring always left him a little more reliant. He didn't mind so much anymore. Six years ago, when he was just trying to get on his feet again, not making steady, upward progress toward marathon running used to infuriate him.

But six years, a lot of therapy, a lot of body acceptance and he was over it. Mostly. Tonight, he was just too tired to care. He had about seventeen hours' worth of project research to finish and finals were just around the corner. There was something wholly exhausting in a way he hadn't anticipated, being a guy in his mid-thirties on a campus full of people, most of whom weren't even old enough to drink yet. He tried to remember that life, and remember that experience was subjective and they had every right to complain about their parents, and their bad weekends, and their break-ups. He had to constantly remind himself that life wasn't a competition, and that he truly *did* feel a measure of gratitude that most of them would never have the struggles he dealt with.

But it was hard sometimes too. Listening to them bitching about dorms and annoying roommates who left towels on the floor, "and oh my god my dorm is like one point eight miles from my first class and there's not even a coffee cart on the way there which means I have to make my own. Like…at *home*."

Sometimes it was too much.

"I'll see you later," Adrian said. He ignored Wes' futile protest and he made his way to Anna's office for his things. He dug around his bag and grabbed his hearing aid. It didn't do much, the IED had fucked his left side beyond repair and all it did was allow him to hear some measure of tones on that side. It helped in traffic though, and on campus, so he used it whenever he was out in public. Hooking it over his malformed ear, he turned it on and grimaced at the muffled tones which were more uncomfortable than anything.

With a sigh, he hooked his bag over his shoulder, then slid his arms into his crutches and began the walk out. Baum Boxing was one of the only places Adrian felt like he wasn't being gawked at as he moved through it. Even if his own issues weren't as prominent as some others, the crutches always drew the eye, drew whispers and curiosity he just wasn't ever in the mood to entertain. Outside the doors, he felt the weight of societal pressure to fit in a box that—even with a purple fucking heart and honorable discharge after eight years of service—he was supposed to fit in.

He lingered near the entrance. He could see Anna's class at the bags. She was standing with the guy—Noah, he'd said—and she had him by the wrist, presumably helping him with how to find the bag on his right side. Adrian was pretty sure the guy had a fake eye with the way he always turned slightly to look at things, and the way he'd missed the water bottle by a few inches. It was probably why Noah was here. Definitely not ex-military—he'd bet most of what he owned on that. But he'd suffered. He had something more than a soft life inside him, and Adrian tried to ignore the draw of it.

After a beat, Anna looked up and grinned, and Adrian hurried for the door lest Noah take notice.

CHAPTER TWO

"**I**s it true?"

Noah looked up from his brisk stride to see his colleague and best friend, Sabrina, making her way across the small patch of grass. She was moving quick enough, the curls of her afro bounced off her shoulder, and her eyes were narrowed and determined. He shifted his laptop bag over his shoulder and raised his eyebrows at her. "Is what true?"

"That Ryan talked you into joining a *boxing* gym?" She gave him a scrutinizing once-over with her narrowed hazel eyes. "You don't look like anyone beat the shit out of you."

He snorted a laugh, shaking his head as he continued toward the far end of campus where he could find a quiet place to get coffee in the old Student Union no one used anymore. "It was a beginner's kickboxing class. There was no sparring. And yes, it's true. And actually, the bag kind of *did* kick my ass a little bit. There was a lot of moving around and I had a hard time with my depth perception, but the teacher was really good."

Anna had lived up to her reputation. She'd taught him to anticipate the recoil of the bag so when it swung on his blind side, he could anticipate where it would land and make contact instead of getting hit. It had taken most of the class to keep from falling on his ass, but by the end he felt more confident.

"And Ryan did that. *Ryan*," Sabrina pressed. She grabbed his arm and stopped him from going further. "Are you two..."

"Jesus, no," he said hurriedly. "Trust me, that is never going to happen again."

She dropped her arm. "Look, you know I'd try not to judge you if you did, and I know I've been kind of harsh about your friendship with him after what he put you through, but you have to understand where I'm coming from here."

Noah didn't have it in him to point out that Ryan had been the only one there for him right after the accident. Sabrina and her wife Esther had been in Europe on a study abroad program and there wasn't much they could do for the four months it took until it was over. When they got back, Esther took a job with admin and had attempted to take over Noah's care, but by then Ryan had gotten Noah through the worst of it.

He'd been fitted for his prosthetic eye by then, and his occupational and speech therapy had him close to where he'd been before the accident. He still stuttered from time to time, and the vertigo had never really gone away, but he had been back on his feet and was able to explain to them that he felt good about being able to get through it mostly on his own.

Sabrina, who had comforted him through the break-up with Ryan, had been less than pleased Noah had let the guy back into his life so readily, but she accepted it. She still worried that Noah would get hurt again, but Noah's feelings for Ryan had settled into something careful and friendly.

"It's actually a really good place. It uh...it caters to disabled vets, mostly," he said, shrugging and shuffling his feet on the pavement. "The owner is one, as was this boxer I met there who helped me with my hand-wraps."

Her eyes took on a light he did not want to see. "Oh *really*..."

"Don't," he said with a groan, pressing his hand to his forehead.

She sighed and patted his arm, letting him know she would let it go. For now. "Oh, before I forget, Charlie was looking for you earlier. Did he find you?"

Noah felt his heart speed up a little, and not in the good way it had done when he was thinking about Adrian. The back of his neck prickled with anxiety at the mention of the assistant professor—the one vying to be the next department head in Classics. Charlie Barnes had been working at the University for ten years. He'd taught a couple of Noah's grad school lectures and had taken a shine to him during those years. Charlie had even written a letter of recommendation for Noah when he applied to work in the department and had not-so-subtly credited himself as the reason Noah was employed there. And, it was becoming more and more obvious, Charlie wanted something more than professional. More than friendship.

It had started simple with invites to coffee and sitting together in meetings. But eventually Charlie had gained confidence and started asking Noah out. In the beginning, Noah had his relationship with Ryan as an excuse, then after that, the split and not being ready. After the accident, Charlie had eyed him warily, but when Noah had come back much like his former self, Charlie had also started to get a little familiar. Noah was running out of reasons to avoid the guy, and it made him nervous. There was just something about him that didn't sit right.

"He didn't, and I really don't have it in me to find another excuse why I can't go out for drinks with him," Noah said tiredly.

Sabrina gave his arm a gentle pat. "That bad, huh?"

"I'd rather not talk about it," Noah admitted. He just did not have the energy.

Sabrina gave him a grin. "So, that boxing class, one of the ways to blow off steam? With a cute guy, maybe?"

"It was a good class," Noah said, feeling weirdly defensive, "and I liked it, and I'll probably use up all the passes Ryan got me. Now, if you'll excuse me, I have three finals to start writing, and a stack of essays to mark, and I need some caffeine."

"Fine," she said, dragging the word out, "but this isn't over. I've seen that look before Noah, and it's been a damn long time, too. You're not getting off that easy."

He wanted to point out he hadn't been getting off at all in recent days, but that would only start her up again and he didn't have time. Hooking his bag up higher on his shoulder, he hurried along the pavement, dodging traffic as he crossed the street, then headed into the old building.

He appreciated the university hadn't shut the old student union down, instead throwing in a bagel shop, a little market, and a diner for anyone who wanted something more peaceful than the University Mall chaos. It was mostly staff who didn't have offices to speak of, and the occasional student having a breakdown over the work load.

Today there was only one table occupied on the patio, a broad man with thick, black hair and short barely-there face scruff similar to Adrian's. Noah shook his head, irritated at himself for seeing the guy everywhere now, and moved to the Bagel Shop queue to order his cinnamon roll and coffee combo.

The student working there whose name he never remembered gave him a wide grin and rang him up without asking. Noah let out a sigh of relief as he took it. "Thank you."

"No worries, Professor Avidan. You look wrecked. Long day?"

Noah laughed. "Something like that. I'll be in for a refill in a bit. Thanks." He walked out, and after a long pause used his elbow to push the patio door open and step out. The guy at the table looked up then, and Noah almost swallowed his tongue. *"Adrian?"* The name fell from his lips without thinking.

Adrian's eyebrows lifted. "From Wes' place, right?" he said. "Noah?"

Noah flushed at what a bare impression he'd made, but he was too startled by the fact that he was actually *there.* Noah usually took his coffee back to his office, but still, he was fairly sure he would have taken notice of Adrian before now.

"Yeah. Hey." He felt like a class-A dumbass and his gaze flickered to the pile of work and laptop Adrian had spread out on the table. "Bad afternoon?" he asked in sympathy.

Adrian sighed, scrubbing a hand down his face. "You could say that. I'm trying to finish up this proposal for funding to get this place updated." Noah lifted his brows and after a moment, Adrian went on. "When I first started here, half the buildings were inaccessible to me. I was using a wheelchair for a while and a bunch of the building entrances are on the second floor. The physics building is the worst. They have an electronic wheelchair ramp, but it was broken almost the entire year. I overheard some of the other students talking about one kid having to change his major because half his classes weren't accessible."

Noah's face fell. He knew exactly what Adrian meant. The university complied—*technically*—with accessibility regulations, but most of the accommodations were absurd. He dealt with enough coming back after his accident. "That's p-pretty amazing, actually. Is there anything I c-can help with?" He wanted to punch himself. He didn't have time to help on some secondary project and it showed with the return of his stutter, giving away his nerves and frustration.

Adrian gave him what Noah assumed was a very rare grin, showing slight dimples in both cheeks. "I'm good. I know someone finishing up her MA in English and she said she'd give it a once-over before it was time to submit."

Noah grinned at the use of grad student time. He remembered paying his own dues very well. "Well if you think of anything..."

"I'll ask." And when Noah hesitated, he said, "I'm sure I'll see you around, but if you have an email..."

"Sure, let me just," he stopped, deciding maybe it was better to just tell Adrian to come to his office when Adrian's phone began to chime.

He groaned, peering at the screen. "Sorry, I have to take this. Just... leave your email or number or..." He shoved a piece of paper at Noah, then jumped up and walked off, his voice low, gruff, and a little frantic.

Noah wanted to blame it on how hectic it was after the midterms, and at least he knew it wasn't a fake call that had dragged Adrian away from him like that. Though it felt a little like a rejection, Adrian had also asked for his number. Which was more personal than an email.

Right? Before he could second guess himself again, he jotted down his cell number and tucked the pen back under the stack of project proposal notes. He was tempted, only for a second, to peek in, but he forced himself to walk away.

Adrian was fifty feet away, pacing at his slow limp, and he caught Noah's eye before Noah went inside and lifted a hand. '*Sorry*,' he mouthed.

Noah waved him off, then made a phone sign with his hand, grinning when Adrian nodded. He wasn't entirely sure the other man was going to call, but at the very least, he could hope.

ADRIAN LET himself into Anna's house, heaving his legs in, sore from having spent the last several hours bent over his current bike job. The thing was still a mess, but it now resembled an actual motorcycle as opposed to the hunk of mangled parts the owner had brought in. He was filthy, covered in grease, his nails ragged stumps, but that was the least of his worries right then. Today had been torture for an entirely different reason.

"I fucked up." Adrian flopped down on his sister's sofa and kicked one leg up on the table. His brace let out a loud thunk and he ignored her wince and glare at the new nick in the wood.

"What did you do?" she asked, blowing on her cup of tea.

"I got that guy's number." He couldn't bring himself to look over, only because he knew she'd have that look on her face, the one that said her baby boy was all grown up and getting himself dates. He didn't want a fucking date. "I ran into him on campus."

Anna smacked him on the thigh repeatedly. "*Wait*. The fucking cute student from class the other night? The newbie?"

Adrian groaned, passing a hand down his face. "Yeah. That one." He crossed his arms over his chest, his eyes straying to the black ink decorating his forearms. He absently traced one of his fingers over the Polynesian design and felt a pang of loss briefly before shoving it away. "I ran into him at the old union and he offered to help me with the ramp proposal."

Anna leaned in with a huge grin across her face, looking so much like their mother he wanted to cry. Or laugh. Maybe both. "And?"

"And I asked for his number. Like a *dipshit*," he groaned.

She smacked him again with the back of her hand and he shoved her away. "This isn't a bad thing, you know. He was really into you. He asked about you before class started, and he kept looking for you after you left. He was so sad when I told him you'd gone home."

Adrian felt something warm in his chest and he pressed the heel of his hand to his sternum. This was such a bad idea, more so now that he had Noah's number. The way his fingers itched to reach for his phone, to hear his voice again. Damn it, he had plans, and this would only fuck them up. Even if Noah was an older student like him—and he wasn't betting on it with the guy's baby face and soft curls—he had no room in his life for heartbreak.

"You don't know it's going to be a disaster unless you try. And it wasn't even that long ago you were saying you might be ready," Anna pointed out.

He grimaced at their stupid twin thing where she seemed to just know what was going on in his head. Pushing himself to sit up a little more, he drew out his phone and drummed his fingers on the screen. "What do I even say? I mean, he offered to help me—it wasn't like, hey call me and we can grab a drink."

"So, you make the offer," she pointed out. "If he's not interested, he'll say so."

"He's probably not even into men, then it'll be awkward as fuck the next time he sees me. I'll just be the creepy gay dude who hit on him. And you'll lose his business at the gym." He was hoping his logic would get her to see reason and help talk himself out of calling.

Instead she laughed. "He's gay. I made a joke about him being able to find a girlfriend with one of the single moms in class and he totally freaked out."

Adrian almost growled, a sudden rush of possessive jealousy gripping him, and he stamped down on it. Hard. "Just because he's not interested in dating a single mom…"

"He literally blurted out, 'I'm gay,' like in a total panic. Then when I was done apologizing profusely for assuming, he told me the guy who signed him up for the classes was his ex."

Adrian's eyebrows shot up. "His ex? His ex gave him a gym pass. Wow that's a dick move."

"He says they're friends, that under no circumstances is he interested in getting together with the guy," she said in a rush, like that might deter him. "I think the guy knows one of the regulars and figured it was a safe place for Noah to work out in spite of the shit he has going on."

"The eye," Adrian said.

She shrugged. "He also has a TBI—residual vertigo, pretty bad stammer, and other shit. Car crash a few years back. He didn't give me a lot of details and you know I didn't ask." She shrugged, then took a long drink of her tea. "Anyway, after that, he made it very obvious he was into all of you," she waved her hand up and down the length of his body.

"Tell me you didn't offer me up like some sort of bachelor auction," he begged.

She punched him again. "I'm not a total asshole, you know. But I casually mentioned that the reason I should have been better about assuming his sexuality is that my twin brother is gay, and it should be second nature by now."

Adrian felt his cheeks heat up. He'd been out since his second tour, though he kept it pretty quiet with his men. But he didn't live a closeted life. Just a lonely one, and he normally didn't mind. But there was something about Noah that got to him, like a fish hook in the gut that was tugging him to shore.

"Just call. Invite him for a drink or something," she said.

"You know I don't do bars," he reminded her. He had a feeling that even thirty years after being out, he still wasn't ever going to be okay with the loud nightlife. Bars meant a panic attack before his first drink was done, and embarrassing himself by tripping over his bum legs as he tried to get to the door before he ended up hurting someone by accident. He'd made the mistake once or twice after he got out, trying desperately to be normal. It took Wes knocking him around the ring a few times before he got his head on straight about not needing to be anyone's normal but his own.

"So invite him to yours," she said, kicking at his leg. "That way you can take your orthotics off, hang with Lemon, drink something you know you're going to like that isn't going to cost you eight bucks a glass. You might actually get to know him that way." She grinned and waggled her brows.

He hated when she made sense. "This is a terrible idea," he said, but he was lifting his phone, and pushing the button, and he tried not to think about how he'd already put Noah's number in there like he knew this moment was inevitable. The truth was, it was a terrible idea, because he didn't just want a drink and conversation, and there was every chance Noah didn't either. Adrian was terrible at casual, but more terrible at serious, and he couldn't see a way out.

And yet...

"Hello?"

"Noah?" Adrian said, then cleared his throat and shooed his sister off. "It's Adrian. You uh...you gave me your number? Before? Do you remember..."

Noah's soft laugh cut him off. "Yes, hi. I wasn't expecting your c-call."

Adrian's face flared bright red. "Oh. I'm sorry, you're probably busy and..."

"Actually, you're saving me from all this work I've been trying to procrastinate on. I just d-didn't have an excuse b-before now. How are you?"

"Good," Adrian said, then fell into an awkward silence. Before it could get too bad, he blurted, "Are you thirsty?"

Noah made a choking sound. "Uh? Like presently?"

"I mean," Adrian said, slapping a hand over his face. "Would you like to have a drink with me?"

Noah let out a soft breath, then said, "I would l-love to. Where at?"

Biting his bottom lip, he released it and said, "I'm not...I don't love bars, you know? But I don't live far from campus. If you maybe want to..."

"Yes," Noah interrupted, and Adrian swore he could hear a grin. "Why don't I p-pick something up. Wine, b-beer, whatever you want. Just t-text me? I'll get it on the way. Oh, and the address."

Adrian couldn't help his own smile at how Noah was just as awkward as he was, but also seemed just as eager to make this mistake. "I'll do that. I'm not home now, I'm at my sister's, but I can head out. How does an hour and a half sound?" It would be enough time to scrub off in the shower, do a spot clean, and spray some freshener around the place so it at least looked like he wasn't a total disaster.

"Hour and a half is perfect. See you soon."

Adrian hung up and sent the text before he could change his mind. He got back a quick okay with a smiley face and tried not to let it get to him. He saw Anna poking her head around the corner with a shit-eating grin, and without looking up, he flipped her off.

"This is going to be so good," she sing-songed.

He didn't believe her, but he was officially too far gone to care.

CHAPTER THREE

Noah stared at his phone for a good minute and thirty seconds before it sank in that his random offer—one that he didn't even mean—to the guy he had the unbelievable hots for suddenly turned into a date. A guy who he was pretty sure was way out of his league. Maybe the guy had a nerd kink, or maybe he just felt bad after his sister confessed how obvious Noah had been pining, but either way, he was getting some kind of date out of it.

And Adrian hadn't been lying, his address was within five minutes of his place, which was plenty of time to hoof it to the farmer's market down the street and pick up some of the beer Adrian had texted. Maybe he'd grab something to eat, too. He didn't know, he'd never really done this before. Prior to Ryan, he'd been a hot-mess grad student who barely had time to think. The two of them had bonded over coffee and dissertation stress and somehow ended up fucking each other in the supply closet in the TA hallway.

That turned into something resembling a relationship, two years of living together, and one cheating boyfriend. Since then, Noah had done his share of hooking up off of Grindr and bar-nights whenever Sabrina or Esther were desperate for a night out, but nothing had ever come of it, and Noah was too busy and too tired to really go looking.

This had fallen into his lap quite unexpectedly and he wasn't sure he felt ready. He'd been on shaky ground since the accident. The last guy had been really into Noah until he found out about his eye, then he couldn't stop staring and eventually excused himself from the date before it could get any further. Noah knew his injuries could have been a lot worse, and a lot more obvious. He could only imagine the shit Adrian got for his scars and his legs, so this was probably a big deal for him.

The nerves didn't make it any easier to stomach, but his anticipation of what might turn into a really good night was enough to get his feet moving. He showered, used an extra layer of deodorant, threw some product into his curls to keep them from frizzing, then put on his most comfy shoes and headed for the door. He brought his laptop bag, discretely stowing his cane inside. Normally he didn't need it, but night time was a little dodgy and, in spite of his resistance, he'd finally given in and had done some training with it.

He never brought it to school, never wanted to show any sign of what his department head could call weakness. He wanted tenure so bad he could taste it, and he knew they couldn't technically discriminate against him for a disability, but he had no problem coming up with plenty of ways they could couch their refusal to offer it.

Still, he didn't fancy a black eye or broken nose because he missed a curb walking home. The night air was cool on his skin, and he made the familiar way through back alleys until he rounded the corner. The farmer's market sign was brightly lit, and the inside even more so. Luckily the place was nearly deserted, so he was able to skim through the beer cooler and come up with whatever pale ale thing Adrian had asked for.

Noah wasn't really much of a drinker, but he was willing to have a little social lubricant for the evening if it made things between himself and Adrian go a little smoother. He added in some vegan faux cheese dip and some crackers, then a bag of mixed roasted nuts, and some covered in chocolate. He knew it was a bit overkill at this point and hurried to check out before he ended up with a damn steak dinner in his basket.

He was a little early when his walking GPS informed him he'd made it to Adrian's place, and he hovered near the entrance. The building was one of the modern places that had just finished being built the year before, with a ground floor entrance and three elevators. He was pretty sure the place was occupied mostly by students, but he supposed for a single professor, it was ideal.

Feeling excited, he pushed inside the lobby, took the elevator to the fourth floor, then found his way down the hall. It was dim and he had to squint through his glasses lens to see the numbers, but eventually he found Adrian's and knocked.

There was a long pause, long enough he started to worry that maybe he'd come too early, or maybe Adrian had even changed his mind. Then he heard slow footsteps and the door swung open. Adrian was there, wearing sweats and a loose t-shirt. It showed off the stark black tattoos on his forearms, his muscles bulging as he held on to the handles of his crutches. His feet were bare and without the braces, and Noah noticed they dragged a little when he stepped back.

"Hey, s-sorry I'm early," he said, stepping inside. He moved over so Adrian could shut the door, and he shuffled his feet awkwardly. "I d-duh-didn't realize I'd g-get here so f-fast." He bit the inside of his cheek. For whatever reason, talking to Adrian was making his stammer almost as bad as right after the accident, and he just wanted to be chill for this unbelievably gorgeous man.

"It's fine," Adrian told him. He looked tense, almost angry about it, but his tone was soft. "I uh…I ordered from that falafel place down the road, I hope that's okay. I didn't know if you'd be hungry, and uh… I hadn't eaten, and I was working at the shop all afternoon…and I'm rambling." He ducked his head, which Noah found absurdly endearing. Enough that he wanted to take the man's face between both of his hands and kiss him.

Instead he gestured to the sofa. "Then you should s-sit. I g-got snacks and everything."

Adrian smiled that same, timid grin which showed off a hint of dimples, and he set his crutches aside before lowering himself down.

It was then Noah noticed the half-moons of grease in Adrian's nail beds and realized he probably hadn't meant work on campus.

"When you s-say w-wuh-work at the shop...?" Noah pressed.

Adrian shrugged. "Oh. I work at a motorcycle repair and detail shop. It's mostly custom stuff for really wealthy people. I have one restoration project I've been working on for about a month now. I don't get a lot of time these days because my class load is kind of heavy this term, but I'm hoping to open my own place soon."

Noah's eyebrows shot up. "Oh, really? S-so teaching's not your l-long-term plan?"

Adrian laughed like he couldn't help himself. "Teaching? God, no. I mean, no offense. That's probably your thing, right? Classics, it's usually a teacher thing."

Noah couldn't help a tiny chuckle, even as his heart raced a little harder and his tongue had that familiar, heavy, sticky feeling which told him every word was going to make him work for it. "I want to d-defend the field and t-talk about archaeology and anthropology and ruh-research and everything, but I'd be l-lying. Yes, most of us are university p-professors. Though m-maybe for me it isn't the buh-b-best idea with my f-f-fucking stammer. I'm sure it's f-fucking terrible to l-listen to. It's n-not usually this bad b-but you make me n-nuh-nervous."

Adrian's grin stayed on his face, soft with a hint of pink in the apples of his cheeks. His five o'clock shadow stood out against the pink and Noah, again, wanted to kiss him, to taste that smile. "For what it's worth, listening to you isn't difficult. And I'm not one to judge careers, trust me, it's just not my area. I used to be an avid rider before my last tour. I've modified a trike for my legs, and it's not as stable as I want it to be, but I'm still working on it."

Noah couldn't help his grin and he felt his heart slow a little bit, the nervous tingles in his fingers easing up. "Yeah? That's amazing. W-would you show me sometime?"

Adrian's grin turned a little shy and he shrugged. He leaned forward, almost like he needed something to do with his hands and dug two of the beers out of the cardboard case. He popped both caps with a twist in the palm of his hand, then handed one over. "I'd love to. I mean, it's not exciting or anything yet. Doesn't go as fast as my bike used to, but it's something. It was one of my goals after I got out of rehab—be able to ride again. My nerve damage means I don't have a lot of feeling or control over my lower legs so it's harder for me, but the first time I was back out on the road, I knew I was gonna be okay."

"That's…wow. Thank you f-for sharing that," Noah said, a little overwhelmed. He knew what it felt like, achieving something that was once so simple, but ten times harder after life had dealt a hard blow.

Adrian shrugged and looked uncomfortable again. "Sorry, I don't do this a lot, and I tend to ramble."

"It's okay," Noah said with a wave of his hand and a soft grin. "When I get going and it's unfamiliar st-stuff, my stammer is almost impossible. I have a TBI and I've d-done really well with my rehab but sometimes when I g-get over excited or n-nervous…" He shrugged and gestured at his mouth, grateful Adrian didn't seem to mind.

"It doesn't bother me," Adrian said seriously, and Noah believed him. Before either of them could say anything else, there was a knock at the door. "Food," Adrian said. He reached for his crutches, and Noah almost stopped him, but realized what a bad idea that would have been.

Instead, he did his best not to stare as Adrian made his way to the door, paid for the food, then came back with the bags hooked on his wrist. "I hope you don't mind. I probably should have asked if you were allergic, or into this, or…"

"It smells amazing," Noah said honestly, then reached for the bags as Adrian got resettled. "This is one of the only p-places around here I c-can eat. I have about a hundred different stomach issues. Jewish c-culture, my mom likes to say," Noah said with a wry grin.

Adrian laughed. "Fair enough. This is just chicken shawarma, some fries, pita. Shit like that."

Noah tore open the boxes, and suddenly the tension felt less. Suddenly it was a couple of guys who were kind of into each other on a nice at-home date without any pressure. Maybe it was the first sips of beer on an empty stomach that lowered his inhibitions, or maybe it was the fact that Adrian understood him better than the way most first dates ever could hope to. Maybe it was Adrian's shy smile and little dimples telling Noah he was glad to be here too, just like this.

Whatever it was, it was nice.

"…so she gets Wes into a headlock," Adrian said, halfway through a story about how Wes and Anna ended up together, "and she tells him she'll only let him go if he stops asking her out. He agrees, then they stand up and she grabs him by the shirt, kisses him, and tells him to pick her up at seven."

Noah laughed, shaking his head. His cheeks hurt from how much he'd been smiling. They'd avoided all talk of work, of students, of anything that was weighing on him and it felt nice. More than nice, it felt perfect. The pair of them had gravitated closer to one another once the food was gone and the beer was empty. And now, when Adrian stretched up, he dropped his hand back down on Noah's thigh and left it there.

It took Noah a moment to find his voice when the almost vicious want rose in him once more. "I think that's sweet."

Adrian laughed. "Yeah. Wes keeps threatening to tell that story to all of Maggie's dates. Their kid," he clarified when Noah gave him a confused look. "She's only four right now, but Wes says that he won't approve of any guy she dates unless she can take him down with her bare hands."

Noah snorted. "I guess every parent has to have goals for their kid."

"Something like that. I think anyone she dates will need a back-bone of steel. Her parents, me, every single person at the studio." Adrian grinned, shaking his head even as his thumb started to rub a slow line along Noah's thigh. After a moment he said, "Hey, your stammer eased up a little. That's good, right?"

"Yeah," Noah breathed out. "I feel…a lot more comfortable. Relaxed." Noah licked his lips, and when he looked up to meet Adrian's gaze, there was heat there. Any other words he meant to say died on his tongue when Adrian's hand crept to the inside of his thigh, and he curled his hands into fists to keep from reaching over to reciprocate. "So," he said, throat dry like the Sahara.

Adrian bit his lip, releasing it in a slow drag. "Is this okay? I want… I want to be clear about my intentions when I asked you over. It was not to shoot the shit and drink beer like friends."

"I was hoping that was the case," Noah told him.

Adrian's cheeks pinked again, and he increased the pressure of his hand against Noah's thigh. "Thank fuck."

Noah wanted to make a pun about fucking, but his brain stuttered at the moment and he couldn't get his tongue to work out the words. Instead, he lifted his hand and traced a line around one of the tattoos on Adrian's forearm. It looked Polynesian style, intricate and meaningful. "Can I ask about this one?"

Something in Adrian's eyes darkened a little, and just when Noah thought he would be rejected, Adrian gave a stiff nod. "He was my buddy. Died in the explosion that fucked me up. His name was Eric— he was from Oahu. He and his uncle designed this piece, and his uncle was going to do it for him when he got out, only he didn't make it home." Adrian swallowed thickly, and just before Noah was about to tell him he didn't need to go on, he said, "He left it to me apparently. A few of us got boxes of his shit, and this one was in there with a note saying that if he couldn't wear it, I should. Not all the guys do shit like that—a lot of them are superstitious and they think if you prepare for your death, it'll happen. Eric wasn't like that. Maybe he knew it was going to happen anyway, who knows. I kept it with me and told myself the day I was able to stand on my own two feet—even if it was just for thirty seconds—I'd get it done. I couldn't fly out to the island to have it done there, but I found a Polynesian guy who does good work here and he put it on me."

Adrian let out a shaky breath when Noah traced his finger around one of the rounded edges. "It's gorgeous, and I think it's the perfect way to remember him."

"He deserved to live as long as I do," Adrian said in a soft voice. "At least this way a piece of him did."

Noah's hand trailed down to Adrian's fingers and carefully curled around them. "If I just killed the mood..."

Adrian let out a small snort, shaking his head. "If I let every moment I thought of a dead friend kill my mood, I'd never get laid." He looked up at Noah then with heat in his dark eyes, and he reached one hand out. It disappeared on Noah's blind side, but a second later he felt a calloused palm cup his cheek. "I really fucking want you."

"I'm good with that. I'm so good with that," Noah said, and then leaned forward to accept Adrian's kiss.

HE COULDN'T BE sure what gave him the ability to relax, or the courage to reach out, but he'd done it. Not only had he talked about himself and his struggles to get back on his bike—to open his shop, to make something of himself—but he'd talked about Eric, and about Anna and Wes. And then he'd leaned over and confessed how much he wanted the man next to him.

He hadn't been that bold in a long time. He'd spent years in the Marines hiding his truth, and then just when he was feeling brave enough to live it, he'd been blown up. His dates since—the ones he'd talked himself into going on—had been total disasters. They were either full of pity, morbid curiosity, or the stupidly romantic who thought they could love all of his problems away.

The one guy he'd bothered to spend the night with had almost been strangled when he tried to kiss Adrian awake in the midst of a PTSD nightmare. He'd fled the moment Adrian was calm, and when Adrian tried to text an apology, his number had been blocked. Par for the course, he supposed.

Except it didn't feel like that now. Noah looked at him with an understanding that Adrian was terrified to take for granted. Noah traced his tattoos and listened to his story about Eric without that overwhelming pity or a sudden move to try and love his pain away. He'd simply absorbed it, had thanked him for sharing, and it was more than Adrian thought he'd ever get from another man.

He couldn't do anything *but* kiss him. It was soft at first, the both of them tentative and a little nervous. Adrian kept one hand on Noah's thigh, and moved the other to clench into a fist until he couldn't take it anymore. He reached up, digging the fingers of his right hand into Noah's curls to confirm if they were as soft as they looked.

They wrapped around the tips of his fingers, and he groaned. Noah took the opportunity to press deeper into the kiss, to open his mouth a little and allow their tongues to brush together. They both tasted like spices, and a little like beer, and the rich taste of another man's mouth which went straight to his dick, making him tent the front of his sweats.

His legs tingled as he tried to move, his nerves shot for the day. He hated the limited mobility of his body in this moment. He wanted nothing more than to stand up, pin Noah against the wall, and fuck him senseless. He couldn't do that, no matter how desperately he wanted to, so instead he shifted his legs until they sat in a V and urged Noah onto his lap.

It took some maneuvering. Adrian was a huge guy, but Noah was no petite twink he picked up in a bar. He was tall, fit, muscular—not Adrian's usual type, and yet everything his body seemed to crave right then. Grabbing him by the ass, he urged the other man to straddle him. The sofa wasn't entirely comfortable, but Noah's knees dug into the backs of the cushions and their groins came into contact.

"Oh, fuck," Adrian gasped. It had been way too long since his dick had touched someone else's, and he was fairly sure he was going to blow his load like some hormonal teenager getting his first hand-job. "I'm...I can't," he thrust up against him.

Noah broke away with a shudder, pressing his forehead against Adrian's. "Yeah. M-me too. *Fuck*...me too." He gave a firm thrust and Adrian's head spun. "We should...I mean, as f-fun as it would be to grind on you until I c-come in my pants, I don't have anything to change into, and your couch kind of sucks."

Adrian laughed gently, pressing his fingers into Noah's hips and gave another thrust, just to enjoy the feel of the friction between them with the barriers of clothes. Once they were naked, that was it, he wouldn't be able to hold back, and he liked that he could at least appear to have some stamina.

"My bedroom is the first door on the right. I might need to lean on you." His legs were all-but useless from the long day, and now from Noah sitting on them. He didn't mind so much taking the help from the other man though. Especially because when Noah braced him with one arm, the other came around to palm at the hard bulge in the front of his sweats.

"Fuck, I can't wait to get this out," Noah said.

Adrian leaned on him hard and appreciated having a lover that could take his weight. He forgot to be careful for Noah though, and murmured an apology when Noah missed the side of the door and crashed into it. "Fuck, I didn't mean to..."

"Happens all the time," Noah interrupted absently. They were in the room and he had turned Adrian, bracing him against the dresser as he began to tug at the hem of his t-shirt. "I don't care. I want you naked."

Adrian closed his hands around Noah's wrists and tugged him in for a filthy, wet kiss. "Yes, me too, but this will go faster if we get ourselves undressed, and I don't want to waste another second of you not naked."

Noah grinned, nipped at Adrian's bottom lip before pulling away. His clothes were more complicated—a belt, jeans, button up shirt, his glasses. Adrian yanked at the elastic waist of his sweats, taking both the bottoms and his boxers off with them. His legs gave way, but he was able to angle himself toward the bed and he had his shirt off as he scooted up to the pillows for a nice view of the other man.

Noah took his time undressing. He was clearly putting on a show, buttons one-by-one at a pace that made Adrian want to growl and yank at his clothes until the buttons ripped off and scattered across the floor. Instead, he occupied his hands by closing his fingers around his hard dick and stroking—not enough to get him off, but enough to keep him interested.

Noah's gaze followed the up and down motion of his hand, and he licked his lips before hurrying to scramble out of his jeans. He kept his socks on, which might have been weird if it had been anyone else, but instead Adrian found it so endearing it actually hurt somewhere behind his ribs. His hands were needy as he pulled Noah on top of him and kissed him again.

"I'm not going to last. I want to be good for you, but I don't think we're going to get much further than this," he admitted. The feeling of their naked cocks brushing together had him teetering too close to the edge. "It's been...a while."

"Me too," Noah said. He brought his hand up to his mouth, gave his palm a wet lick, then closed his hand around them both. He couldn't quite fit, but the grip was strong enough Adrian felt it all the way down to his toes. "Fuck...f-fuck," Noah breathed out. "Your dick is fucking b-buh-beautiful, feels so guh-good. I want it in me s-soon, okay? In my m-mouth, in my ass, juh-j-just...I...I have t-to..."

Adrian hadn't known what to expect—the babbling, the stuttering all seemed so natural right then, so Noah, and so perfect. It was enough to drive him to the edge. The feel of Noah's cock sliding against his, the wet palm stroking him, having another man on top of him who wanted him just because he found him attractive.

He curled into himself a little, eyes squeezing shut, and he pressed an open mouth to the crook of Noah's neck as he came with a short, heavy grunt. Noah followed seconds later, his hand slowing, his come mingling with Adrian's on the soft hair of his belly. Their breathing was equally matched, rapid and a little hitched at the ends, and soon the cool breeze from the fan tickled at the pinpricks of sweat on his temples, along his shoulders, at the edge of his hairline.

Noah came to himself not long after, rolling to the side and grimacing a little at the wetness between them. But where it had been awkward in the past with his fumbling encounters, this felt right. It was soft and sweet, and his heart gave a tiny lurch when Adrian reached in the space between them and tangled their fingers together.

"We didn't exactly set boundaries," Noah said quietly, his face turned up to the darkened ceiling. "What we wanted out of this."

"I'm not great with casual," Adrian said, deciding there was no point in holding anything back. "But I'm still kind of a mess and honestly I probably always will be a little bit. I have PTSD that isn't going away. Ever."

"I understand," Noah said, and Adrian believed him.

"I don't really know what I'm capable of doing. I wasn't looking for anything when you showed up at the ring the other night." Adrian pushed himself onto his side and found Noah's face pointed toward him. His prosthetic eye was turned in a little bit more than the other, but his sighted eye was fixed right on Adrian's. Unable to stop himself, Adrian reached a hand up and traced a finger along the edge of Noah's jaw. "I like you though. This was not in my plans, and I need structure, but I'm willing to try. If you...I mean, I haven't asked if you..."

"I do," Noah said, cutting off the start to Adrian's insecure rambling. "I've done casual, but it's not what I want. I don't have a lot of time. My class load is pretty heavy for the next two semesters at least and probably for the foreseeable future. The department is a little in disarray and they put a lot of pressure on us, but I'm willing to make time."

"I understand," Adrian told him quietly. "I have my classes, I have the garage, and I have my family. But there's space enough to carve out for you."

Noah let his face fall into a relaxed grin. "Then I guess we're on the same page."

Adrian leaned in to seal it with a kiss, slow and gentle. "I'd invite you to stay, but when it's new and different I tend to have nightmares, and I don't want you to get hurt."

Noah shook his head. "I understand, and actually I have a meeting tomorrow morning at six because the head of the Classics Department is a fucking sadist who has it in for me, and my children, and my children's children."

Adrian laughed, and briefly wondered at the differences between being a classics student and business. His professors, the heads of his department, only gave a shit that your ass was in the seat at the start of class, didn't move until it was over, and that all your shit was turned in on time. They were really in different worlds, and yet

Adrian couldn't help himself but imagine the two of them making it work.

"I can walk you home," he said finally.

Noah smiled but shook his head. "You're clearly done for the night, and it's literally a whole five-minute walk if I take it at an easy stroll. You can walk me to the door, though."

Adrian conceded. It felt a little like a blow to his manhood, or at the very least his ability to be an attentive partner. His first instinct was to insist, was to push himself, but then he realized Noah's response was what he needed. He acknowledged Adrian's limitations without treating him like an infant. He didn't offer to stay, to tuck him in, to make it better. He just offered a compromise.

The two of them kissed a few lazy moments longer, then finally broke apart to clean up. Adrian fetched a wet flannel from the bathroom, then let Lemon out of the back room before returning to Noah's side. Looking up from the bed where he was struggling into his jeans, Noah startled at the sight of the retriever.

"Holy shit, you have a dog," he said flatly.

Adrian reached out and put his hand on Lemon's back. "She's my support dog. I swear she's docile and everything. I forgot to ask you if you were allergic or…"

"It's fine," Noah said, smiling as he stood up and crossed the distance between them. "She's gorgeous. I was never allowed to have pets when I was a kid. Though she's not a pet, right?"

Adrian shook his head. "No, but she's mostly off-duty when we're in the house. You can pet her."

Noah took the immediate invitation to lean in and pat her gently. Lemon was eager for more affection and wasted no time in licking Noah's face and burrowing against him. With a laugh, Noah buried his face along her back and scrubbed along her sides.

"Holy shit, I love her," he said.

Adrian felt his heart swell even more and knew he was in serious trouble. It had been a handful of hours, and here he was, falling way too hard, way too fast, with no way to hit the brakes. And yet, he felt no compulsion to do so. There were no barriers to cross between them. They were on even footing, even if their lives were different. He would take it.

Noah eventually rose from Lemon's side to give Adrian a kiss and cuddle of his own. Then they reluctantly parted and made their way to the living room where Noah fetched his bag and Adrian his crutches. His legs weren't cooperating well, but he strapped on his braces so he could at least walk Noah to the street.

"You don't need to," Noah said.

Adrian sniffed. "My mother would skin me alive if she knew I let a date show himself out. Just let me do this."

Noah rolled his eyes but let his hand rest at Adrian's waist in the elevator as they rode down. They made it to the street, most of the lamps out since it was just past midnight, and Noah sighed as he gazed up, then at his bag.

"You okay?" Adrian asked.

Noah hesitated, then nodded and reached into the zipper. Adrian felt a small jolt of surprise to see a folded white cane in his hand. "I've always had shitty vision and losing an eye didn't help. My therapist suggested this at night to help keep me from falling on my face." He unfolded it, then gave it a couple of taps on the ground. The tip was metal, a small pinging sound echoing off the brick building. "It's taken some time to get used to."

Adrian realized what Noah was really saying. He was adjusting to something outwardly visible declaring himself different, declaring himself an object to be stared at, considered, assumed. He knew how much it sucked. Letting go of one crutch, Adrian drew him close. "I love it. Mostly because it means you'll get home in one piece and nothing will stand in the way later this week when I have actual stamina to fuck you."

Noah sucked in a breath, then let out a tiny groan and turned his head to kiss Adrian. "Okay, you've convinced me. I'll be extra careful." He hesitated, then asked, "When can I see you again?"

Adrian considered, then said, "Any chance you can make class on Thursday night? I have a private session with a new vet around the time Anna has class. We can get some food after, go back to mine and...relax."

"Netflix and chill?" Noah said with a wink. "That sounds perfect, and I can totally make that work."

Adrian kissed him one final time before stepping away. "Get the hell out of here before I lose my ability to let you go. You have an early meeting and if you stay, there's no way you're getting any sleep."

Noah groaned. "I hate being responsible. Text me, okay?"

"You know I will." Adrian backed up a few paces and watched Noah turn, put the cane in front of him, and begin his careful trek back to his place. It was only when he turned the corner that Adrian finally went inside, and he hoped surrounded by the smell of them together now seeped into his sheets, he'd be able to rest.

CHAPTER FOUR

He felt a little ridiculous as he walked into the building, a hum in the back of his throat, his coffee in hand. He wanted to burst into song—and not just because he'd been laid, but because it had been so fucking good he couldn't stop thinking about it. He'd jerked himself off in the shower that morning remembering the way Adrian's cock felt sliding against his, and he almost missed two green lights on the walk to campus because he'd been lost in echo of Adrian's dark eyes.

He didn't burst into song, nor did he start humming, but he could feel an ache in his cheeks from his smile that would not leave. Stepping into the room, Noah glanced around and saw a couple of the other professors already there. A small, pathetic array of supermarket bagels and store-brand spreads were laid out, and he was grateful he'd gotten himself something before heading in. He got a nod from a couple of the older guys, and then he spotted the newest and youngest professor, Trevor Bane, who was eyeing him with a half-smirk.

"Good night?" he asked when Noah made his way over.

Noah sipped his coffee primly. "It was my usual."

"Yeah, I'm gonna say that your usual doesn't usually have you walking into work with a love bite on your neck," Trevor said, dipping his head in low so he didn't draw attention.

Noah's cheeks immediately flared white-hot and his hand flew to his shoulder. He'd felt sore there, but he'd been in such a damn rush he hadn't stopped in front of the mirror for more than a second. The collar of his sweater had fallen to the side and when he pressed on his skin, it hurt. Like a bruise. Like a love bite in the exact same shape as Adrian's mouth.

How had he not noticed?

"Uh," he said.

Trevor laughed, shaking his head and clapping Noah on the shoulder. "It's about time, man. Some of us were getting seriously worried you were just going to start adopting cats."

Noah pursed his lips and sipped his coffee again as he tried to compose himself. "Can we not make a big deal out of this? It's really new."

Trevor put his hands up in surrender. "Of course, man. No worries. Who is he, though? Where did you meet?"

"We actually met at Baum's," Noah confessed. "I had a couple of kickboxing passes and his sister teaches the beginning class. He works here. I don't think he's full-time, but he teaches over at the Business School."

Trevor looked mildly impressed and let out a low whistle. "Nice. I know a couple of the guys over there, chill dudes. Maybe I know him?"

Noah half considered keeping it quiet, but he figured it would be out soon enough if this actually went somewhere. And with the way he was feeling... "His name is Adrian...but I just realized I never got his last name." He was a little mortified by that, but Trevor didn't seem to care. Then again, Trevor was the kind of guy who took home a new partner every time he went out. He found commitment an archaic relic of religious institution and wanted no part of it, according to what Trevor shared with him during a drunken night a few months prior.

"You gonna see him again?"

Noah couldn't help his smile. "Yeah, we have a second date planned for Thursday. Just need to get through the hell that is Wednesday staff meetings and I can unleash all my frustration on a heavy bag…"

"Then some heavy dick," Trevor said with a wink.

Noah rolled his eyes and looked away, shifting so Trevor was totally in his blind spot. The guy knew what Noah was doing and laughed, nudging Noah with his knee, but kept quiet. Noah enjoyed the rest of his coffee as they waited for their boss to arrive—who was naturally late but acted as though the rest of the department should be flattered that he bothered to show up to the meeting he himself had called.

At five till, Charlie strolled through the door, his light eyes narrowed and scanning the room until the came to rest on Noah's form, and he smiled. Noah shifted uncomfortably, giving the guy a nod without drawing too much attention. He realized that if this thing with Adrian was actually going somewhere, it meant he'd have an excuse to give to Charlie once again. Maybe it would take the edge off now that he could say he was spoken for, and Charlie would turn his attention elsewhere.

"You look chipper this morning," Charlie said as he slid into the seat next to Noah. "Good news?"

Noah bit his lip, not wanting to say anything just yet, not until he spoke to Adrian. "Nothing special, just had a nice, relaxing night."

Trevor snorted. "Right. *Relaxing.* Our boy finally got laid."

Noah wanted to punch Trevor in the face, but before he could retaliate, Professor Lowe entered the room with a sneer. "Nice of everyone to make it on time," he said as though his staff were the ones who had walked in the door late. Noah settled back in his seat and did his best not to acknowledge the fact that all of Charlie's attention was on him now.

THE MEETING DRAGGED out for ages. Lowe was trying to pull the department together after a fall out where Classics and Religious Studies had been forced to absorb each other and the department heads had been demoted. The departments had all blamed each other, enrollment was down, and frankly Noah couldn't bring himself to give a single shit. He had a fairly full enrollment in each of his classes which meant he was in no danger of having them cancelled just yet. He wasn't vying for head of the department—just tenure to secure his future and plump his CV should he choose to look for work elsewhere.

He let his mind wander to Adrian, to the way he held Noah, the way he kissed him, the way he fucked. They hadn't done more than rub off on each other, but it had felt so fucking good if he let himself linger in those thoughts, he was going to have a situation happening in his trousers. He forced his mind onto other things. On the scars Adrian bore which almost looked like tattoos, on the dark ink he wore on his forearms, on the shapes and symbols over his fit chest. He even took a moment to remember the first time he'd seen Adrian, and the way he'd held his ground in the ring without any assistance and had bested his sister.

Noah was falling deep and fast, and though it should be a problem, he couldn't bring himself to worry. He startled a little when Lowe called the meeting to an end and groaned as he pushed to his feet. He was hoping Charlie had moved on, but when an arm grabbed him as he made his way into the corridor, he knew he had no such luck.

"You shouldn't let Trevor spread rumors about you like that," Charlie said, turning Noah to face him. "I mean, not that most people will care, but I know you're going for tenure and..."

Noah flushed a little and glanced away. "Being in a relationship isn't going to disqualify me."

Charlie made a small, choking noise. *"Relationship?"*

Noah let out a tiny sigh. "It's...new. I'm not entirely sure what it is, but I'd rather not discuss it just yet."

"I understand," Charlie said, his voice suddenly ice old. "It's only, when I invited you out not last week you told me you still weren't ready to date. I didn't realize you had changed your mind in such a short span of time. I only regret I missed the window."

Noah licked his lips, regretting every lie he'd ever told to this man. He knew he should have been straight forward from the start, but Charlie made it so damn difficult most of the time. "It just happened, okay? I wasn't out searching for a date. We met under…unusual circumstances and we hit it off. Sometimes you just can't control when you connect with someone."

"Clearly," he said. He gave Noah a firm once-over, then turned on his heel and left.

Though Noah wanted to believe that was the end of it, he had a feeling Charlie wasn't going to let this go so easily.

CHAPTER FIVE

"...**A**nd tomorrow we have a quiz. Prepare to do some short translations and then identifying various forms of middle-passive verbs we've been working on for this module. If you have any questions..."

Noah almost groaned aloud at the sight of Derek Jones' hand raising into the air. He was good student, in both of Noah's classes, but it was clear the kid was angling for a letter of recommendation and Noah desperately wanted to tell him he'd just write it so he'd be left alone.

"Professor, will there be a study guide for this?" he asked.

Noah almost pinched the bridge of his nose. "As with the other classes all term, you can use the Greek-to-English sentences at the end of the chapter as a guide for what you'll find on the quiz, and for practice you can work on English-to-Greek. In fact, if you work on the first five sentences in chapters seventeen and eighteen and turn them in before the quiz tomorrow, I'll give you some extra credit points."

That at least got the class writing it down before they threw their books in their bag and headed out. Noah held his breath, expecting a few of the stragglers to want to chat with him. The last thing in the world he wanted was to delay the walk to his office. He had two hours of office-hours and then he had to race home and get ready for his kickboxing lesson. And then...

And then there was Adrian.

Luckily, everyone seemed as eager to end their week as he did. Most of his students didn't have classes on Fridays, and Noah was looking forward to a long night tonight and maybe even a chance to sleep in. And, if Adrian had time, maybe being able to see him again over the weekend. He didn't want to push, didn't want to hope for more, but they'd been texting every so often over the last twenty-four hours. If he was reading the tone right, Adrian was as excited for this night as he was.

Gathering his bag, Noah started out, then felt a wave of dizziness. The familiar pressure shift in his ears indicated it was about to get ugly, and he made a bee-line for the elevators before it hit him full on. The vertigo was intense, and with only one eye working, he had trouble keeping his balance. The short walk to his office now seemed like a hundred miles, and by the time he stumbled to one of the low brick walls near the front of the building, he was close to falling over.

Digging his phone out of his pocket, he peered at the time and realized that Sabrina had classes and Esther was long-gone. His finger hovered over Ryan's name at first. Ryan worked only half a mile from the main campus and had rescued Noah more than once from an attack of vertigo. But his second though had him scrolling up to the As. To Adrian's name.

It rang three times before Adrian picked up. "I wasn't expecting to hear from you yet."

Noah flushed. "I know, I'm so sorry. I uh...I was wondering if you were busy right now. I never thought to ask when your classes were, but I'm...sort of having a little trouble."

"I'm actually at the garage right now," Adrian said with some regret in his voice. "I'm not far though, how can I help?"

Noah felt his flush retreat into something soft in the center of his chest. "You know what, it's not a big deal, really. I'll just..."

"Noah," Adrian said very softly. The busy background noise faded into nothing, and that was oddly soothing to Noah's spinning head. "Just tell me. You don't sound like it's no big deal."

"It's just...I'm having some vertigo right now. It's nothing major, it happens all the time. But my balance is a little off and I was trying to make it to office hours but..."

"I can be there in five," Adrian said. Noah could hear keys suddenly, and then the clinking sound of a crutch. "Where are you?"

"The Modern Languages building. My Greek class just got out."

"And you want me to get you to what building?"

Noah shook his head, knowing he'd be totally useless to any of the students who needed him. "I'm going to cancel, it's fine. I'll just send out an email. You really don't mind?"

"Not even a little bit," Adrian said. "Hang tight, okay?"

"Thank you," Noah breathed. He heard a hum of acquiescence before the line went dead, and Noah squinted his eye at the screen as he pulled up his email. Luckily, he had a pre-written template for all this, and quickly sent out the mass email to his students, promising to make it up with an extra day the following week. That done, he hunkered down on the bench, pressing his hand to his sighted eye as he waited.

Five minutes went by, then ten, and just before he started to really panic, he heard Adrian's gait on the pavement. He looked up to see the man walking toward him, leaning heavily on a cane. Noah attempted to stand, but his world spun, and he fell back onto his ass. It was humiliating, even if Adrian likely understood exactly how it felt not to be able to get up on your own, and he bit his lip as he tried to keep himself in check.

"I'm really sorry about this. Jesus. I don't think I'll be able to make it tonight, and I feel awful."

Adrian shook his head as he extended his hand and gently eased Noah to his feet. He was unsteady, but having Adrian's large, strong body pressed against his side was a god-send. He wrapped his arm around Adrian's waist and they began the slow stroll toward the parking lot.

"I can't cancel my private session tonight," he told Noah quietly as they pushed through throngs of students, "but what if I grab dinner when I'm done and take it back to your place? I mean, if you're up for it, I really want to see you."

Noah swore he could fly in that moment, which was absurd. He was a grown man with a Ph.D. and here he was acting like a fifteen-year-old getting asked to the prom. It was just dinner and an admission that Adrian didn't mind his company, not a damn marriage proposal. And yet, he couldn't stop smiling. "I would love that."

Some tension drained out of Adrian's body, the muscles under Noah's hand going slightly more lax. Neither of them said anything else as they walked to a sleek, black car which Adrian unlocked with the push of a button.

"I thought you drove a trike?" Noah asked, easing into the seat. He startled when Lemon shoved her head between the seats and gave him a lick on the cheek.

Adrian laughed. "I do, but I wasn't sure that was the best way to get you home if your head was spinning. Plus, I thought Lemon might help."

"She does," Noah said, and turned his head so he could look at Adrian properly as he ran his fingers through Lemon's soft fur. Adrian had been right, he was almost immediately soothed by her. "But I do want a ride on it someday."

"I can make that happen," Adrian promised, then put the car into gear and started on the short drive to get Noah home.

ADRIAN STRIPPED HIS GLOVES OFF, touching his aching jaw where it was stretched with his grin. It had been a fairly massive triumph for Cole to get that hit in. The guy was fighting totally blind, having lost both eyes to an infection after a chemical explosion on his last deployment with the British Royal Army. He'd come to the States for treatment, and had been cleared from rehab for nearly six months now and had happened upon Baum's on a friend's recommendation. Wes was a little hesitant about training the guy—he didn't have experience with visual impairments like that and never a completely blind person. He hadn't been wrong when he was giving Adrian shit about him not working there, but he also didn't push back when Adrian volunteered to take up the guy's training.

It had been six weeks, two nights per week, and Cole finally got the better of him. "Alright, mate?" Cole asked, sitting on the edge of the ring to strip off his wraps.

Adrian lowered himself down next to the guy and nudged him. "Not bad. That's going to leave a decent mark."

"Am I meant to apologize?" Cole asked with a half-grin.

Adrian snorted. "I'll let you figure that one out on your own. Anyway, I'd love to stay and chat, but I actually have somewhere to be."

"Yeah, you seemed a little distracted, and I was pretty sure I over-heard Wes talking about you getting your dick wet tonight," Cole said. He pushed himself off the ring and to the floor, then made a clicking noise, calling his guide dog over.

Adrian groaned as he reached for his braces. "Wes needs to keep his fucking mouth shut."

"It's true, then?" Cole turned toward him with a wide grin. He didn't wear prosthetics since his sockets were still dealing with flare-up infections from the work that needed to be done, but he still gave Adrian the impression he was giving him a wide-eyed, innocent stare.

"Not that it's anyone's *fucking business around here*," Adrian said, raising his voice because he knew Wes was probably listening in, "but yes, I have a date. Actually, you probably would have met him tonight. He takes Anna's class, but he had to cancel last minute."

"Maybe next time?" Cole chanced.

Adrian bristled for a second. He wasn't used to people wanting to be friendly with him outside of the ring, or outside of his team back when he had one. But the guys at Baum's were different. They retained that military loyalty to each other, but with something a little deeper. They understood one another, understood the struggle and the pain and the adjustment to a new normal. They didn't really get along with the other patrons, but vets like him? It was almost a given.

Adrian didn't have a lot of room for new people, but he liked Cole all the same. "I'm sure he'll be around. I'll see if I can get him to come in Tuesday." He gave the guy a clap on the shoulder, then grabbed his cane and headed out.

It was the simple fact that he cared what Noah thought that had him scrubbing down and rinsing off in the shower before he tapped an order on his app to order food, then grabbing Lemon from Wes' office and heading for his car. He contemplated dropping Lemon off at home and taking the trike on the off-chance Noah would be feeling up for a ride later, but he figured something during the day—when it was warm and sunny, and they could appreciate a nice view—would be a better intro to the open road.

The rich smells of curry filled his car on the short drive over to Noah's building. He found street parking not far off, and though it wasn't often he did it, he thanked his disabled parking tag that allowed him to stay close. The building was locked, so he buzzed the door and Noah wasted no time letting him in.

He took the elevator up, and he couldn't suppress a grin when he saw Noah waiting for him in the doorway, one shoulder braced on the frame. "I thought you'd be later."

"Sorry if I'm interrupting," Adrian began.

Noah rolled his eyes playfully, grabbing Adrian by the front of his shirt to drag him in. "I was getting lonely. And hungry. What did you get?"

"Tikka masala, some chana, roti," Adrian said absently, his gaze focused on Noah's bottom lip which was a little shiny from being bitten, and just the faintest bit swollen. He swallowed back his desire to drop the food, grab the other man by his front, and kiss him.

"That sounds amazing. I got a decent nap in and that seemed to help." He took the bags from Adrian's hand, and before Adrian could protest, put his hand there instead. It was impossible to complain about that.

They headed into Noah's living room and Adrian got his first real look around. Earlier that day, he'd dropped Noah off at the door, then had to dash to make it back to the garage to finish up on his work for the day. Now he was able to take it in, and he was surprised by just how *Noah* it was.

And he was struck by how he was able to recognize it.

Noah had four black metal bookshelves, two on either side of a large window, and both were crammed full. Most of them looked like old library editions, though Adrian could tell a good portion were textbooks from past semesters. There were photos in little frames stuck to the sides with magnets, but he wasn't close enough to get a good look at the people in them.

On the far wall was the sofa, over-stuffed and an almost corduroy-like fabric—straight out of the seventies but looked more than comfortable. The table in front of it was laden with what looked like work, stacks of paper, an open laptop, and a really thick binder-like book off to the side with blank sheets.

"We can sit here. I'll just move all my crap," Noah said, shutting his laptop and shuffling his papers off to the side. "Do you want me to get a blanket for Lemon to lay on?"

He shook his head with a smile and gave Lemon the lay-down gesture. She complied and curled up on the floor near the far end of the sofa. Adrian hooked his cane along the back of the cushions before he sat, and he peered down at Noah's stuff. "Man, this semester has you drowning or what?"

Noah laughed. "No, no. This is mostly a side project. I mean, I have this study guide to finish up for finals—I wanted to get a jump on it before things got too crazy, and there was a quiz in my Greek class which I have to deal with the aftermath—it's middle-passive verbs which I think are intimidating only until everyone realizes we still have aorist and plu-perfect to cover, which means fourth and fifth principal parts, and that's when the breakdowns begin."

"Okay I literally understood about ten percent of what you just said," Adrian admitted.

Noah laughed. "Sorry, I get a little nerdy about this stuff. And I've been eyeballs deep in academia for long enough today, I'd kind of like to forget."

Adrian grinned as he started to unpack the food. "Fair enough. Talk to me about your hobby?"

To his surprise, Noah flushed and glanced away. "It's stupid."

"I have a hard time believing that," Adrian said.

With a shrug, Noah ripped a corner of his roti and nibbled the bits of garlic baked on the top. "It's just…right after I got fitted for my prosthetic," he tapped the side of his eye, "the prosthetist made this comment about how I needed to take extra care of my sighted eye because I didn't have a backup any longer. I had panic attacks for three weeks straight—I wanted to wear protective lenses, didn't want to leave my house. It took me about six months before I was able to ride in a car again." He ripped more roti off and stuffed some into his mouth, chewing a moment before he went on. "Then I decided to stop being so worked up over a hypothetical, but the only way I could do it was by taking precautions."

Adrian frowned. "What do you mean?"

"I mean, I'm not totally blind. I don't need a cane most of the time, and I can still see just fine with my glasses. But I now know for a fact anything can happen, and I wasn't prepared for this," he tapped his eye again. "But I could be prepared for losing my vision totally."

"So…"

"So I'm learning braille," he finally said with a shrug. He fell quiet a moment as he reached for one of the containers of the curry dish and rice, and he stirred them together with his fork. After taking a bite, he sighed and said, "I've done cane training and I'm learning braille, and I mean, I'm not living like I *will* lose the rest of my vision someday, but I'm allowing myself to accept the possibility of it happening. Crazy, right?"

"I don't think it's crazy," Adrian said softly, after a long pause as he considered what Noah was saying.

"I know you can't actually prepare for something like that, but at least I'll have coping skills if it does go that way, right? That's…it's how I deal with my anxiety."

"I don't think it's crazy," Adrian said again. "I think it makes a lot of sense for someone who has already been through trauma and loss."

Noah's mouth quirked into a half smile. "Thanks. I can't tell you what it means that you get it. My friends try to understand, but they think I'm over compensating and they get a little annoyed with me sometimes. I love them, but…"

Adrian laughed quietly as he took up his own dish of food. "No, I get it. Like the guys at my garage? They're great. Loyal dudes, always have my back. But they don't entirely understand what it's like to live with this. Not just my legs," he said, biting his lip for a second. "All the shit in my head. They think it's going to get better, that one day I won't be overwhelmed by all the noise and chaos on busy days. I don't have to deal with that at Baum's, and it feels safe."

Noah's half-smile quirked into a full grin. "How did your session go?"

"Oh," Adrian said and huffed a little, hiding his own grin back. "Actually, it went well. I've been working with this guy for a while— *he's* totally blind, coincidentally."

Noah's cheeks pinked a little. "Yeah? And he's boxing?"

"Damn good at it. Clocked me good tonight." Adrian turned his face fully so Noah had a full view of his blossoming bruise. "I was proud of him. I don't know when or if he'll be ready to face anyone in competition, but he's quick and he's really learning to hone vibration and sound. Helps that I'm slow as fuck on my feet, but I'm willing to bet he'd make a good match for Anna one of these days."

"That's," Noah said, then stopped and laughed. "I don't think I'll ever be at a level where I could match Anna."

Adrian couldn't help a tiny grin as he reached for Noah's hand. Their fingers linked, and he rubbed his thumb over the side of Noah's wrist. "Do you want to get into that kind of shape? Because you know I could help you."

"That would mean going rounds with you, wouldn't it?" Noah said, then took a breath and put on a very brave face as he leaned in and said in a very low tone, "I think I'd rather take a very different sort of pounding from you."

Adrian's moan ripped from his chest before he could stop it, and he curled his hand around Noah's wrist, tugging him fully into his lap.

"You can't just say things like that and not expect me to do this." With that, he dragged his hands down, cupping Noah's ass as the other man straddled his thighs.

Noah bit his lip and looked right into his eyes. "I didn't."

Adrian couldn't do anything else besides kiss him. It was messy, rougher than the night before, demanding with a wet, hot tongue and biting lips. One hand drifted from Noah's ass to his hair, fingers digging into those curls Adrian loved to feel so much, and he tugged just a little. Noah gasped, the bulge in the front of his joggers getting even harder, and he ground down against Adrian's matching erection.

"I want you so fucking much," Adrian groaned against Noah's lips.

"You've got me," Noah said, like a promise Adrian hadn't been prepared to hear. "You've got me, and I want everything with you. But first…" He managed to disengage himself from Adrian's hands, though Adrian struggled to let him go, but he didn't go far. Instead, he crouched between the V in Adrian's thighs, using a firm grip to spread his legs even wider. "Okay?" he asked, looking up into Adrian's flushed face.

Adrian licked his lips, then nodded, not capable of speech right then. He knew what was coming and the anticipation was making his head spin. As Noah's hands crept to his waistband, Adrian's hand cupped his cheek, thumb grazing Noah's plush bottom lip. God, those lips were going to look so fucking good wrapped around him, stretched around his cock, cheeks swollen with the girth of him. Adrian couldn't help a small thrust as Noah finally worked his bottoms and boxers down toward his thighs, then pooling at his calves.

Noah's hands were warm and so fucking soft as they brushed up the fine hair over Adrian's legs. The scar tissue was sensitive and went right to his dick, a sharp contrast between pain and pleasure that he wasn't sure he wanted more or less of. But he didn't have time to consider it. Not when Noah reached into his pocket, pulled out a condom, and ripped the packet with his teeth.

"I want to do this bare soon. Soon as we can be certain it's safe," he murmured. He gripped the base of Adrian's dick in a firm hold, giving him a couple experimental strokes. Adrian's head fell back, eyes rolling upward, and he let out a ragged sigh at the thought of doing this without any barriers between them. It was too early now, too soon, not enough definition of what this was between them, but there was a promise on the horizon and for now, that was enough.

"Please," Adrian managed to choke out.

Noah wasted no more time rolling the condom on, following the downward slide of his hand with his mouth. Wet-hot heat enveloped him, and Adrian almost spilled right then. It had been too long since someone he connected with had touched him like this. It had been a long time since Adrian felt wanted as a whole, and not out of pity, or in spite of the way he'd come back. Noah made him feel like a person, like the man he'd been before his life was irrevocably changed, and he knew he couldn't squander it.

He knew he'd be willing to make promises and carve out pieces of him just to keep it.

Blowing out a fresh puff of air, trying to retain some control, Adrian lifted his head and forced himself to look down. Noah was going at him with vigor, with his eyes squeezed shut and a look of pleasure on his face like *he* was the one being sucked off. His lips stretched so prettily over Adrian's length, red and a little wet. Spit gathered in the corners of his mouth, and Adrian brushed his thumb through it before rubbing it in a circle around Noah's tight lips.

Noah moaned and Adrian thrust himself upward without thinking. When Noah made a slight choking noise, Adrian cupped his cheek in apology, but almost lost his head again when he felt the bulge of himself in Noah's mouth against his palm. He swallowed thickly. "I'm not going to last, baby. Fuck, I'm going to blow in seconds. You're so fucking good, your fucking mouth…" His rambling died off as he began shallow thrusting, chasing the warm, intense build making his balls draw up tight and his face flush red-hot.

Noah used one hand to stroke at the base of his cock where his mouth couldn't reach, the other slipping behind his balls to play with his taint. It was all Adrian needed to let go, to spill into the condom. Somewhere in the back of his head he realized that sometime—maybe soon—he'd be able to spill it all straight into Noah's mouth, and watch him swallow it down. The abstract thought penetrated his lusty haze and his dick gave one last valiant twitch to empty what remained in his balls.

When Noah sat up, he was panting, pink in the cheeks as he rubbed at his jaw. "Fuck, you are so hot."

Adrian started to gather himself, pulling Noah into his arms. His hand went for Noah's own erection, expecting to find a bulge there to take care of, only he found Noah's soft dick and a wet spot. "Holy shit, did you...?"

"Like I said," Noah murmured, pressing a kiss to the scarred side of Adrian's neck, "you are so hot."

It wasn't the first time Noah had lost control like that, but before it had been a matter of youth, inexperience, and anticipation. With Adrian, it was different. Adrian had breezed into the apartment freshly showered from the gym, the sleeveless shirt showing off his muscles which hadn't yet relaxed from his boxing session. There were flecks of motorcycle grease under his nails, and there was lust in his eyes like he wanted to devour Noah right where he sat.

Noah hadn't felt wanted like that in a long time. Maybe ever, if he really considered it. His relationship with Ryan had been comfortable and happy, and he hadn't ever felt like they were lacking, but there hadn't been anything like this. Maybe it was the fact that they were young grad students just trying to get by that robbed them of their ability to find that kind of passion, but he doubted it. The way Ryan had looked at the *dog-walker* when Noah walked in on them was more intense and sexual than he'd ever seen Ryan look at *him*.

Chances were, Noah just hadn't experienced anyone who got him worked up that way. At least, not until Adrian had breezed into his life. Noah still didn't know his last name, what classes he was teaching, what his life was like before the military, but he could still feel an intensity between them he couldn't put words to, and he wasn't willing to give up on.

They'd eventually made it to the bed, trading lazy hand-jobs thanks to their sleepy lack of energy, and now Noah found himself full in more ways than one, curled up on his side with his eye fixed on Adrian's profile. They were both shirtless and Noah was tracing absent lines around Adrian's ink.

"Can I ask you something?" Noah said in the still quiet of their afterglow.

Adrian turned his head, the left corner of his mouth quirked up in a smile. "Go for it."

"Is it weird we fucked in front of your dog?"

Adrian's head fell back, his entire body shaking with laughter. He turned his head on the pillow and found Lemon fast asleep on her side right near the edge. "I don't think she noticed."

Noah grinned and shrugged, laying his cheek back down against Adrian's chest. "Can I ask you something else?"

"You can ask me anything. Always."

"What's your last name?"

Adrian blinked, then covered his face with a laugh. "We never did give those, did we?"

Noah shrugged, grinning back at him. "I guess when you don't meet in a traditional way, those things slip through the cracks. I understand if you want to wait a little, get to know me better…"

Adrian quieted him by rolling over and pressing a warm kiss to the side of his neck, just under his ear. "It's Flores." He rolled the R as the name danced off his tongue and Noah shivered. He'd always had a thing for accents and languages—maybe being a polyglot or maybe it was just his thing, but his face went warm. "Can I ask yours?"

Noah grinned and reached up with his hand, carefully touching the edge of Adrian's five o'clock shadow, curving his finger around a patch of scar tissue where the hair wouldn't grow. "It's Avidan," speaking it the way his parents did, though he'd never really been able to nail down a Hebrew accent enough to make his mother happy. Still, it brought a little bit of light into Adrian's eyes.

"I've never heard that one before. Where's it from?"

"Israel," Noah said, his fingers drifting down to Adrian's. They hooked together at the first knuckle, and Adrian's thumb began to rub gently along his skin. "They moved here when my older brother was two."

"First gen," Adrian said. He pulled Noah's hand to his lips and nipped gently at his fingertips. "Me too. My mom was pregnant with me and Anna when my dad got a job at NYU."

"Where from?" Noah asked.

Adrian shrugged. "My mom was from Stockholm, but when she was twenty-five, her best friend got a job in Manila. She followed her and started working at the hospital there where she met my dad. He and his friends had been fucking around at the beach and he bashed his face on a rock. She sewed him up and he left her his number and she gave him a chance in spite of him being a clumsy dipshit."

"Well thank God for that," Noah said quietly, squeezing Adrian's hand. "Means you're here."

Adrian chuckled again, the sound still soft and sweet. After a moment, he rolled over and pinned Noah down, kissing him in quick, firm pecks peppered across his lips. "So now we know that. You curious about anything else?"

"Well, everything," Noah said. He reached up to push his hand through Adrian's short hair. He loved the way it felt against the pads of his fingers, slightly coarse, thick, gorgeous. He rubbed a lock of it between his thumb and forefinger.

"Ask me anything," Adrian said, his voice almost a whisper, like he was afraid to disturb the quiet between them.

Noah's hand drifted down, curling around Adrian's malformed ear. At that, Adrian winced a little and Noah pulled his hand back. "I'm sorry. Does that bother you?"

Licking his lips, Adrian tensed like he might pull away, then shook his head and dropped his forehead to Noah's collarbone. "It's not you."

"Does it hurt? I don't want to…"

"It's not that," Adrian interrupted. He took a breath, then looked up. "People tend to have a morbid fascination with the way I look now. And I get that the scars are part of me—you can't see me without them, and frankly I don't think I'd want anyone to pretend like they weren't there. But sometimes it just becomes all about them."

Noah bit his lip, feeling a little bit of shame coursing through him. He was curious, and he liked touching them, but only because they were part of this man he was falling for. But the last thing he wanted to do was make Adrian feel more self-conscious about them. "That's not why I like touching your face, but I do get it. Right after my accident, when I got fitted with my eye, my friends kept asking me to take it out, kept pushing me to wear it less. They were kind of obsessed with what it looked like underneath. My ex…"

"The one who bought you the passes to Baum's?" Adrian asked with a hint of something tense in his voice.

Noah almost smiled because he was pretty sure the tension was jealousy. "Yeah, Ryan. We'd been broken up for a while before the car accident, but he was there for me during the recovery. After my implant surgery, he kept trying to like—surprise me, I guess? Get the jump on me when I didn't have it in. I think he thought there would be some grotesque hole in my face. Finally I just gave in and pulled the eye out and showed him and he was almost disappointed. It doesn't look like anything, really," Noah added. "The implant is kind of white, and round. You can't see into my brain or anything like that."

Adrian chuckled and shook his head. "I know that. I've seen guys missing literally half their faces, I know what's reality and what's expectation."

"Right," Noah said, blowing out a puff of air. He dragged a hand down his face with a short laugh. "This conversation got weird."

"Not exactly the most romantic post-fucking pillow talk," Adrian conceded, but he was smiling all the same, still hovered over Noah's torso making him feel safe and wanted. "I like it, though. I like that I can be real with you and there's no expectation. No pity."

Noah smiled and reached his head up for a kiss. "Is there any chance you can stay tonight?"

Adrian's sweet expression fell, and his gaze darted to the side. "I want to. Noah, you have no idea how badly I want to, but the last time

I tried to sleep with someone else in the room, it didn't go well. For me or them. It's not never, okay? Just...I don't think I'm ready yet."

"We can work up to it," Noah said, calling on his earlier promise that he would do everything in his power to understand. "As long as it's okay that I ask from time to time. I will never, ever make you feel bad when the answer is no."

"Even ten years from now, when I'm having a terrible night and have to sleep on the couch because I'm afraid I'll hurt you?" Adrian asked quietly.

Noah had no idea what to do with the emotions that question conjured up in him. The idea Adrian was even abstractly considering ten years from now, that they still might have this. He dug his hands into Adrian's hair and tugged him in for a long, slow kiss. "Yes," he murmured against the other man's lips. "Even twenty years from now. Maybe even a hundred."

Adrian laughed. "Forward thinking, Mr. Kurzweil, but I don't think I want to live that long."

Noah's grin stretched his face enough his cheeks ached with it. "I can't even tell you how much I love that you just referenced him. I mean, I'm not a science guy at all, but I've had classes derailed for the entire hour and fifteen minutes debating the ethics and morality of singularity and how it relates to the Classical period's strive to reach immortality through heroics. One student gave an impassioned speech about how modern tech inventions is the new hero's journey. Didn't do much for everyone's percentage on their finals, but it was a good topic."

Adrian laughed again, burying his face in Noah's neck, kissing his warm skin there. "Are you busy tomorrow?"

Noah's heart thudded against his ribs. "I can find some free time. What are you thinking?"

"That I have my niece on Fridays, and I'd like you to meet her," Adrian said, meeting Noah's gaze with all the seriousness in the world. "She'd really like you."

Noah felt his throat go a little tight. "Yeah? Wes and Anna's kid?"

"That's her. Maggie," Adrian said, then his mouth softened into the proud uncle grin that made Noah want to melt into the sheets. That man was already too much, and the sight of him spoiling a little toddler... god, Noah was in trouble. "We usually do movies and the park, sometimes ice cream or pizza."

"Well," Noah said slowly as Adrian finally rolled onto his side, staying tucked in close, "I can't do dairy, but going to the movies and the park sounds great. As long as it's not 3D."

Adrian blinked, then flushed. "Shit. Right. I mean, she's four so anything she wants to see is just going to be brightly lit Disney shit. No 3D. But I need to try and remember that."

"It's fine, really," Noah said, giving him an easy smile. "I can do Disney shit."

Adrian gave a firm nod. "Okay. Then I'll pick you up around one." He sighed, then peered at the clock and groaned as he pushed himself up to sit. "I should get going."

Noah sat up with him, moving slowly to his dresser for a pair of clean sweats and a t-shirt. When he looked back over, Adrian had already put himself back in his workout clothes and was strapping his braces over his socks. He glanced up at Noah, smiling in that shy way that made Noah want to pin him back to the sheets and spend another hour making out like teenagers.

Instead he bent down for Adrian's shoes and handed them over. "Will your sister and Wes be okay that I'm tagging along on this uncle-niece day?"

Adrian snorted, shaking his head as he pushed up to stand. Reaching out, he dragged Noah in close, cupping his face to kiss him before he answered. "They're going to be thrilled. Anna basically threatened my life if I didn't at least try to get to know you. She could tell I was into it before I even realized I was."

"Thank god for her, then," Noah said with a laugh.

Adrian gave him a small shove back, grabbed his wallet and keys from the nightstand, then called Lemon to his side. "Mm, yeah, I am never, ever telling her you said that." He winked and started out the door with Noah close at his heels. "Talk soon?"

"Text me when you get home," Noah said.

Adrian rolled his eyes but turned for a last kiss. "If you insist." They lingered in a chaste press of lips that felt so much bigger than a simple goodbye. When Noah shut the door, he pressed his forehead to it and listened to Adrian's slow gait and the gentle clink of the dog leash until he couldn't hear it any longer.

CHAPTER SIX

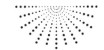

Jolted awake by his phone, Noah wanted to fling it across the room. But somewhere in his sleeping brain he realized it had been going off. A lot. Trying to make his eye functional, he saw several emails, text, and missed call alerts on the screen. Before he could even attempt to read them, Sabrina's name flashed up on the screen with another call.

"What the fuck, someone had better be dead," Noah bit.

"God, I thought you might be. I've called six times," she all-but yelled at him. "There's an all-hands meeting for STEM and Humanities and you need to be there."

Noah sat up, more awake than he had been. "What? What are you talking about?"

"There's been a department purge and three people just got fired," Sabrina gasped, sounding out of breath. "Esther gave me a heads up, but we're having some stupid fucking coaching session for all the faculty." There was a pause, then she said, "That's not all, though. Trevor was one of the guys who was let go."

Noah felt the blood drain from his face. He hadn't been very close to Trevor, but he'd known him since he started, and he'd always liked the guy. "W-what the hell happened?"

"There was an anonymous tip about some of the faculty dating students," Sabrina said quietly. "I guess they've been investigating for a while and they were able to confirm three people who were engaged in relationships with their students."

"Holy shit," Noah breathed out, dragging a hand down his face. "I mean, for f-fuh-fuck's sake, these people are kids. What the...you know what, n-never mind. God, but *Trevor*, though?"

"I don't know the details," she confessed. He heard her cover the mouthpiece of her phone and order a coffee before she was back. "I'm sure he'll get in touch with you at some point. I can't see the guy going after some nineteen-year-old, but I don't think the University is using age as a basis, you know?"

Noah knew. Of course he knew. He'd gone through his extensive training about why you can't date students, about the cost, about the fact that you held power over their academics. He wasn't ignorant, he'd had plenty of attractive people pass through his classes, but he'd never, *ever* been tempted to cross the line. Losing his job, losing his chance at tenure—having that kind of mark on his record—wasn't ever going to be worth a quick fuck.

"What time is the meeting?"

"Eleven. It's supposed to go until four, and they're having it catered which probably means fake Mexican from that horrible place down the road."

Noah grimaced, then the realization of it hit him and he groaned, dropping his head. "Fuck. That's the worst timing ever. God, I can't b-believe this is happening."

"What are you talking about?" Sabrina demanded. "You're literally never busy on Fridays."

"Yeah, except I have a d-date today. I was supposed to go to the movies and the park with him and his niece. I was m-meeting family, it's a big deal." Then he realized Adrian may have to be there. "Is the School of Business called in?" he asked.

"Uh, no, I don't think so, but I don't have all the details. I'm really sorry, man. I know this is new, but I'm sure he'll understand. Hell, he might be dragged into this mess too."

Noah pinched the bridge of his nose, nodding. "Yeah. Yeah, I should c-call him and check in, let him know I have to reschedule."

"Alright, I'll meet you there, okay? We'll get through it. One day of bullshit listening to the suits talk to us like we're twelve, then we can go back to our lives."

Noah wanted to laugh, only the suits apparently *had* to do this because his colleagues were fucking morons. Honestly, he wanted to grab Trevor by the front of his shirt and shake reason into him. What the hell was he thinking? In a million years, Noah wouldn't have pegged Trevor to take advantage of his students, and at the very *least*, take that kind of risk with his job. Now he was fucked, and it would be a miracle if he could find an institution anywhere that would take him.

Taking a breath, Noah got up to relieve himself and splash water on his face before thumbing through his contacts. He'd texted with Adrian for a while the night before, then had gone to sleep early, excited for his date. Meeting the family was big—meeting one of the kids even more so because that implied trust—it implied something on a level of serious that Noah wasn't going to take for granted.

He was certain Adrian would understand the circumstances. Even if he hadn't been called in to this mess, he had sat through the same HR seminars Noah had when he'd been hired. He'd get it.

It rang three times before Adrian picked up, sounding sleepy but calm. "Hey. I wasn't expecting to hear from you yet."

"I'm sorry. Shit, I woke you, didn't I?" Noah asked.

"No, I was up, just being lazy. You okay? You sound a little tense."

Noah shook his head as he pressed his hand to his forehead and spoke slow enough to control his stammer. "It's...did you get the call? About the all-hands meeting?"

"All-hands meeting?" Adrian asked, a frown in his voice.

"There were apparently some instances of misconduct in a couple of the departments; some of the professors were let go because of relationships with students." It was the most he wanted to give away if Adrian hadn't been informed. The last thing he needed was to get himself into trouble for sharing information without the go-ahead.

"Oh god," Adrian said softly. "Were the students punished?"

"I would imagine there's an investigation at least. I'm not entirely familiar with the process, but depending on the circumstances, I'd say yes. I know someone who was involved and I just…" Noah let out a frustrated sigh. "I don't know why he'd make that choice, why put your entire future at risk like that?" He stopped himself before he got carried away. "Unfortunately, the entire Classics department and at least Astrophysics are being called in for an ethics seminar. Mandatory."

"Oh," Adrian said, and understanding dawned in his tone. "Today."

"Yeah. Fuck. I'm so sorry, I wanted to meet up with you so badly, you have no idea." His tone was begging Adrian to understand.

"Hey, it's not your fault," Adrian said. "We can reschedule. I have Maggie all the time, and I'm not going anywhere, okay? Just let me know if you need anything. Maybe we can grab dinner later."

"I would like that," Noah said. Relief hit him like a punch to the gut. He wasn't sure why he was expecting anything less than that, but it felt especially good to hear it. "Text you when they let me out?"

"I can't wait. See you later." Adrian hung up first, and Noah flopped back onto his bed, covering his face with his hands.

The day was officially a shit-show, but he was hoping by the end of the night, things would get a little better.

"AND THE STUDENTS in that department are being dragged into an ethics seminar?" Anna asked with a frown on her face. "That's weird."

"Is it?" Adrian asked. He handed Maggie the Barbie he'd been 'babysitting' for the last five minutes as she set up the Barbie house with her new furniture. Lemon seemed to sense his frustration because she lifted her head and draped it over his thigh. Adrian felt something in his chest unknot and he dug his fingers into her coat.

"It doesn't make sense that it's mandatory. Unless he was involved somehow."

Adrian bit his lip and let his fingers drag over Lemon's floppy ears.

"Well, he said one of his friends was involved, so maybe because of that? I don't know, but I trust him that he's telling the truth. Why would he lie about something like that? It'll be all over campus by Monday."

"Yeah," she agreed, and sounded a little less suspicious. "That's true. It's just weird, but then again, it's been a long damn time since I was a student. Things have probably changed."

"Thanks," he said dryly.

Anna looked a little chagrinned as she reached out to squeeze his wrist. "You know I'm not taking a dig at your age, babe. I'm fucking proud of you for doing this. You've been working your ass off and I know it feels weird to be in some place with a bunch of kids you're nearly old enough to have fathered, but it takes a lot of strength to do something brand new."

He was a little irritated at her words. He appreciated that she believed in him, but she had the worst habit of talking to him like he was her daughter's age. Anna had been the one taking the most care of him when he'd gotten out of hospital, and although she was already married to Wes and familiar with life after deployment and injury, she mothered him long after he needed it. She meant well, but he was exhausted with well-meaning infantilizing.

"Anyway, he and I are getting dinner this evening to make up for it, and I told him he can hang with me and Mags next week."

"Imma show him my Barbies," Maggie said, looking up with a grin. "Tiyo, will he like Barbies wiff me?"

"I think he'll love playing Barbies with you, *kaanakin*," he said and reached for her. He gave her smacking kisses until she giggled and he let her go. He looked up at his sister who was smiling softly at him and he tried not to sigh. "What?"

"Just...you're happy, and it's been a while. You're willing to give this guy the benefit of the doubt and I wasn't sure I was ever going to see that. Even before the explosion you were..." She hesitated.

"An asshole?" he offered.

Maggie gave him a scandalized look. "Tiyo!"

"*Paumanhin, kaanakin*," he said, offering her an apology. He laughed when she shrugged and went back to playing. "Look, I know I've never been the easiest guy to get along with, and I know it's worse now."

"It's not," Anna started, but he held up his hand.

"It is, and I don't want to beat around the bush here, okay? I am who I am, and I don't need you to walk on egg shells with me. I like this guy and I am willing to give him the benefit of the doubt. I can safely say I've never felt like this before and I'm willing to risk a lot to see where it goes. And for fuck's sake *please* don't cry."

"I can't help it," she said with a sniff, then leaned forward and punched him in his arm. "And stop fucking cussing in front of my kid!"

He grinned at her, feeling like he might have just triumphed a little.

CHAPTER SEVEN

I
t was almost five in the afternoon by the time Noah finally
texted. Though he was trying to keep control of his anxiety over
it—and trying not to give into his sister's second guessing—he
had been starting to wonder if Noah would get in touch with him
at all.

Instead of replying, Adrian picked up his phone and hit Noah's
name, pressing the phone a little too tightly to his working ear. "Hey,"
Noah said, sounding exhausted but happy to hear from him. "How
was your afternoon?"

"Probably less productive than yours," Adrian said, unable to hold
back his grin. "Was it rough?"

"It made me feel like I was seventeen-year-old flipping burgers and
having to watch a sexual harassment at work video for five fucking
hours—and they served the worst lunch, most of which I couldn't eat
because everything was covered in cheese." Noah sighed quietly. "I
really hope your day was better than mine."

"I played Barbies with my niece and had to deal with my sister
getting all emotional over the fact that I like someone," he said, feeling
utterly unafraid to be open with this man.

There was a little awe in Noah's voice when he replied, "Is that right? That's...sweet."

"It's something. Mostly annoying, but also pretty great. So, you're starving? Can I take you out?" He gnawed on his lip as Noah silently contemplated his answer. "Or, I can bring something over since you're clearly exhausted?"

"Actually, I'd love to get out if you don't mind," Noah told him. "I know you said loud restaurants are a little rough for you so if it's too much..."

"I know a couple places that aren't far," Adrian said, more than willing to compromise if it helped bring a better end to Noah's bad day. "They're usually quiet, have good food, and are some of the few places I can eat in peace. We could take the trike if your head is up for it, maybe cruise a little after? I always find that clears my head when things have gone to shit." He knew he was rambling, but Noah had a way of getting him all twisted up and as much as he should have hated it, he didn't.

Noah laughed softly. "Fine, but I'm also going to eat a fucking pop tart while I'm waiting, and you are not allowed to judge me."

Adrian laughed, the sound booming from his chest as he grabbed his collapsible cane to store in his compartment. His legs weren't half bad today, but he wanted to be able to give this to Noah without taking any risks. "No judgement here, especially since the other day I was in a rush with a pile of shit to finish and I ended up eating a can of Maggie's cold spaghettios. Like out of the can."

"So we can agree not to judge each other's poor choices," Noah said.

"Deal." Adrian glanced back at his coffee table, at all the homework he had due, and the proposal which had a deadline just around the corner, and yet he felt no guilt leaving home and letting himself have this. Maybe it couldn't be all the time, but it could be some of the time, and he could live with that. "I'll be there in five."

"Sounds good."

The line went dead, and Adrian stowed his phone and cane in his travel compartment before revving the engine and taking off. It was less than five minutes before he pulled up to Noah's building and grinned when he saw the man waiting for him at the curb. He was licking the last bit of blueberry filling off his fingers and swiped his palms on his jeans before walking over.

He looked delicious as ever, his hair a little wild from his long day, his arms bare, shirt stretched over his fit chest. His jeans filled out in all the right places, and his smile showed the faint dimples in both cheeks.

"God, you are a sight for sore eyes," Noah said, then grimaced. "Well...eye."

Adrian rolled his own and gave the seat behind him a pat. "Climb on up. I'll take it slow, but you can grab the helmet back there if you want it."

Noah clearly did, jamming the thing on his head, and Adrian twisted in the seat to help secure it. He understood his fear—Noah had confessed his apprehension and deep desire to protect his remaining sight, even though he'd dedicated himself to learning to cope should he ever lose it. Adrian had never been like that, had never planned for the what ifs, even now. In the future, he'd probably lose complete mobility in his legs. He wouldn't end his life on two feet— his doctors had made that perfectly clear. But he was making the most of his walking time while he had it and he hadn't felt compelled to live an abstract, future life that hadn't happened yet.

Still, he respected Noah for his dedication, wanted to cup his hands around the other man and protect him from anything else in the world that could hurt him. And he knew it was fast and he knew it could blow up in his face far too easily. Yet, he recalled Wes telling him once about Anna, "When you know, you know, man. There's no two ways about it."

He'd always thought the guy was full of shit, just making him feel bad for how he never really connected with people. Now he understood. Adrian was no stranger to hook ups, to dates, to fucking, but with Noah, it was an entirely different universe.

"Hang on," he told him, then started the engine. Noah's arms closed around him tight, his body pressed in a hard line behind his. It would take all of his concentration to keep his focus on dinner and relaxation rather than finding a secluded spot off the side of the road to fuck on the trike's seat. But he could do it. For Noah, and because he knew this was so much *more*, he could do it.

THE SANDWICH SHOP fifteen minutes from campus was as empty as it ever was. Most of their clientele were to-go orders, which meant Adrian could always get a table, and wouldn't have to try and focus over the din of chatter and obnoxious mood music most restaurants pumped through loud speakers, which meant he wouldn't have to struggle with his deaf ear and spend half his time guessing what the person was trying to say.

Noah was a little shaky as he stepped off the trike, but that was common for someone who hadn't ridden before. When Adrian was sure it was just a little adrenaline and not a vertigo attack, he linked their hands together and they made their way inside. He took a moment to appreciate how quickly Noah adjusted his own stride to match his, how he didn't make a public acknowledgement that he was doing something for Adrian.

It just...was. And it was really fucking nice.

He waved at Sheri, his usual server, and then dragged Noah to his favorite booth with the window overlooking the street. He didn't like people, but he did enjoy watching them. They were near downtown, near the art district, and it was a good place to sit and see the weirdness of the world pass by without anyone asking him to be part of it.

"I like the atmosphere," Noah remarked as they sat.

Adrian pulled two of the laminated menus from the holder by the wall and handed it over. "Me too. A lot of places are so chaotic, my anxiety can't handle it, even when I have Lemon with me. But they know me here. They don't bother me, they keep the music down, no one tries to make small talk."

"Except the pain in the ass nerd sitting across from you," Noah said with a wink.

Adrian shook his head with a half-grin. "We haven't gotten far enough for any asses to feel pain. Yet. Though I'm looking forward to it."

"Wow. Dirty," Noah said, then grinned. "I like it. Now let's order so I can actually focus and feel like a person."

Adrian had his usual and didn't bother looking at the menu, but he offered Noah a couple pointers, and within ten minutes they both had sandwiches and soup sitting in front of them.

"God, ambrosia," Noah said, groaning around a mouthful of avocado, chicken, and vegan mayo. "If I wasn't making out with this sandwich right now, I'd be making out with your face."

Adrian chuckled and took a few bites of his soup. "It's good, then?"

"I mean, right now hunger is my sole driving force and I think almost anything would be good. But yes. Honestly, I needed this more than I could say."

"Then I'm glad I could help." Adrian took a bite of his own food, then asked, "So really, how bad was it?"

"It was just long," Noah said. "We had to listen to some weirdo with a skinny ponytail talk about how his own experience with learning things the hard way has made him an expert in his field. Which basically means he used to be a teacher who fucked some of his students and paid for it. Now he fancies himself a protector-of-morality public speaker or some shit." He rolled his eyes and took another bite, talking through a half-full mouth. "It was just a refresher about how student-teacher relationships can ruin lives, even if both parties are consenting adults. The balance of power dynamic has no way to protect a student, blah blah, like we haven't heard it a thousand times." Noah's face fell a little and he stirred his spoon in his soup without taking a bite. "I still don't understand how Trevor got wrapped up in that mess, though. I didn't expect that. I don't know the circumstances, so I don't want to judge or anything, but his life is fucked."

"And he was expelled?"

Noah blinked up at him. "What? God, no. Trevor was a *professor*. He taught History of Ancient Rome, and Latin up through the four hundreds where they tackle the Vulgate. He wasn't planning on being here long, either. He had his sights set somewhere in the Boston Theological Institute group, but now..."

Adrian was startled to hear that. The way Noah had spoken, he assumed the guy had been a *friend*, friend, not a professor he was probably vying to get a letter of recommendation from. Or maybe he was a professor turned friend since he was pretty sure the Classics department was small, and he assumed they all ended up knowing each other pretty well. Hell, he didn't even know what year Noah was in. Though he didn't think now was the time to grill him on it.

"So, what happens? Did they tell you?"

Noah sighed. "Well, the three people they fired will probably end up in public education unless they can find a way to spin it. They didn't give us the circumstances, obviously, so it's hard to tell. I think maybe mitigating circumstances—like if they weren't dating one of their students, just *a* student. Or maybe a grad student? That might help them if they're looking for work."

"What about the students?" Adrian asked softly.

Noah shrugged. "They didn't go into that much either, but Sabrina—my best friend—she thinks if they can prove they were coerced or taken advantage of, they'll be able to stay. Otherwise they'll be forced to take failing marks on their classes and transfer to another institution." Noah rubbed at his temple. "It just doesn't seem worth it, you know? It's hard to see how putting yourself—your future—in that kind of jeopardy is worth whatever kind of lay they were getting."

Adrian couldn't help but agree, even if he was considering what he'd said to his sister. What if it were him and Noah in that position? Would he be willing to risk it? He needed that degree to start up his own shop—needed to prove he could do this on his own, to finish something and make a life for himself. "I guess if they were in love," Adrian said softly.

"Most of these people are infants. Barely nineteen, maybe twenty. They don't know shit about love and if they think some forty-year-old professor getting his midlife crisis kicks with someone who still remembers prom like it was yesterday—because it almost was—then they're clearly not ready to be in love."

Adrian couldn't help but laugh. "Okay, that's fair. I mean, I know the struggle of being an older student. I joined the Marines when I was really young, and I didn't get the chance right away to do all that college shit at the age most people did. It's hard not to look around and think, 'you people don't know what the fuck you're talking about.' But I guess it feels a little strange to think of someone's life getting totally derailed just because they made a bad choice."

"Dubious consent," Noah said with a shrug. "If the person has power over you, can you really consent? It's...complicated, I guess. The adult world masquerades as something that actually knows what the fuck it's doing so kids in high school aren't shit-scared of graduation day. Then they slowly ease into the idea that no matter how old we get, we still don't know up from down."

Adrian grinned and though it was awkward with his brace, managed to play a little footsie with Noah under the table. "I think that's enough deep shit for the day, huh? Why don't we go for a ride?"

NOAH COULDN'T GET ENOUGH of being on the trike with Adrian in front of him. He hadn't expected to feel so safe out in the open like that, but with his arms secured around Adrian's waist, it felt like he could fly off and land in one piece. Normally, taking a risk would have sent him over the edge. He tried to get back some of his confidence after the accident, but every time he moved outside of his usual routine, he felt that little bit of panic crawling up his spine. *What if it happens again? What if I get hurt? What if I lose my other eye?*

The therapist he'd seen after the accident told him it was normal. She said overcompensating was just part of the process, and eventually it would get easier. She hadn't been wrong, but Noah *had* started to wonder if he'd ever let himself step outside of his comfort zone. As they whipped up a tall hill heading for the edge of town, Noah smiled at the thought of how proud she might be.

This was more than just risk taking with his body, it was risk taking with his entire life. Adrian had the capacity to throw it all out of balance, and for the first time in years, Noah wasn't afraid of where that might lead, or what it might change.

When the trike rolled to a stop at the top of the hill, Adrian killed the engine and offered a hand to help Noah down. He was less shaky than he'd been at the sandwich shop, and he was able to stand on his own as Adrian swung his leg over the side. He didn't get off the trike, though, and he didn't let go of Noah. Instead, he spread his legs into a V and tugged Noah between them.

With gentle, pressing hands, Adrian turned Noah, exposing him to the view beyond. It wasn't that easy to see. Even with his glasses, it was late, and the sun was setting in the distance. The darkness made everything blur, the city lights melding together, and there was the utter and complete absence of anything on one side which always startled him whenever he was given a massive panoramic view. But it didn't feel overwhelming then. With Adrian behind him, his chin resting just over Noah's shoulder, he just felt content.

"It's beautiful," Noah said quietly.

"It's one of the few places that can calm my head some days, when nothing else works," Adrian murmured, then kissed the edge of his ear. "I was hoping you'd like it."

Noah did. There weren't really words for how it was making him feel—not just the view, but the pieces of himself Adrian was sharing, because Noah could tell the guy was intensely private. Noah had no idea what Adrian had seen, what he'd been through, but the trauma of it was evident in every aspect of Adrian's life. Noah understood what a gift it was to be allowed in like this.

With a small sigh, he tilted his head back against Adrian's shoulder and glanced up. Even with his corrective lens, he couldn't quite make out the sky the way he used to. It was fuzzy shapes and faint twinkles now, and he let himself mourn it a bit.

"My dad used to take me stargazing when I was little," he said, his voice feeling a little harsh in the intense silence. "My vision was always poor but he'd take me out to an open field, miles and miles away from the city. I think he'd always wanted to get into astronomy, but he didn't really have the head for it. Still, his telescope was probably his most favorite thing in the world."

Adrian hummed, his hand drawing lazy circles along Noah's side. "Does he still go now?"

Noah felt a little wrench in his chest, swallowing past a tiny lump in his throat, and shook his head. "He died eleven years ago. Sometimes I would go on my own, sometimes on the anniversary my brother went with me. But...I haven't done it since my accident."

Adrian breathed out, heavy and warm against his neck, and he nuzzled against the warm skin there. "I don't know what it's like to lose a parent. Not yet, anyway. But I can only imagine the emptiness. I'm sorry, Noah."

Noah shrugged, the apology somehow feeling better than any expression of sympathy he'd ever gotten. "Thanks. It's...I mean, it's not *fine*. I'm left with my mother who spends her days trying to convince me gay is just a phase and if I just attend temple more regularly, I'll meet a nice Jewish girl and settled down to give her some grandchildren."

He felt Adrian give a full-body wince. "Rough."

Noah snorted. "Yeah. I love her. I mean, of course I love her, but it gets exhausting trying to convince her to just love me for me and not the man she thinks I could be. I think my biggest regret was not coming out before my dad died. I can't say for sure he'd have been okay with it, but I like to think he would have."

Adrian raised his hand slowly, then dug his fingers into Noah's curls and gently raked his blunt nails along his scalp. "My parents really struggled with me too. They're...better now. Mostly. But we aren't as close as we were when Anna and I were kids. I changed a lot after the service. I was stationed in New York after my first tour and I think they could tell I wasn't ever going to be the same guy as I had been when I first signed up."

Noah turned in Adrian's arms, dislodging the other man's grip, but not going far. He just wanted to be able to look at him as best he could. "I've never been a risk-taker. Hell, my accident wasn't anything more than being in the wrong place at the wrong time, and I've been even more terrified after that. Your life, your past, it...it kind of scares me, because I can't imagine ever having the courage to do something like that. But..." He paused, licking his lips as Adrian's eyes watched him with soft curiosity and so little judgement it made Noah ache. "But you make me feel brave. And I know that sounds stupid to a man who literally risked his life and limbs over and over but..."

"It doesn't sound stupid," Adrian said. He brought one hand up, cupping Noah's cheek and holding him steady. "I've seen and done a lot of things that have made grown men piss themselves with fear, but trusting someone with my heart, is hands-down the scariest thing I have ever done." He hesitated, then said, "But it doesn't feel like a risk with you. I know we just started whatever this is, but I felt like you should know."

Noah couldn't answer with words, he had none in that moment, so he went up on his toes and pressed his mouth to Adrian's. He was welcomed with parted lips and a searching tongue. Adrian's hand moved to his waist, tugging him close so their chests touched, and Noah felt the passion and intensity in that kiss. It was a little scary, and a lot beautiful, and everything he hoped it would be.

When they finally parted, Adrian pressed his brow to Noah's. "I don't know where we're going, exactly, but I feel like we're on the right path."

Noah grinned at him and closed his eyes, allowing himself to take comfort in darkness where he'd been so afraid before. "Me too. And I trust you."

CHAPTER EIGHT

Wiping sweat from his brow, Noah rolled his shoulders and didn't miss the way Anna was grinning at him. A mixture of pride and a little mischief in her smile. Noah didn't always see the resemblance in the twins. Adrian favored his mother's side, broad, tall, square-jawed and bulky from his Nordic lineage where Anna was smaller, curvy but lithe in her frame and more rounded features. But they had the same eyes, and the same sense of stubborn pride, and the same absurd sense of humor Noah had been getting to know over the last few weeks.

The controversy on campus had finally died down, and though Lowe was breathing down Noah's neck about keeping enrollment retention up and ensuring enough people in his classes were maintaining As and Bs, it wasn't anything new. Charlie was shorter with him now, less likely to corner him in corridors and at his office, but he was counting that as a win. Noah knew he should have just been up front with the guy, but the damage was done and maybe this time the guy would take the hint.

Noah had more important things to focus on—like trying to win the university's favor so he could secure his position there which would make him comfortable for a long time. He hadn't exactly set his sights on tenure here—every academic like him dreamed of Oxford, Harvard, Duke—but he wasn't foolish enough to think his name would go down with the greats. He'd never discovered anything, and his greatest accomplishment was having been invited to do six months on Crete at the Minoan ruins.

It was enough though. Things finally felt like they were enough. His job remained the same pain in the ass, but he was three weeks into an official relationship with Adrian—even if their time together was growing more and more sparse. Finals were approaching, and with that the final deadline for Adrian's accessibility proposal and Noah had to assume whatever exams the School of Business leveled out for end of term. Plus, his garage was getting busier, and he still had his client at the gym.

But Noah also knew it wasn't forever. They'd have six weeks over winter break, another semester, and then the summer. Noah had already decided he wouldn't be taking on any summer courses, wanting to spend some time working on a couple book concepts with his downtime. He had thirty grand in savings which would easily see him over those three months, and maybe even secure him a few days away.

Maybe even with Adrian, if they got that far.

"You did good tonight," Anna said, clapping him on the shoulder when the last of the other students filed out.

"Yeah, that bag never saw me coming," Noah said with a short laugh. "Really though, this has been great for my stress. This semester has been worse than others and I swear it's the only thing that's keeping me together before winter break."

"Yeah, I remember it *un*-fondly," she said with a wink. "All that stress eating and cramming and not sleeping. It's a wonder I passed anything."

Noah chuckled. "Literally every conversation I've walked in on for the past three weeks. But it's almost over and I..." He trailed off when he saw Adrian and his client walking out of the back boxing room. The guy was holding Adrian's shoulder with one hand, and the leash of his guide dog in the other, and they were talking softly.

Adrian shook his head at something, then he laughed, the smile lighting up the whole room and Noah felt his heart thud.

"Wow. You're like a fucking Disney movie prince," Anna said, nudging him in the side. "I don't think it's possible to be more obvious apart from spontaneous violins playing."

Noah flushed and rubbed the back of his neck with a shrug. "I like him," he said slowly. "I...yeah. I like him."

"Good, he likes you too. I haven't seen him this happy in a long time."

Noah turned to her. "Is this where you give me the shovel talk?"

Rolling her eyes, she shoved at him again. "I don't think I need to. You know I could take anyone in this gym, especially little kickboxing newbies. What I'd really like to do is have you over for dinner."

Noah blinked at her. "Really?"

She nodded. "Wes has been up Adrian's ass to ask you, but I think he's afraid you'll turn him down."

Noah almost choked on his own tongue. "What?"

Anna shook her head sadly. "He's a little bit of a dipshit, and he has a hard time accepting when things are good in his life. So fuck it, I'm the twin, it's my job to cross lines. How about this weekend?"

Noah worried his bottom lip. He had fifteen research papers to grade, but then again, he had a small arsenal of grad students looking for favor too. If he shuffled off seven or eight, he could clear a few hours. "Yeah. Count me in. But you have to break it to Adrian."

She laughed and rolled her eyes a little. "Trust me, I have no problem with that. That asshole doesn't scare me. So, what do you say? Saturday."

"Perfect," Noah said. He glanced up through the window again and saw Adrian making his way over to them and his heart started beating rapidly behind his ribs. He was so gone for this man, so damn gone and it was probably going to freak the guy out if he made himself obvious.

Licking his lips, he finished unwrapping his hands and just managed to drop the wraps on his bag when Adrian breezed through the door and came right for him. He was leaning on his cane heavily, holding Lemon's leash around his wrist, but he was moving quickly and had his free hand around Noah's waist in seconds.

"Hey, you," Adrian murmured in his ear, kissing his jaw gently.

Noah felt his entire body heat up and was only vaguely aware of Anna slipping out of the room. "Have a good session?"

"Yes," he replied, moving his face to give him a swift kiss on the mouth. "Go for a ride with me tonight. I'll have Anna take Lemon back to my place and we can take the trike. I'm feeling a little amped, but I want to be with you. Say yes."

"Yes," Noah said without a second of hesitation. "I just need to change first."

Adrian nodded. "Go. I'm going to talk with Wes for a few minutes so take your time. Meet you out front in ten?"

Noah nodded, then gathered his things and headed for the shower. Luckily, he was one of two men in the beginner's kickboxing class, so around that time he had the locker room to himself and could take his time. He used the body wash dispenser on the wall, and the woodsy scent always reminded him of Adrian which, on nights they didn't get to see each other, was a way to take him home. He didn't linger, though. The promise of riding with Adrian, holding him close and letting the wind whip around them as they tore through the quiet streets of city's outskirts was enough motivation to get him moving.

He'd been feeling good these past few weeks in spite of the stress, and he planned to take full advantage of it while he could. With finals looming, he was going to be swamped until just before the winter break. It would cut into his Chanukah celebration with his mom—though in all honesty it had been a long time since he'd been able to see her for any of the holidays—but it meant seeing the new year in with a clean slate and this time, a new boyfriend.

That, he thought to himself, was well worth it.

Dressing in a hoodie he'd tucked in his bag, he tugged his shoes on, then shoved his bag into his locker and fit the lock on snug. He was glad to come back for it later if it meant no burden when he climbed on the trike behind Adrian. He made his way out front and saw the lights turned low. It was near closing, and only one of the personal trainers was left, swiping down benches with a towel and disinfectant. Noah gave him a nod before heading out front, and he felt his heart do a little staccato pattern against his ribs when he found Adrian leaning against it, a leather jacket on, looking like walking sex in his tight jeans.

"Ready?" he asked as Noah approached.

Noah nodded, swallowing thickly and biting his tongue from all the dirty things he wanted to say right then. Adrian seemed to tell though, if the smirk on his face was anything to go by. He held out a hand and helped Noah mount the bike before climbing on. He pulled Noah snug against him, revved the engine, and tore off down the street.

THEY ROLLED TO A STOP AND, when the engine cut, Noah's ears rang in the sudden silence. The hilltop overlooking the city was far from most neighborhoods, barely room for two cars to pass, and perfect for a night like this. It was cold, the air crisp and dry with the promise of an intense winter. The sky beyond was pitch black, mottled by a sea of stars. Noah always had trouble with them at night, seeing more of a smudged galaxy than anything else, but it had its own beauty attached to it.

He swung his leg over the trike and steadied himself as Adrian climbed off and held on to the seat to keep himself steady. Perching his backside against it, he pulled Noah against him, spreading his legs into a close V and held him there. His arms cinched around his waist and Noah could feel warm breath puffing against his neck.

"Gorgeous," Noah murmured as he looked at the city beyond them.

"Yes, you are," Adrian whispered, then kissed the back of his ear, a little wet with parted lips and a hint of tongue. "You are so fucking gorgeous."

"You really know how to charm a guy."

"*A* guy," Adrian emphasized. "One. *You.* I'm only interested in charming you."

Jesus, Noah thought, letting his head fall back against Adrian's shoulder. It was like a movie, like he was in some gay romcom being swept off his feet in a manner of days, in ways that should not have worked and yet...

And yet.

Here they were. He pressed his palm over the back of Adrian's hand that was holding him tight and let his fingers slot between the other man's. It was cold, but Adrian's skin was warm, and sent tingles all the way up to his elbow. "I've never felt like this before," he finally said. "I don't exactly have a world of experience, but I know this is different."

"It is," Adrian told him. "Maybe it'll wear off someday and we'll start to feel like everyone else, but I hope that doesn't happen for a long time."

Noah huffed a laugh through his nose, shaking his head against Adrian's collarbone. "Me too. Because trust me, I am boring as fuck. Just some classics nerd drowning in papers and getting all stupid excited every time they find some old shitty Aesop manuscript."

Adrian chuckled against his ear. "I find your nerdy excitement hot as fuck. And I hope after the break I get to see more of it because three days in the last couple of weeks has not been enough."

"I know," Noah said from behind a sigh. "I have every intention of making as much time for you as possible."

Adrian spun him, hands on his hips, then dragged their bodies together for a slow kiss. "Let's go grab dinner, okay? Take it to go, because I know we have shit tomorrow, but I have plans. I have things I want to do to you and I'm willing to risk a little fatigue if it means I can take my time."

Noah's entire body felt like it was going to erupt into flames. They hadn't gone very far yet—they just hadn't the time—but the promise of what Adrian was implying, it went straight to his dick, plumping up the front of his sweats. "Uh. Yes. Yeah. I'm...we could do that." Honestly a good dicking would make a world of difference in his mood the next day, he was damn sure of that.

"Then let's get going," Adrian said, releasing him so fast, Noah stumbled a little.

With a laugh, he shoved at Adrian's shoulder before climbing back onto the trike and grabbed his waist when Adrian followed suit. "I also plan to cook for you over break," he said before Adrian started the bike up. "I'm not amazing or anything, but I enjoy it and it'll be nice to have the time."

"I can't wait to taste anything you want to put in my mouth," Adrian said, and laughed, revving the engine to drown out Noah's loud, exasperated groan.

CHAPTER NINE

The places near campus were a little full that night. Students from all walks of life were grabbing comfort food to soothe their pre-final nerves, and Adrian definitely considered himself one of them. Though it wasn't the food tonight that was going to ease the way into the exams he had coming up.

No, it was the man on his arm, the one holding his waist as they queued up to get some of the Thai take-away Noah said he was craving. They weren't all over each other, not nearly as bad as the twenty-somethings who seemed seconds away from taking their clothes off and touching genitals right there in the restaurant, but there was something profoundly erotic, yet also grounding, at the way Noah held a possessive hand around him.

Adrian wanted to crowd him up against the counter right there and kiss him stupid. Instead he handed off the to-go cups to Noah and said, "Fill these up and I'll pay."

Noah looked like he wanted to argue, but eventually sighed and did as he asked while Adrian smiled and dug his student ID out of his wallet for his discount. Adrian had it all paid for and the sacks of fragrant noodles and soup on his arm by the time Noah was done.

Together they decided to walk the rest of the way to Noah's place since it was closer.

Noah held his arm to help navigate the dark streets, and they didn't say much as they headed off, but they didn't need to. A need was simmering between the two of them, and Adrian swore he could feel the bottle of lube and box of condoms pressing against his side through his jacket pocket. He wasn't sure they'd actually get that far tonight, but he wanted it. Whether it was himself in Noah, or Noah in him, he didn't care. He just wanted the connection to the man he was falling head over heels for.

"Let me move my shit around," Noah said as they stepped inside his place. It was warm from the running heat, and the coffee table where they usually sat was positively covered in papers and old looking books.

"Research?" Adrian asked as he settled on the couch and reached down to take his braces off.

Noah looked up, a faint blush on his cheeks making his freckles stand out against his pale skin. "Oh uh. Sort of, yeah? We can talk about it later though, because if I get started, I won't stop. It's kind of consuming my brain right now."

Adrian laughed, remembering full well the research papers he had due in his previous core classes. "Fair enough. No academic talk until after the food and sex."

Noah bit down on his lower lip and looked like he was barely holding himself back as he finally cleared a space for food. They slid down to the floor, Adrian groaning in relief at being able to flex his feet out, and he let Noah dish the portions out as they got comfortable.

"So," Adrian said as he twirled noodles around his fork, "how is Anna's class? I haven't been able to watch lately."

"It's good." Noah sipped a little of his soup and shrugged. "I wish I could go more often, but I've been so swamped with everything. I told her to count on me more once the semester was over. I'll need to buy more passes soon."

Adrian leaned over and nipped at his jaw, his hunger for Noah's body starting to eclipse the hunger for food. "Wes will give you the friends and family discount."

"He doesn't need to do that," Noah started to protest.

Adrian set his plate down and reached for Noah's jaw, turning his face so their gazes connected. "I know," he said, his voice heavy with meaning. "I know he doesn't." Then he tipped Noah's head up by the chin and their mouths connected.

There was a desperation to that kiss, lips parting, tongues dancing together almost frantically. Noah's teeth were sharp as they grazed his lower lip, Adrian's head spinning a little when Noah pulled back with biting, sucking pecks.

"I want you. Fuck, I want you so badly."

"Yes," Adrian said. He reached down and cupped Noah's rock-hard erection, stroking up and down with the heel of his palm. "Do you want me to fuck you? Or do you want to fuck me?"

Noah groaned and pulled him into another kiss before he seemed capable of words. "I w-want you in me," he finally said. "I want you in m-me, and I want you to f-fuck me so hard I f-feel it all week."

Adrian almost lost it right there, his dick giving a valiant effort to shoot his load in the front of his jeans as he listened to Noah so worked up, he was stammering on his words. He pulled back from Noah, squeezing his eyes shut until he had control. "Careful, sweet-heart, I have less than a thread of control right now."

"Exactly how I like you," Noah said, his voice hot with promise, and a lot calmer. "Come on, my room isn't too much of a mess and I want to be comfortable when I get down on my hands and knees for you."

Adrian needed a second more before he had the strength to stand up, and he thanked everything he knew to be holy that the evening's work out hadn't been too stressful on his legs and he was able to make it down the short hall without falling over.

It was a near thing though, mostly because when he reached the doorway, Noah already had his joggers puddled around his ankles, and he was stroking his dick with a fast, tight motion.

"God," Adrian gasped. He was frustrated with how clumsy his

fingers were, how his legs just didn't want to cooperate as he struggled out of his jeans—and what a dumbass he was for putting that on
instead of something he could slip out of. But eventually he freed
himself from his cotton prison. Eventually he was stark naked and
bracing himself on Noah's desk with one hand and gripping his dick
with his other.

"You are so sexy," Noah said, drinking him in as he lounged back
on the bed.

Adrian licked his lips. "My jacket," he said, his voice slightly strangled with want. "Condom, lube—in the front pocket. I want you to
prep yourself and I want to watch."

There was a glint in Noah's eyes, something a little devious, a little
smug. He slid to the floor and retrieved the items from Adrian's
jacket, but before he climbed back onto the bed, he pulled something
from under it. A small, sleek box about the length of his forearm.
Adrian had three guesses what was inside, and the first two didn't
count.

His dick started to throb a little as he watched Noah's clever
fingers pop the top open and reveal a thick, rubber dildo. It was sili-
cone, a light blue color, fake veins and ridges, and it was just a little
smaller than Adrian's own.

"*Fuck*." The word tumbled from his lips and he saw Noah's lips curl
up at the edges as he climbed back onto the bed and poured lube in
his hand.

"Is this w-what you had in m-mind?" Noah asked. He laid back,
spreading his legs, and carefully drew the tip to his hole. He didn't
push in, just let the wet end of it rub in a slow circle. Adrian's eyes
were fixed hard on the way Noah's cock jumped with every brush
against him.

"No," Adrian admitted in a strangled voice. "No, but you have the
best fucking ideas." He pushed off from the desk and took the three
nearly impossible steps to the edge of the bed. He pressed his knee
to it, then lowered down so he had full view of Noah teasing
himself.

"Tell m-me what you w-want," Noah told him.

Adrian's head spun. "Push it against you. Hard. Just enough to breech, but don't go in past the head."

Noah's legs fell a little wider and Adrian could see the strain in Noah's arm as he obeyed. He watched like a hawk as the blue head of the dildo pushed. There was a little resistance, but with a small groan, Noah managed the feat. Adrian's cock jumped in his hand, and he squeezed the base of it to keep control.

"Good," he grunted. He had never been so turned on in his life. "Good. Push in slow and steady, fuck yourself. Not too hard, baby. Just to spread you open, just to get you ready for me. Can you do that?"

"Yeah," Noah groaned, arching his hips a little as he did what he was told. "Yeah I c-cuh-can...god, I can. Yes. I w-want this to be your cock, Adrian. I w-want you in me."

Adrian couldn't stop himself from touching, from reaching over and sliding a flat palm up the inside of Noah's thigh. "Soon. Soon, okay? Just get yourself nice and ready."

Noah nodded and seemed to be incapable of speech right then as he pumped the dildo in and out of his ass. It took all of Adrian's self-control not to come, and not to pull the dildo out immediately and replace it with his aching cock. He watched for what felt like a near eternity until he saw a flush rising along Noah's neck and knew it was time.

"Okay, okay. Are you ready for me?" Adrian asked.

Noah nodded, biting his lip as he gently pulled the dildo out and tossed it to the side. He pushed up on his elbows, his eyes hooded and his eye dilated. "How d-do you...what's easier f-for you? How c-can we do this so it's good?"

Adrian nearly swooned at how Noah could be so worked up, but still so aware of the situation, concerned not just about getting them off but about making it good. He didn't know which deity to thank for sending him this man, but he was ready to praise each and every one just to be safe. After a moment of considering his own limitations, he dragged his hand up the outside of Noah's thigh. "On your side, okay? Let me take you that way."

Noah nodded, shuffling onto the pillows and he rolled onto his side, sticking his ass out in an invitation. Adrian had to take several deep breaths before he grabbed a condom and, with shaking hands, managed to roll it on. He poured a dollop of lube into his palm, spreading it around, then took his slick fingers and pushed them into Noah's waiting ass.

"God. So ready for me. *Fuck*," he groaned. He gave Noah's prostate a few good fucks with his hand before pulling away and pushing the tip of his cock in. There was a little resistance, then a lot of give, and it only took a moment before he was fully sheathed in the tight, hot ass. "You feel so good, god, baby you feel," he said, words a struggle.

Noah seemed beyond them completely, moaning, nodding, reaching back with scrambling fingers for Adrian's ass to pull him closer, to encourage his thrusts to come harder, quicker. The only sound left was the slapping of skin, was the quiet, muffled groans, was Adrian's harsh puffs of breath against the back of Noah's neck as he fucked himself into a frenzy.

His orgasm was building with a swiftness he had only half expected, and it was by instinct alone that he reached around to Noah's front and began to stroke him in time with his own motions. Noah groaned, his head falling backward against Adrian's shoulder, and Adrian craned his neck to kiss him as his balls pulled up tight.

He moaned right into Noah's mouth, his thrusts erratic and fierce. His hand would have stuttered, but Noah closed his own around it and guided the motion until he shuddered and came all over the sheets. As Noah's grip eased up on him, Adrian pulled away, peppering kisses across the back of Noah's naked shoulder.

His heart was racing, his fingers trembling a little with the come-down, but he felt a warm wash of contentment he had never experienced before. He found himself pulling Noah close to him, clinging tight, wanting something more, something deeper. Tonight was not the night to test himself, to experiment with his ability to let someone in while he was at his most vulnerable, but he wanted it soon.

He needed it, and with Noah.

"Thank you," Noah murmured, pulling Adrian's hand up to his lips.

His mouth was dry as it pressed against the back of his hand, and Adrian closed his eyes against the emotions flooding through his chest.

"I..." The words died on his tongue, the things he wanted to say faltering because it was just too early. "I'm...fuck, Noah. I'm really falling for you."

Noah turned and Adrian could see the brightness of his smile, the expression mirroring the feelings he felt thrumming in his chest. His hand came up to cup Adrian's cheek, thumb stroking against his flushed skin. "I know. I feel the same way. It's early and we have a lot to learn about each other, but I like this. I want this."

Adrian pulled Noah's hand to his mouth and kissed the center of his palm. "When the semester is over, I want to try to sleep together. I don't know if it'll go well—I'm worried but..."

"I want to take the risk," Noah said in a rush. He squeezed his hand over Adrian's tight. "You've told me the truth and I know what might happen, but I want to take the risk. I want to be able to wake up with you sometimes, and I'd like to start trying now."

Adrian let his eyes drift closed, then opened them slowly and leaned in for a last kiss. "Then we try."

They cleaned up shortly after, Adrian wanting to linger and maybe have a shower, trade lazy blow jobs, and talk. But he knew Noah had a lot of work to get done, and Adrian had a lot of studying to do. There were twelve days left in the semester, then dead week, then finals, and *then* they would have time to take risks and learn more about each other.

Noah walked him down to the lobby, kissing him at the door before turning away, and Adrian took a moment to bask in it before gripping his cane tight and heading out. Just as the door swung open, his shoulder hit a man who had been lingering and he looked up to see cold, almost angry blue eyes staring at him.

Adrian immediately bristled. He was used to people staring, to having strange reactions to the scars on his face, to the way he walked, the mobility aids, but there was something more to it. The guy was handsome at first—symmetrical features, full lips, a broad build—but there was something that didn't sit right about him.

"Sorry," the guy said after a beat.

Adrian shook his head. "No worries, man." He moved past him and though he refused to look back, he could feel the stranger's eyes on him as he headed toward the shop near where he'd parked his trike.

CHAPTER TEN

"Can I…can I haff it, tiyo? Can I play wiff it?" Maggie bounced on the balls of her feet, trying to reach the hastily cobbled-together model Anna had clutched in her hands. She held it deftly over her head, to keep it from wandering, destructive fingers as Adrian let go of one crutch handle and gently pulled Maggie away from his hard work.

"Not right now, okay? I need that for my meeting later today, and remember, we talked about it? It's not a toy."

Maggie pouted. "But…"

"No buts," Anna said, her voice a little sharp. She ignored when Maggie's eyes went watery. "You were told, and you need to be a good listener or we can't get froyo later with tiyo."

That pulled Maggie away from the edge of her impending tantrum, though she crossed her arms and made a quiet, disgruntled noise and turned her nose up. Adrian bit the inside of his cheek to keep from laughing and turned his eyes on his sister. "You know that's all you, right?"

"I'm sorry, but no. You're the baby and you always have been and she one-hundred percent gets it from you." She grinned at him and pulled the model closer to her chest. "Anyway, she'll forget all about it once we drop it off."

Adrian lifted his right crutch and jabbed the tip at the door to the building across the small walkway. "It's in there. My meeting is at three, so I can meet you after that."

Maggie hurried over to open the door for the pair of them, and Adrian went in first, Anna trailing behind him. "What do you have to do today?" she asked, her voice carrying just a little in the near-empty lobby.

Adrian sighed and turned to face her. "I have to turn in two papers this afternoon, so I'm going to skip the garage today and do my final pass around lunch. Other than that, my professors are giving us a pretty easy last few days, mostly just finals prep."

"Well don't stress," she told him. "You're going to do fine, and your meeting will go great, and you're almost done."

Adrian nodded, then turned and nearly ran into someone standing too close for comfort. He took a stumbling step back and looked into a face he recognized from somewhere, but he couldn't put his finger on it.

The guy was tall and attractive, but his eyes were cold, and it hit him. He was the guy he'd nearly run into the night before when he was coming out of Noah's building. He could tell the stranger was sizing him up, his look calculating. He found himself wishing he'd brought Lemon, but he'd been feeling so good that morning, he let Wes take her to the gym, and he was desperately regretting that now as anxiety started to creep up his spine.

"Sorry," he said after a second. "You just look like the pair of you could use a set of hands and I'm guessing you're going up to meet with Dr. Parker?"

Adrian felt something uncomfortable in his stomach, but the guy's offer seemed sincere. "Ah. Yes, I have a meeting for a..."

"Proposal. I know, I've been sitting in on them with him all afternoon since Dr. Agarwal had a family emergency. I'm more than happy to help. I'm Dr. Barnes." He held out his hand to shake, not deterred by the fact that Adrian was holding crutch handles.

The last thing in the world Adrian wanted to do right then was touch this man's hand, but Maggie was getting restless and he could see Anna was tired and ready to go. He released the handle of his crutch and offered his hand over. "Adrian Flores."

"Student in the School of Business, right?" he asked, giving his hand a hard shake.

Adrian pulled back and adjusted his hold on his crutches. "That's right. My proposal is regarding the accessibility issues around campus from the buildings who haven't been updated in the last decade."

Dr. Barnes let out a low whistle. "That's..." His gaze flickered down to Adrian's feet where his braces could be seen, outlined by his tight jeans, then he looked back up. "I can see it's an issue important to you."

At his condescending tone, Anna stepped forward with her eyes blazing, but Adrian took the lead, not wanting to compromise his chance at getting his proposal through. "It is. I struggled quite a bit when I first started here, and it's been almost four years, but it hasn't gotten any better. I think it's a worthy cause."

"Absolutely," Dr. Barnes said. He plucked the model from Anna's hands before she was aware of what he was doing. "I'm happy to assist."

Anna gave him a careful, dark look before turning back to her brother. "You good here?"

"I'm good," he assured her. "I'll text you after my meeting."

She looked hesitant, but eventually gathered Maggie up and they headed out the door. When it swung shut, he turned back to Dr. Barnes. "I don't actually have my meeting until three, but Dr. Parker said I could drop this off since it's not easy for me to carry around."

"Of course," Dr. Barnes said, his tone breezy but his eyes still intense. "We can take the staff elevator there, right around the corner. I'm sure he'll be excited to get a good look at it before the meeting. It's a very intricate design." He reached for his badge and swiped it at a small, black box on the wall and the doors immediately opened with a soft ping.

Adrian went in first, then used his crutch to hold the door for Dr.

Barnes. "Design is definitely not my forte," he said, answering the man's disingenuous comment, "but I figured it would do for what I was trying to get across."

Dr. Barnes laughed, but the jovial expression on his face didn't reach his eyes. "So, you said you were in the School of Business, right?"

Adrian bristled. "Yes, I'm a senior there. I came back after a couple military tours and I'm working on my degree to establish a shop."

Dr. Barnes whistled again. "That's brave. I mean…not a lot of people have the guts to change their entire lives like that. You're to be commended."

For whatever reason, Adrian didn't believe him. "Thank you," he said anyway. Then to be polite he said, "Where do you teach?"

"Oh, I'm in the Classics department," Dr. Barnes said, and Adrian's eyes widened at the thought of this ass teaching Noah. "In fact, I think that's where I've seen you before."

Before Adrian could ask, the doors opened and Dr. Barnes headed out, making a bee-line for a door at the far end. It took Adrian a moment to catch up with him, and Dr. Barnes came to a stop outside of a door with a small plaque reading *Meeting Room 504*.

"Are you taking Classical Greek?" he asked.

Adrian blinked. "Sorry, no. I took Spanish for my language, but I finished that a few semesters ago."

Dr. Barnes shook his head. "It's only, I know I've seen you around with Dr. Avidan, so I just assumed."

It was like someone had thrown freezing water over Adrian's head and it took him a moment to shake free of the shock. "I'm…sorry. *Dr. Avidan? You mean Noah Avidan?*"

Dr. Barnes' lips stretched into a smile which might have been friendly on anyone else, but on him looked sinister and Adrian's knuckles suddenly itched to connect with the man's face. "Yes. Dr. Noah Avidan. I thought I saw you two together the other night."

Adrian swallowed thickly, realizing now what was happening, and his head threatened to spin right off his neck. Luckily, he'd always been a quick thinker, no matter how much a situation had knocked him off guard. It's what made him so effective as a lieutenant, and what made him a damn good boxer, even with legs that didn't always cooperate. "He offered to assist me in writing the proposal. We met at my brother in law's boxing studio where he's taking lessons."

That seemed to throw him off. "Oh. He's...boxing?"

Adrian let himself smile, even as waves of fear and betrayal coursed through him. Noah was a professor. A *professor*? A fucking university professor with a *doctorate*. "My brother-in-law's place specializes in people who need accommodations. It's mostly ex-military like myself, but it works well for people like No—Dr. Avidan," he corrected, even if it killed him to do it, "who have balance issues and visual impairments. One of my strongest students is totally blind and I feel for anyone who goes up against him."

"Oh. You're an instructor there?" The guy seemed a little off kilter for the first time as he gazed down at Adrian's legs again, which gave Adrian a little wave of pleasure.

"Like I said, my brother-in-law is really good at what he does. Then again, I was a Marine for nearly a decade. It would take more than a few damaged nerves to take me down. Anyway, I should probably get this inside before I'm late."

"Right," Dr. Barnes said, his arrogance rising again. "You have class, of course. I wouldn't want to keep you."

NOAH CLOSED out his IM and sat back, scrubbing at his face. He was deliciously sore, just like he'd begged Adrian for in bed, and he loved it. It had been way too long since he'd been uncomfortable sitting in a chair, and knowing it was the man he was head-over-heels for who had given it to him made it even better.

Sabrina and Esther had both seen right through him and had been giving him endless shit, but he didn't much care. The semester was crawling to an end, Charlie had finally backed off, and even Lowe hadn't said much. He had classes that afternoon, then he would be spending the rest of the week finishing up writing his finals. Then there was a long stretch of vacation in front of him—one which he planned to spend as much time as he could between the sheets with a hot, muscular body wrapped around him, and a thick cock deep inside his...

His head snapped up when he heard familiar sounds. A soft clinking nose, and a dull thud he couldn't mistake. His heart raced just a little as his eyes fixed on his office door. Then, as if by his own will alone, Adrian appeared. He looked as gorgeous as he ever did, dressed in a tight Henley and form-fitting jeans. He was wearing his crutches which meant last night had taken a toll on him too, and he felt a momentary wash of guilt.

It was replaced with concern though, only seconds later, because Adrian didn't look pleased to see him. His face was pale, his cheeks mottled with deep color, and his mouth was drawn in a thin line as he crossed the threshold of the office door.

"You're a professor," he ground out. His hands on his crutch handles were so tense, his knuckles had gone yellow-white and Noah could make out the flecks of motorcycle grease staining them. "You're a fucking..." In the midst of Noah's utter confusion, Adrian stopped himself, turned, then swung the door shut with the tip of his crutch. It shut with a purposeful click, and then Adrian abandoned the crutches in favor of bracing his hands on the top of Noah's desk and leaning forward toward him. "You're. A fucking. Professor."

Noah blinked, pushing his chair back slightly. "Uh. Is this a joke or..."

"Does it fucking look like I'm joking, *Professor Avidan?*" Adrian hissed through clenched teeth.

Noah had never seen him like this before and a small spike of fear raced up his back. He gripped the arms of his chair and pushed to his feet. "Adrian, what are you freaking out about? You knew I worked here."

"You're not a student," was all Adrian said, his tone completely flat.

It took only a moment to hit him, really, because Noah's brain was a little slower than it used to be, but not by that much. His knees went weak and he sank back down as he felt all the blood drain from his face. "Oh my god," he whispered. "Oh my g-god, *no*."

Adrian licked his lips, then leaned back, groping for the guest chair behind him. He fell down with a heavy thud and looked at Noah with shattered eyes. "You're a professor."

"And you're a st-student," Noah countered. He shook his head, swallowing thickly. "You're...how the hell is that puh-p-possible? Your sister told me you w-worked here!"

Adrian's hand slapped on the desk, making Noah jump. "There's no fucking way she told you I was a professor! I work at a *garage*, I'm barely four years cognizant enough after the explosion to actually *get* a degree!"

"She did," Noah started to argue, but against his will, the memory came flooding back to him.

'I'm at the University.'

'Oh shit, Adrian too.'

What a fool he'd been. He hadn't been clear at all with her, and he knew he looked young, he knew people always assumed he was a student. He just didn't think... "This is all my f-fault," he said, his voice cracking. "I juh-j-just assumed, and we nuh-n-never...fuck, we n-never really talked about anything p-personal. I am such a f-fucking idiot." He covered his face and heard Adrian make a soft noise.

"It wasn't all you. At the end of the day, neither one of us really wanted to talk about whatever was stressing us out. I assumed you were...god, at worst a grad student. I didn't know. I wouldn't have ever..."

Noah dropped his hands and forced himself to look at Adrian. "P-please don't say that. Fuck, please d-don't..." His heart felt like it was being ripped out of his chest. He couldn't stand the thought of Adrian walking away, of all of this falling apart when he was finally feeling wanted, and needed, and happy.

Adrian swallowed thickly, looking just as wrecked as Noah felt. He scrubbed both hands over his face, then dragged them into his hair and let out a shuddering breath. "A bunch of professors were just fired for doing what we're doing."

Noah opened his mouth to argue, to say their situation was different, that it wasn't anything like this, but he forced himself to hold his tongue. Yes, most of the people who were fired were dating their own students—decades younger, using their privilege and power to entice impressionable young minds into entering something they were unprepared for. What Noah and Adrian had wasn't that. Noah had no influence over Adrian's future as a student. Adrian was two years older than he was, for fuck's sake, and they hadn't even met on campus.

And yet, the circumstances couldn't be changed. There was no grey area when it came to something like this.

Noah licked his lips and did everything in his power to keep his speech measured. "How did you figure it out?" Because god, how had he missed the signs? How much longer before he would have realized Adrian wasn't teaching there?

"I met a friend of yours," Adrian said, and his tone, if possible, sounded even more bitter. "Dr. Barnes."

Noah nearly choked on his own tongue. "Oh g-god. Charlie?"

Adrian blinked at him. "That's the asshole who was giving you shit after your break-up? The one who wouldn't stop asking you out?" He let out a bitter laugh and shook his head. "I really should have punched him." After a beat, taking a few deep breaths, Adrian looked up at him again. "Anna was helping me carry the model for my proposal. I have a meeting at three to give my presentation for the building upgrades. He was there in the lobby and offered to walk me up. He said he's been sitting in on the meetings in place of Dr. Agarwal." Adrian stopped abruptly and then gave another frustrated laugh. "Shit. *Shit*, he very obviously knows who I am and what we're doing."

Noah wanted to assure him that Charlie would never use his position to do anything like that, but he couldn't because he wasn't sure that was true. Charlie was arrogant and persistent, and Noah had a feeling he'd use whatever advantages he could to ensure Noah was single again.

"So, he confronted you?" Noah pressed.

Adrian shook his head. "Not directly, no. But he made it a point to use your title, *Dr.* Avidan. Asked if we were friends. I told him we met at Baum's where you were taking kickboxing and left it at that. I didn't give anything away, but he knows. Shit, Noah. He *knows.* I'm going to lose everything, aren't I? And you're going to get fired, and we'll both be..."

"Stop," Noah said quietly, holding up his hand. "No one has proof of anything right now. We've never used our university emails to speak with each other, and you're not in any of my classes so no one can do anything to prove I've used my power to influence your grades in any way. Charlie has his word and whatever stupid fucking vendetta he has because I won't go out with him."

"He was two words away from getting a fucking rabbit punch and being left unconscious on the floor," Adrian all-but growled.

It was inappropriate timing, but Noah felt a small twitch in his groin not only at the sound of Adrian's low voice, but at how protective he was still. Even after all this. But it was only a moment, because the weight of it all crashed down on him and he knew they couldn't carry on like this. Charlie would be watching him like a hawk, and it would only take one slip-up.

"What are we going to do?" Adrian asked softly.

Noah swallowed thickly. "I d-don't..."

"We have to end it," Adrian cut in, and he shook his head, looking gutted. "Noah, I can't lose this. I'm so fucking close and I've worked so fucking hard. And I couldn't live with myself if I ruined your entire career, either."

Noah wanted to beg him not to go there, to say he'd throw himself on the sword, to take the fall because the risk was worth it. But it wasn't just about him, and he couldn't afford to set his entire future ablaze for something so new and fragile.

"What year are you?" he asked, feeling like the world's worst person that he didn't even know.

"I've got one semester left," Adrian told him. "Then I graduate."

Noah licked his lips. "Okay. Okay so...that's just a few months."

Adrian blinked at him, his mouth working like he meant to say something, but no sound came out. Noah's heart was beating so rapidly, he could feel it in his fingertips, in his temples, in his throat. All he wanted in the world was to reach across the desk, pull Adrian into his arms, and hold him there until Adrian said he wanted this just as much. But there was something playing in the other man's eyes that said it wouldn't be that easy.

"Noah," he said softly, shaking his head.

Noah felt his heart threaten to crack. "Please," he whispered. "Please d-do not give up on this yet."

"I don't want to. Shit, Noah…" He pressed his hand over his face and let out a shaking breath. "How the hell can we do this? It might already be too late."

"It isn't," Noah said, mostly because he would do everything in his power to protect Adrian from retribution, and he would be taking care of this, doing damage control as quickly as he could. "Please j-just…don't make any rash d-decisions."

Adrian bit his lip, then glanced behind him. "Coming here was a mistake. Fuck, Noah. What if he sees me coming out of here? That's only going to confirm what he thinks he knows."

"He won't see you," Noah said firmly. "I'm going to head t-to his office and if he's there, I'll take him out and s-see how I can head this off. I'll send you an all c-clear, and we can meet later, okay? We can figure this out."

Adrian licked his lips, then finally—finally—gave a nod. "Okay."

It wasn't everything Noah needed to hear, but it wasn't nothing. It was a promise that they could try, that he wasn't about to lose the first good thing that had happened to him in a long, long time.

CHAPTER ELEVEN

True to his word, Noah managed to orchestrate Adrian's escape without incident. The text told him Dr. Barnes was out for the day—Noah confirmed he wasn't sitting in the proposal meetings anymore and had left campus. It didn't help Adrian feel any better, but he was able to make a hasty retreat without being noticed and further incriminating himself.

His head was still reeling from Barnes' reveal about Noah. He wanted to be angry, wanted to blame Noah for not telling him, but it was just as much his own fault for keeping tight-lipped on his life. And Noah had been protecting himself, too. He suffered just as much as Adrian had post-accident which had irrevocably changed his life, and he didn't blame the man for withholding personal details. They'd only been dating a few weeks as it was, and logically he shouldn't be hurting this much over something that was barely a blip on his own timeline.

And yet. And yet, the thought of never seeing Noah again, of ending this for good, felt like he was ripping his own heart out and setting it on fire. How was it possible that just hours before, he was inside Noah, wrapped around him, pushing into him and feeling more connected to a person than he ever had in his life? He'd been thinking that four letter word, his tongue curling toward the front of his teeth aching to say it as he held Noah's body against his. As Wes liked to brag to him, when you knew, you knew. And Adrian swore he knew.

But how was he going to reconcile this? How could they make it work? Yes, it was only a few months and if they had to hit the brakes, he could do that. He'd waited a lot longer for a lot less and Noah was worth it. But if they picked up where they left off the moment he graduated, it could arouse suspicion. This Charlie guy was clearly vindictive—there had been a manic, cruel glint in his eye when he revealed the truth about Noah. He was trying to hurt them both, which meant if they got together and Charlie noticed, they could be investigated. Noah's job would still be in jeopardy, even if Adrian got away with it.

He couldn't profess to care that much about a person and put them at risk like that. But the way Noah had begged him? It had taken every ounce of Adrian's self-restraint, and then some, to keep from not launching himself over the desk and pulling Noah into his arms.

Without really being aware of it, Adrian had his phone out and was dialing his sister. He'd already missed his first class and it was creeping toward his second, and he knew he wasn't going to make it. He was hard-pressed to care, really.

"Hey, don't you have class?" Anna said by way of answer.

"Where are you right now?" His chest was tight, and he started to feel far off, dissociation creeping up on him. His hands tingled and he gripped his phone hard enough to feel the bite against his palm.

"Uh, Wes and I were taking Maggie to get some pizza, why?"

Adrian gnawed on his lip, then checked his watch. It was barely noon, which meant he had three hours before his proposal and he couldn't miss that, but he wasn't going to be able to be productive with anything else that day. "Can I meet you? Things just went to shit, and I need…something."

"Of course," Anna said in a rush. "We're actually not far, we're going to that little place over on Sixth? You know, right next to the Children's Museum? Adrian, are you okay?"

"I'll be there," Adrian said, not answering her last question. "Bring

Lemon. See you." He shoved his phone into his pocket and limped his way toward the motorcycle parking.

Adrian pulled into the parking lot of the pizza place and saw his family in the window. Anna was in a booth next to Wes, and Maggie was across from them, bouncing a little on the seat. Adrian allowed himself a small smile, a second to forget all the other shit and just be grateful he still had this. It was the one thing that got him through recovery—knowing he had people he desperately loved to come home to. For a short while, Noah had started to feel like he was being lumped in with them—but now…

He let himself in and nodded to the hostess before heading for their table. Maggie gave an excited yell and shifted over to make room for her uncle as Adrian set his crutches under the table and eased himself down. He almost sobbed with relief when Lemon's head popped up from under the table, and she wedged herself between his legs as his hands buried in her coat. His head tipped forward and he felt like he could breathe for the first time in hours.

"God, you look like shit," Wes told him pointedly.

Maggie gave him an offended look. "Daddeeee, bad word!"

Wes rolled his eyes then dug a handful of coins out of his pocket. "Want to go play on the dance machine?"

She shrieked and leapt over her uncle, taking the coins and walking a few feet away to the busted but brightly lit Dance Dance Revolution machine the restaurant kept around for some reason. Adrian had a perfect view of her which let him both relax and turn some of his attention on his sister and brother-in-law.

"Spill," Anna told him.

Adrian worked his jaw, pulled Lemon a little higher up on his lap, then said, "Noah is a fucking professor. Did you know that?"

She blinked and Wes frowned.

"Uh," Wes said, "yeah? I mean, it was on his paperwork he filed at the gym. Why? Is that a problem for you?"

Adrian curled his hands into fists. "Well, it's against the University bylaws for one, which means he could get fired and I could get expelled."

"*Fuck*," Wes breathed out.

"Yeah but," Anna said slowly, twirling her straw around in her iced tea, "he's not *your* professor. He's not even in the same department."

"That doesn't matter," Adrian said miserably, then launched into the drama at the university over the past few weeks. He gave every detail, until his jaw hurt, and he never wanted to say another word again. His hands were shaking a little and he felt his anxiety rising. His PTSD would be at a hair-trigger after all this, and it made him nervous. "We're going to talk later," he finished up. "I don't know where or how but…" He trailed off and Lemon turned her head to lick the side of his hand.

"Our place," Anna said firmly. When Adrian gave her a look, she shook her head. "No, I'm serious. Have him take an Uber or something and Wes and I will take Maggie out to visit her bubbie. Wes' mom has been bugging us to have dinner with her anyway, so it's a good excuse. That way you two can talk it out and if some asshole is pulling a stakeout around Noah's building, he won't catch him leaving or you going in."

Adrian swallowed thickly, then nodded. "I'll send him the address, tell him to come right from work." He pulled out his phone but couldn't make his fingers move. He let out a small groan and dropped his forehead to the table for a moment, turned slightly so he could still see Maggie who was bouncing on the light-up floor. "I liked him. Fuck, I thought this was going so well. I don't know who I pissed off up there, but I'm starting to take all this a little personally."

Anna laughed quietly and reached over to pet his short hair. "Look, you're not losing anything, Adrian. And you have to let Noah make that call after you graduate. If he's willing to take the risk…"

"He'd resent me. If anything happened, he'd resent me." Lifting up, he groaned and shook his head. "Fuck, I need to beat the shit out of something."

"Come over right after your meeting and you can use my basement," Wes told him. "I'll take Lemon over there now, and you can work yourself exhausted and stay down there in the guest room. If it's a rough night—which we both know it will be—you can be as loud as you need and it won't wake up Maggie."

There were a lot of times Adrian was grateful that Wes understood what it was like after the military, after all that pain and trauma, and this was no exception. Wes had already had the downstairs, sound-proof room built by the time he started dating Anna, and he still used it from time to time. A lot less than Adrian would need it, probably, but if anything, it just proved that someday Adrian wouldn't feel like this as often as he did now.

"Thanks," he finally muttered.

Shortly after, the food arrived and, even though he didn't have an appetite, he got a drink and nibbled on the crusts Maggie didn't want. Before he knew it, it was time for him to go. Despite Noah telling him that Charlie had left the proposal panel, Adrian didn't feel entirely confident that he was safe.

"It'll be fine," Anna said, kissing his cheek as she walked him to his trike. "Just take a breath, get this part over with, then come over and work yourself tired. Okay?"

He leaned in and kissed her cheek, profoundly grateful for her as both a person and as a twin sister. "I love you."

"I know, dipshit," she said, and punched his arm.

The normalcy of it made a world of difference. He shoved her back, then stowed his crutches and got on the bike.

ADRIAN LOVED BEING RIGHT MOST of the time. But not always. Not right then.

"I'm sorry, Mr. Flores, but I'm afraid we're already going in another direction. I regret we weren't able to hear your proposal as it does seem a worthy cause, but there were a lot of those today." The woman speaking was someone Adrian didn't know, but the tone in her voice said that he didn't need to. Charlie had done his work there.

Adrian's jaw clenched as he nodded, and he wished to god he could put his fist through something right there. "I appreciate the consideration."

"Do you want to take your model with you?" she asked.

He let out a bitter laugh as he waved one crutch. "Unfortunately, I'm not able to get it down with me and carry these. So…feel free to just trash it. It's not worth anything to me anyway." Turning on his heel, he'd give anything right then to make a swift exit, but his legs wouldn't allow it. It felt like the universe was making a spectacle of him, mocking him now at every turn, reminding him that he'd survived the blast, but it would make living through it a painful reminder that he hadn't ever really escaped.

He was shaking by the time he made it to the trike, and he had just enough energy for one thing.

> Adrian: I need to cancel tonight. I'm not sure when I can see you again, but now isn't a great time. I'm sorry, but this really isn't going to work out for either of us. I'll contact you when I can.

It ripped him to shreds to hit send, but he had no choice. The avalanche had begun, and there was no telling what kind of devastation would be left after Charlie was done.

CHAPTER TWELVE

Noah stared at his phone, then at the door to his office which felt like the only barrier between him and the void that had become his life. He could count back the hours to where things had been good—damn near perfect—and he couldn't begin to describe the pain now blooming in his chest.

Not only had Charlie done this simply because he was too much of a weak coward to accept that someone didn't want him, but he'd done it so perfectly, Adrian was giving up without even trying. Noah wanted to cry but forced himself to keep the tears at bay. Instead, he picked up his office phone and dialed a number he probably shouldn't have.

"Well, well, well," Ryan's voice sounded on the other end.

Noah opened his mouth and tried to speak, but his voice was at a harsh whisper. He could feel his tongue sticking to the roof of his mouth, his stammer threatening to silence even the shortest words. "I," he started. "I nuh-n-nuh…"

"Noah?" Ryan's voice was flooded with worry. "Where are you?"

"M-my… *office*," he managed.

"I'll be there in fifteen. Do not fucking leave." The line went dead, and Noah let the phone fall back into its cradle. The sound was painful as he sat back, letting his head fall against the top of his seat.

Somehow, he'd managed to get through his classes that day, though his lectures had been tough when his mouth didn't want to obey his brain's commands. But it was the promise of seeing Adrian, of finding a way to make it work that had kept him going.

Now...

Now he didn't have that. He had a text telling him Adrian was out and wasn't going to give him a chance. His throat went hot and tight, and he breathed through it. He wanted to stand up and punch something, and he also wanted to curl up under his desk and cry himself to sleep. It would solve nothing, and the last thing he wanted was Charlie to find him like this, but he had no idea how to control these feelings.

By the time Ryan had betrayed him, things had gone so stale it had been more of a dull ache of resignation than any real devastation. He'd been hurt, yes, but not enough that he wasn't willing to be friends the moment Ryan suggested it. With Adrian, it was so much more. And maybe it was because it was new, but he didn't think that was the case. In truth, he was falling in love harder than he ever had, and it had been ripped from his fingers before he even had a chance to tell the other man how he felt.

Time seemed to reach a crawling pace and it felt like an eternity before he heard footsteps in the hall. Ryan entered, looking as dapper as he ever did in his work suit and perfectly combed hair. Ryan was the sort of man built for standing in front of a jury and making impassioned speeches to guarantee convictions. He'd been working for the state attorney's office since he passed the bar and had steadily worked his way up over the years.

He looked every part a man who belonged in that world and nowhere near someone like Noah whose life was falling apart. And yet, here he was, and Noah had to appreciate that regardless of their past, he could still trust this man.

Ryan took one look at his face and closed the door, locked it, then twisted the blinds shut. "Who am I murdering?"

Noah licked his lips, then said, "Adrian is a st-student."

Ryan blinked at him, then let out a quiet, "Shit," before crossing the room, grabbing the chair, and plunking it down directly next to Noah's and grabbing his hand. The touch immediately calmed him, and he felt his tongue start to unstick.

After a beat, Noah rubbed a hand down his face, breathed out, then said, "Charlie found out."

"Double shit."

Noah couldn't help his laugh after that one. "Yep. Quadruple shit, even. I d-don't know how he found out, but he cornered Adrian during his p-proposal meeting today and dropped the bomb. Adrian showed up here freaking out—naturally, of course. He thought I was a student. We were both so f-f-fucking stupid."

"Well," Ryan said slowly, his voice placating, "I am curious how the fuck you two have been inside each other and had no idea what your professions are, but I also know you can be a secretive dipshit, so it doesn't entirely surprise me."

"Thanks," Noah muttered dryly.

Ryan shook his head, giving Noah's fingers a gentle squeeze. "What did he say?"

"He said he c-can't risk dating me if it means losing his degree and me l-losing my job. I thought..." His voice broke and he cleared his throat. "I told him we c-could just hold off until he graduated and then...suh-see where we were at. He seemed like he was okay with it. I thought he was willing to accept a c-compromise, but he texted me a little while ago and ended it." Noah gestured to his phone and didn't stop Ryan when the other man reached for it and flicked the screen on.

Noah wasn't sure what it said about him as a person that Ryan still knew his password to get in. He watched as Ryan read through the most recent text, then sighed and looked up at him.

"Something happened."

"I just told you," Noah began, but Ryan shook his head and held up his hand.

"No, I mean between the time he left here and sent you this

message. Something happened. Trust me, Noah, he didn't walk away from you willingly. I kicked my own ass for years after we split up because I made a fucking terrible mistake and didn't realize what I was losing until I lost it."

"Ryan," Noah said softly, the confession hitting him right in the chest. He didn't love Ryan again, couldn't, but it still affected him all the same.

"I got over it and got one of the best friendships I could ever hope to have. I wouldn't trade that for the world," Ryan told him, stroking his thumb over Noah's knuckles. "But listen to me when I tell you that Adrian didn't send this lightly. Something else happened and you should find out what."

Noah licked his lips, then said, "He p-probably won't answer my calls."

"Well, he might answer mine," Ryan said, then pulled out his own phone. When Noah hesitated, Ryan waggled it at him. "The worst he can do is not pick up. And the best is, he will, and you'll get a chance to see if there's something to salvage. Only an idiot would let you go, Noah, and you need to know now if the guy is worth waiting for."

Noah knew his ex was right, and it was the promise of a maybe alone that had him reaching for the device to dial.

ADRIAN SWIPED his hand across his brow, his entire body aching, knuckles bruised and stinging from going at the bag without gloves, with every ounce of his pain and frustration. He'd gone to Wes and Anna's, only to find them gone which was a blessing in disguise. At first, he had craved human interaction, but he quickly realized the silence was exactly what he needed. He wouldn't have known what to say anyway, how to tell them that something that important—not only to him, but to other disabled students on campus—had been ripped from him simply because a guy had a rejection grudge.

Adrian briefly entertained the thought of tracking down Dr. Barnes and offering him a trade—never see Noah again in exchange for having his proposal heard. But it was a momentary, mad idea which only would have ended with Adrian putting his fist straight into the man's gut, over and over until he begged for mercy. Adrian didn't take this lightly, and it was by sheer will alone that he put his focus into beating the shit out of equipment than actual, human flesh.

The work-out had helped, though he would have preferred to go a few rounds with Cole or even Wes. Having a living opponent who could make him work for it was always better than a steady bag. But it was something at least. He limped over to the shelf to grab his water when he noticed his phone screen light up.

He prickled, momentarily terrified it might be Noah, and only afraid because he wasn't sure what he'd do. The only thing in the world he wanted right then was to hear his voice, to listen to his soothing tones assure him that it was going to be alright, that they'd somehow find a way to make it all work. It was also the last thing he wanted because if Dr. Barnes had already gone this far, there was no telling what he was forcing Noah to endure, and Adrian couldn't be responsible for anything more happening. His conscience couldn't take it.

Luckily, it wasn't Noah. It was an unknown number—probably someone from the gym and Adrian realized he wouldn't mind another student if Wes was trying to set him up with someone. He quickly swiped the screen to answer the call. "This is Adrian Flores."

There was a beat of silence, and Adrian swore in that moment he recognized the puff of air. He was confirmed correct when Noah's voice spoke quietly on the other end. "Please d-don't hang up."

Adrian licked his lips. "You can't do this, you can't call me. What if Dr. Barnes finds a way to…"

"I'm on Ryan's phone," Noah said swiftly.

The sound of Noah's ex-boyfriend's name on his lips, knowing that Ryan was giving Noah comfort over this, sent his head into an irrational jealous spin. His hand clenched at his side, the other on his phone, and he swore he felt the glass casing start to give. "Oh. Well,s I'm glad you two were able to reconnect and…"

"Don't," Noah snapped, and though it irritated Adrian, he knew he had no right to say something like that. "I called him after your text because I was thrown for a loop. When you left here, you said you were willing to try, and that was the only thing that got me through the day. Then I get this text and I…" His voice broke and Adrian hated himself so much for putting Noah through this. "Ryan convinced me to c-call you, said that there had to be m-more. Something from b-beyond this afternoon when you saw Charlie. So, will you tell me, p-please? I deserve to at least understand why you're giving me up so easily."

Adrian turned toward the wall, pressing his forehead against the cool brick hard enough it bit into his skin. He needed the pain to keep focused, to keep steady, because with Noah, it was too easy to let go and put himself into the caring hands of the other man. He turned and sank to the ground, letting out a whoosh of air when Lemon immediately laid across his lap. Her presence gave him the courage to find his words. "I," he started, then took a breath. "My proposal was rejected."

"Shit," Noah breathed out. "Shit, I'm so sorry. Was Charlie there?"

"No," Adrian said, and was unable to help his humorless laugh as he scratched his blunt nails along the side of Lemon's head. "No, but he sure as hell left his calling card. I was stopped by some woman before I could even get into the meeting room and she told me they decided to go in a different direction." He pressed his forehead to the back of his hand and let his body shudder with his fury and anguish. "The answers weren't supposed to come in until mid-January, so they didn't have a direction. But I know why it happened."

"I'm going to k-kill him. I'm going to rip his fuh-fucking throat out and use his skull as a goddamn c-cuh-candy dish," Noah said, his voice strange as he spoke through clenched teeth.

In spite of himself, and probably because Noah couldn't see him right then, he smiled. He couldn't help it. Noah was a spitfire—he was brave and intelligent and so strong, and Adrian wanted nothing more than to keep him close. "You won't kill him because it means jail and no more teaching your nerdy Greek shit."

Noah was silent a moment, then said, "Might be worth it if it means you won't get fucked over."

Adrian shook his head closing his eyes tight. "It wouldn't be. Trust me, you can't throw your life away over something so short—something without a guarantee." Saying the words gutted him, his heart twisting into a knot because it was the last thing he ever thought he'd be saying to this man, but he knew he couldn't live with Noah's future being ruined over this. Over him. He sure as shit wasn't worth it. He curled one arm around Lemon and pulled her close, feeling only slightly soothed when her tongue darted out and licked along the inside of his arm.

"Can I see you?" Noah asked. "An hour, that's it, and if we c-can't figure it out, if you really want to break up, I swear I'll never call you again."

Adrian felt his eyes get hot at the idea of never speaking to Noah again, and considering the depths of his feelings, no matter how new they were, he owed them that chance. Maybe there was a miracle solution. "I..." He leaned forward and buried herself in Lemon's fur.

"I can't let him win," Noah said after Adrian's hesitation. "I've been to hell and back and I'm not about to let some asshole like Charlie Barnes dictate my life. He doesn't have that right."

"I'm at my sister's place," Adrian said by way of answer, and he heard Noah's small sigh of relief. "Do you have a pen? I'd rather not text anything right now."

"Of course. I'm r-ready whenever you are, and I'll have Ryan drive me over." Noah said, his voice a little on the desperate side.

Adrian rattled off the address and felt a profound sense of relief knowing that whatever happened after this, at least he'd get a private moment with Noah. Even if it ended up being their last. "I'm in the basement, so I'll have the door unlocked so you can just come down. The door is through the kitchen, with a small hanging chalk board in the center of it."

"I'll be there. Please don't leave," Noah begged. Adrian bristled, but realized Noah had every right to doubt him.

"I won't bail on you," Adrian promised. "Just...hurry."

They ended the call and he managed to limp over to the sofa before collapsing down on his back. He pressed his hands over his face, taking several deep, shaking breaths as he tried to keep himself calm. Normally when he was like this, going a few rounds with the bag helped soothe his nerves, but right now it wasn't enough. Right now, all he wanted was Noah's arms around him, his soft mouth pressed to his, and the sound of his voice speaking quietly in his ear telling him it was going to be fine.

Three weeks. Three fucking weeks and his entire life had been rearranged by this man, and now he was expected to contemplate living without him.

CHAPTER THIRTEEN

He wanted to pretend like he hadn't spent the last twenty minutes listening to every creak and groan of the house above him, but that would have made him the worst liar. Adrian jumped at every tiny noise, ready to climb to his feet the moment Noah appeared, but time moved at a crawl and he was certain that a disaster had occurred and somehow Noah had decided it wasn't worth it after all.

And then the door creaked open. "Adrian? Are you down here?"

At the sound of his voice, knowing he was steps away, Adrian felt his entire body react. His heart raced, his hands began to sweat, even his dick swelled just a little at the anticipation that Noah was close enough to kiss, to touch, to make his again. He couldn't let himself go there, but he did push himself up to sit, dislodging his dog who hopped to the floor with a small huff.

"I'm on the sofa."

Noah made his way down, his steps careful when Adrian could finally see him, and he realized how dark it was. There was only the dim halogen light hanging above the makeshift ring, and it did little to help anyone navigate the space. Still, everything was so damn overwhelming, he couldn't bring himself to do more than stare as Noah walked over.

"Ryan's still upstairs, I hope that's okay?" Noah asked quietly. He lowered himself a cushion away from Adrian and wrung his hands together between his spread knees.

"It's totally fine. Anna and Wes are out dropping Maggie off with Wes' mom, and they knew you were coming," Adrian told him. "They'll be back in a bit."

Noah smiled just a little, and fuck, Adrian wanted to lean over and kiss him more than anything else in the world. After a beat of awkward silence, Noah let out a small sigh and shook his head. "I want to tell you that I can fix this, that I can make Charlie stop whatever he's doing and make it right again, but I don't know how. I've never been in this position before." He looked up at Adrian and the pain was obvious on his face.

Adrian clenched his hands into fists. He felt a tug on some of the scars on his arm, the strange numbness that hadn't gone away even after all this time. Part of him wished that scarring would have extended to his heart, protecting him from having to feel any of this. "I don't want you to ever resent me," he answered honestly. "If you and I keep this up and you get fired…"

"I know," Noah said through a breathy sigh, then made sure he was looking directly at Adrian when he said, "but I would never blame you. You didn't do this, Adrian. This is a vindictive asshole who has never been able to take no for an answer. I don't know what he thinks he'll accomplish with all this? Does he think I'm going to swoon and jump into his arms simply because I'm not allowed to openly date you?"

"He probably just wants you to suffer," Adrian told him softly.

Noah's face fell a little and Adrian again wanted to pummel the asshole for putting that look on Noah's face. How dare he? How fucking *dare* he? "I don't want to let him win."

Adrian dragged his lower lip between his teeth, then released it slowly and said, "I don't know how to let you go, Noah. I don't want to. I want to say that if I'd known the truth, I wouldn't have taken the risk, but the moment I saw you…"

"Me too," Noah said quietly. His hand twitched, then he seemed to throw caution to the wind as he reached over and pushed his fingers between Adrian's. "I love my job, Adrian. I dedicated years to my education, and I worked harder than I ever thought I could after my accident, so I didn't lose what I had. I've fought my boss every step of the way because he thinks people with disabilities shouldn't be allowed in higher education, and I refused to let him convince me I didn't belong. But the second I laid eyes on you, I knew you were different. I knew you were worth the risk."

Adrian felt his throat tighten a little as he rubbed his thumb over the edge of Noah's. "So, what do we do? I can't lose my degree this close to being finished. I can open the shop without it, but I've worked really hard and I need to prove I'm capable."

Noah squeezed his hand. "You don't need a piece of paper to tell you that you're capable of doing amazing things, Adrian. But I also know how you feel. Every step of my education gave me something important, something I carry with me every day, and I don't want you to lose that, either. I can't say I know what to do, but I can say I'm willing to do everything in my power to have both."

"And if we can't?" Adrian challenged, because there was no sense in pretending like it wasn't a strong possibility they'd be forced to choose.

"Then we make that decision when we have no other options left. Okay?" Noah begged, tugging a little on his hand. "I want to give this some time. We can cool off, see each other less. I'll take classes at the gym when you're not there. No more texting or calling."

"I don't want to cut you out of my life, even if it's only for a few months," Adrian admitted. "It sounds like hell."

"We'll figure it out. We can use your sister and brother-in-law as go-betweens. I have Ryan to help me," he said, and though hearing Ryan's name still made Adrian bristle, he was starting to soften toward the ex who had made an unexpected effort to help them. "Sixteen weeks of spring semester. Then you walk, and you're done, and we don't have to hide." Noah clenched his jaw, then said, "I don't owe Charlie anything. He is not entitled to any piece of me, any control over me. I won't let him take this."

Adrian couldn't stop himself then. He pulled and pulled until Noah was spread across his lap, until he had him pinned to the sofa and their mouths pushing and pulling in a desperate kiss. He nearly sobbed with relief, with knowing this wasn't the last kiss—not yet. Maybe not ever. Noah was damn determined, and Adrian was willing to match that with his own resolve to keep this man and his future alive.

When Adrian finally broke away, leaving Noah dazed under him, he cupped his boyfriend's cheek and rubbed a thumb over Noah's puffy bottom lip. "I want you to stay, but it's not a good idea. I'm really worked up right now and I don't think tonight's going to go easy on me."

Noah closed his hand around Adrian's wrist and held him firm, turning his face to nuzzle and kiss at his palm. "I'm so sorry. I wish there was something I could do. But look, we can plan a get-away during break, okay? I'm not teaching any of the winter courses, and I don't have to explain where I'm going, or why, or with whom, to anyone. We can find some vacation house somewhere and just take some time to be us."

Adrian closed his eyes, leaning in, and he nosed along Noah's soft cheek. "I would love that." It would be tricky. His stress would make sleep difficult, his mood unpredictable, and he was forced to constantly be aware of whether or not a place was accessible. His life post-military meant he could never just hop in the car and go, just throw caution to the wind and explore without a care. But the look on Noah's face, and the very idea of being able to be with him without prying eyes, meant everything.

"Let's do it," he murmured, then nuzzled their mouths together, smudging a kiss across Noah's lips. "Let me find somewhere, you pick the dates, and we'll make it work."

Noah's entire body relaxed a fraction and he brought both hands to Adrian's waist, holding him tight. "Thank you. Thank you for taking a chance on me."

Adrian looked at him, his eyes soft, his heart hurting but full of promise, and he couldn't help but smile. "I really didn't have a choice."

NOAH SHIFTED in the passenger seat of Ryan's car, a little uncomfortable still from the scene in the kitchen. Ryan was a shameless flirt, and Noah hadn't expected anything less, but to walk in finding Anna giggling and Ryan feeling up Wes' bicep in a way that was far more suggestive than innocent was a lot to take in.

Years ago—hell, even months ago—he might have been jealous. It was still a sore spot for him that he'd never been able to capture Ryan's attention like that, not even when they were together. But with Adrian, all of that fell by the wayside. It wasn't the flirting, it was the fact that Wes and Anna were married, and it was the fact that they were related to his boyfriend and Ryan was his ex.

"Okay, you two worked it out, why do you look like someone pissed in your cheerios?" Ryan demanded as he turned the corner toward Noah's apartment.

Noah sighed, dragging a hand down his face. "For one," he said, his voice tense now that he was no longer in Adrian's presence, "I have no idea how the fuck I'm going to deal with Charlie. The guy had Adrian's project tanked and I have no idea what other bullshit he's going to come up with. I would not put it past the guy to try and blackmail me."

Ryan's jaw twitched. "Feel free to remind him that your very protective best friend works for the state attorney's office and knows full well that blackmail is illegal."

"And then he'll feel free to remind me that I'm currently dating a student and will legally get fired for it," Noah pointed out.

Ryan scoffed. "He has no proof. He's trying to freak you out so you'll give in and be a miserable fuck like him. But he doesn't seem to understand you're too fucking amazing to ever let a shithead like that drag you down."

Noah felt a small wash of affection for his friend and managed a smile. "I appreciate it, but I also can't take the risk. I know you'd do anything to help me, but you're not exactly in the position to do that. And let's face it, it is against policy to be dating a student."

"It's not like you knew," Ryan pointed out. He bypassed Noah's apartment and turned down a second street which meant he wasn't heading to Noah's. He was heading to his own place down the freeway, and Noah didn't hate the idea. If Charlie had been staking out his apartment the other night, there was every chance he was watching him now.

"No, and that defense will work for the weeks that led up to finding out," Noah told him with a shrug. "But we can't get caught even speaking to each other in passing from now on."

Ryan gave him a pained look. "I get it. And I'm not advocating for you to break the rules here, babe. It's only a handful of weeks and then you're done. You won't have to worry about this shit again, and I know you can do that."

"I know I can too. I just…I don't trust Charlie. He's underhanded and devious and I think he's going to try to get everything out of this that he can." He leaned his head against the window, his sighted eye staring out at the blur of city lights as the sun started to set. "I'm afraid."

Ryan made a small noise but offered no assurances which Noah appreciated. Right now, there was no telling what Charlie would try next, and Noah couldn't drop his guard.

Ryan led the way into his condo, up two flights of stairs and at the very back of the hall. It was far more luxurious than the house they'd shared together—a testament to how far he'd come from the law-school, stressed out student Noah had tried to navigate a relationship with. The place was warm, heated wood floors, leather furniture, stainless steel and marble kitchen.

The first time Noah had seen it, he'd been seething with jealousy. He'd been trying to make ends meet on a part-time professor's salary living in a shitty studio and eating like a freshman in the dorms. But he'd made his choice—his parents had warned him about his choice in careers, told him there was no place to make money in the world of academics. He hadn't cared—still didn't, even if things weren't going his way.

He brushed past Ryan who was emptying his pockets into the bowl on the little stand by the door, and he collapsed on the plush sofa. Massaging his temples, he tried to regain a little bit of his control, even if the idea of Charlie and everything the guy was doing had threatened to turn everything upside down.

He didn't look up again until he heard Ryan clear his throat, and he realized his ex was standing on his blind side, holding out a bottle of beer. "You need this."

Noah snatched it from him, grateful Ryan had thought to open it, and he took a long drink. "Yeah. I really fucking do. And probably about six more."

Ryan laughed as he sat down on the opposite end of the sofa and kicked his now-bare feet up on the table. "I have plenty. Rhys was here last weekend from some trip to Portland and stocked me up on that hipster shit you like so much. There's a case in the fridge and one in the pantry."

"I knew I always liked your brother better than you," Noah said, taking another pull from the bottle.

"Thank god he was straight or you'd have left me a lot earlier," Ryan said with a wink. After a moment of silence, he said, "So what's number two?"

Noah blinked at him, frowning. "What?"

"In the car when I asked why it looked like someone had pissed in your cheerios, you said firstly. Which implies there was a second reason why you looked like you were in mourning in spite of winning your boyfriend back."

Noah sighed, pressing the side of the bottle to his temple. "It's nothing." Which was a lie, and Ryan saw right through it. He kicked out a leg and hit Noah's thigh with the ball of his foot until Noah swore and shoved him away. "Just…could you maybe not flirt with Adrian's family like that?"

Ryan's eyebrows flew up into his hairline. "Are you jealous?"

"Jesus, no," Noah spat, setting his beer down hard enough to make a little foam rise to the opening. "Trust me, I haven't given two shits about what you do in your personal time in years. But for fuck's sake, they're married and Adrian's family, and things are unstable as it is. I don't need Adrian to think my ex is some kind of homewrecker, okay?"

Ryan looked at him a long time, then burst into laughter, his head falling back. "Oh my god. Noah, I'm not…it was harmless flirting. I've known them for a damn long time and we just…have that sort of rela-tionship. And for the record, they both came onto me first. I was sitting like a good boy with my hands in my lap like I was at fucking temple, Wes touched my abs."

Noah choked on his own tongue a little. "He what?"

"He bet his wife that I had been keeping up with my ab-work, she bet against it, and he asked me if I could prove her wrong. Which duh, of course I can. So I lifted my shirt and he touched me. I might be an asshole—we both have come to terms with that, and I might not have done right by you with Max but…"

Noah winced at the sound of the guy's name, even if it had been a one-and-done thing. "Right."

Ryan leaned in, grabbing for his hand. "I've grown up a lot since then, okay? Nothing will ever happen there that will hurt anyone. The three of us were worried about you and Adrian and we were just trying to ease the tension. I'm not interested in fucking with anyone's life. I know first hand how awful that feels—and it was my own damn fault. I would never do that to someone else."

Noah immediately felt guilty and he turned his hand palm-up so they could link fingers. "I'm sorry. Shit, I keep punishing you for something I should be over."

Ryan shook his head as he squeezed Noah's hand. "You don't ever have to get over that."

"Yeah," Noah said, "I do. You and I are definitely better off as friends, and it wasn't a great way to figure that out, but you've been there for me when my own family couldn't be bothered to get on a fucking plane while I was recovering from losing an eye. You've made amends and I need to stop assuming you're going to fuck things up."

"I appreciate it," Ryan said, then grinned at him.

BY MIDNIGHT, Noah had finally exhausted himself enough he was fairly sure he could sleep. He'd turned down Ryan's offer of an all-night comfort cuddle in favor of the guest room and was just slipping between the sheets when his phone went off.

For a brief, stunned minute, he thought maybe Adrian had changed his mind and wanted to talk to him. Then he picked it up and swiped the screen and his heart sank down into his gut.

> Charlie: We should get coffee tomorrow.

Noah's hands started to shake, and he dropped the phone face-down on the duvet, afraid to touch it. In spite of it being all in text, he could hear the command in Charlie's words, the underlying threat of something else. It wasn't a request. He could ignore him—it was midnight after all, and he couldn't possibly be expected to answer every text.

His phone buzzed again.

> Charlie: It's in your best interest. I'll be at the Fluted Friar tomorrow around nine. Sleep well, see you then.

Noah's entire body tensed, his stomach twisting with nerves. He was up before he realized what he was doing and crossing over the warm wood floors to the closed bedroom door. He didn't knock, having seen Ryan in nearly every compromising position over their years as lovers and then friends, and walked right in. Luckily, Ryan was sitting up in his bed with his phone, glasses sitting low on his nose, and he looked up, not entirely startled to see Noah there.

"Change your mind?" he asked with a small grin.

Noah wordlessly held his phone out, trying to ignore the welling panic threatening to take him to his knees. He felt a sense of relief the moment the phone was out of his hands, like someone else was carrying his burden, if only for a moment. He took a few shuffling steps over, then lowered himself on the bed and his eye fixed down at his bare feet as he heard Ryan's sharp intake of breath.

"Is he fucking serious?"

Noah turned his head to look over. "Seems like it."

"You're not going," Ryan said, and he set the phone down. "You can't let him take advantage of you like this. The moment he thinks he has power over you..."

Noah swallowed, then shook his head. "If I pretend like he doesn't exist, like none of this is happening, there's no telling how far he'll take it. If I show up looking weak, he'll walk all over me. But if I show up and tell him that he has no power over me..."

"I don't like it," Ryan interrupted, reaching for Noah's hand. "I *really* don't fucking like this. You need to call Adrian."

Noah felt his heart clench and he shook his head. "Hell no. Ryan, he's barely willing to consider a relationship in the *future*. If I tell him this asshole is harassing me at midnight with vague threats, he's going to cut me off completely and tell me it's for my own good."

"Have you considered that maybe it is for your own good?" Ryan asked, his voice a little hesitant. When Noah's eyes narrowed, Ryan held up his hands in defense. "I want you to be happy. Fuck's sake, Noah, you're one of the most important people in my life and there's not a heaven nor an earth I wouldn't move to make that happen, but is this really worth all the trouble? You barely know this guy."

Noah didn't know how to explain it to him, how right it felt, how different. He wasn't a fool, he wasn't some young, inexperienced, barely-legal person trying to navigate his first relationship. He had enough experience to tell when something felt special, and Adrian was that. He was worth fighting for. He was worth all of this.

"I just need you to trust me," Noah said, and saw it in Ryan's eyes when he acquiesced. "I don't know exactly what I'm going to do with Charlie, but I'm not letting him hurt Adrian, and I will not let Adrian walk away. I can do this."

Ryan hesitated, then nodded and set Noah's phone down on his nightstand. "Get the fuck in my bed and lay down. And do not touch your phone, no matter how much you want to. I'm taking that over tonight and you're going to rest." When Noah's mouth fell open to protest, Ryan shook his head. "I'm not an idiot, I know you're not going to sleep, but you are going to lay here quietly with someone who loves you, and tomorrow you're going to face this moron down and tell him under no circumstances does he have power."

Noah felt a crushing wave of gratitude for his friend, but it was all too much after the events of the last twenty-four hours. So instead of expressing himself, he merely nodded, climbed under the covers, and let Ryan's arms fall around him. Ryan had been right—Noah was not sleeping—but at the very least, he'd get a few moments of peace.

CHAPTER FOURTEEN

A drian hit send on his final paper, waiting for the little ping to let him know the file had been accepted. He felt a moment of relief, then the crushing weight of the day hit him again, and he had to take several breaths to calm himself down. It was four in the morning, the sun wasn't close to up yet, but he hadn't been able to sleep more than twenty minutes at a stretch. He was plagued with nightmares—images from his past and images from his present coming together to form one gigantic, abstract monster threatening to suffocate him.

Eventually he gave up on trying, and spent the rest of the early morning hours finishing up his final assignments for the semester. All he had left then was to take his exams to end this term, and then finish his last sixteen weeks at school. Once that was done, he would walk the stage, take his diploma in hand, and start his life again.

All that stood between his uncertain present and a hopeful future was a handful of weeks.

He had always known taking on this new endeavor, finding a life outside of the military with a body he was no longer familiar with, would be one of his biggest challenges. He had anticipated meeting with resistance along the way—people who didn't understand him, people who were unwilling to allow him the space he needed to recover. Hell, even people who wouldn't understand that his new normal was something that would last forever. But he hadn't even begun to anticipate this.

He had always allowed himself a small glimmer of hope that he might meet someone and fall in love. Being gay in the Marines had been hell in itself, trying to keep quiet even when it was technically acceptable, and he knew he would never be allowed to be completely open. Then he'd been injured and disfigured, and he'd come home to find his best friend creating a life for all of them where they could just be themselves.

He hadn't been expecting to meet someone when Noah walked into his life, but his heart was open to it. He had just started dropping his walls and feeling like maybe there was something to look forward to when it all came crashing down. It was just his luck and if it hadn't been so fucking painful, he might have laughed.

All he could do now was comfort himself with the echo of Noah in his arms just hours before, and the determination in his lover's face that he wouldn't let one asshole get in their way. If Noah had been hesitant at all, if he hadn't shown with every ounce of him that he was willing to take risks, Adrian would have fled. But it was the look on Noah's face that set Adrian's own expression into one of grim determination, and with his stubborn nature, he would give Noah that extra push he needed to make this work.

He just wasn't sure he could take much more.

With a sigh, Adrian got to his feet, shuffling to the bathroom at a pace that frustrated him. The stress had taken its toll and he was pretty sure he'd be in his chair for most of the day, once he could get to it. He washed up, then grabbed his crutches and used the lift to reach the ground floor. He could hear sounds of the early morning, and he felt a moment of relief that Maggie was still with Wes' mom and Adrian wouldn't be expected to put on the face of happy uncle for a little while.

He found Anna and Wes in the kitchen talking quietly over coffee, Wes leaning on his walker which meant last night had been rough on him too for whatever reason. Anna got up from her stool to get a mug for Adrian's tea, then pointed firmly to the bar stool at the end of the breakfast bar.

"Wes got bagels this morning," she said, elbowing a paper bag toward him. "We figured you might be in need of some comfort food."

Adrian sighed but didn't deny it. He was normally strict about what he ate, especially in the mornings and especially when his muscles were weak, but right now he just wanted to wrap up in some carbs and let himself wallow.

"Did you hear from Noah last night?"

Adrian blinked at her, frowning. "You mean after he left?"

She exchanged a glance with her husband and Adrian immediately knew there was something they weren't tell him. "We just know it was tense when he left last night."

"I'm working it out," he told her, his eyes narrowed. "Though feel free to explain what I don't know yet."

Anna bit down on her bottom lip, slightly to the left which was one of her tells, and he was prepared to leap to his feet—damn his legs —and pin her to the counter until she gave away all her state secrets. "Ryan said there was some drama last night after they got back to his place," she finally said, clearly reading Adrian's mood.

Adrian felt his heart sink toward his stomach and his shaking fingers curled around the paper bag full of food he now couldn't even begin to stomach. "He didn't say anything." His voice came out flat, and he felt a momentary flash of irritation when he saw pity on his sister's face.

"He will," she said after a beat. "Ryan didn't give us any details, he just said that there was some drama last night and that Noah was taking care of it this morning."

As if the drama itself had been summoned, Adrian's phone pinged with an email and he reached for it, ignoring his sister's look. He saw the message was from the university online system and he swiped it open, his eyes registering the words before his brain caught up.

Flores, Adrian

Student ID: A289482

This is an automatic message to inform you that your account is currently disabled. A plagiarism investigation is pending on assignment number 0786. You will be contacted by a University Representative within 72 hours. If you do not hear from anyone by then, please call the number at the bottom of this email.

His ears buzzed, and when he looked up, he realized Anna and Wes were both trying to talk to him, but he couldn't hear over the white-noise in his head. The phone fell to the counter, and the clatter was the first real sound that penetrated his shock.

"...going on. You look like you're going to pass out. Do you need me to grab you a Xanax? Adrian, talk to me, please."

His eyes lifted to meet the worried gaze of his sister. "I think I know what the drama is now. And I have no idea how the fuck Noah's going to be able to fix it."

NOAH HAD NEVER BEEN sick in public. Even the drunkest most wild nights during his early university years, he'd never lost it. But reaching for the door handle outside of Fluted Friar, it was a close thing. It was five till nine and he could already see Charlie seated at the back of the café, a large cappuccino mug between his hands. He'd spotted Noah's hesitance and his smirk widened, which made the twisting and churning in Noah's stomach even worse.

But he wouldn't give this man the satisfaction. He would not be cowed, would not be coerced, would not be tortured in his own life simply because Charlie was a man with no scruples and no ability to accept that someone didn't want him. He straightened his shoulders, then pulled the door open and walked in.

Charlie made a sweeping gesture with his right hand toward the empty chair, and Noah took a few breaths as he crossed over in an attempt to keep his tongue from getting locked up. The last thing he wanted to do was let his brain injury dictate the way this conversation was going to go. He needed to be articulate, firm, and brave. The latter two could come easy, but the first…

"Did you want something to drink?" Charlie asked, much in the same tone as he would have asked at a staff meeting or casual lunch.

Noah almost balked at him, but instead shook his head. "M-my," he started, then forced himself to breathe again. "My friend and I had an early breakfast this morning."

"By friend, I'm assuming you don't mean Adrian Flores," Charlie said. Clearly he was ready to cut right to the heart of the matter.

"I mean Ryan," Noah said, deliberate and slow. "You remember him? My ex?"

"Right. The lawyer," Charlie said. There was a sneer in the words, but maybe just a flash of worry as he remembered Noah was not some nobody who couldn't find backup if he needed it.

"I was at his place last night. But I'm not going into detail, you're not here to make small talk," Noah pointed out.

Charlie laughed quietly, shaking his head before taking a sip of his drink. "No, and of course I don't want to torture your poor brain with having to get out too many words. I know how hard that is for you most days."

Noah clenched his hands into fists but forced himself to stay silent.

After a beat, Charlie sighed. "When Trevor was let go after he was found in Thirsty's grinding up on some junior Delta-Pi, I wasn't really surprised. Hell, I don't think any of us were."

Noah was, though, and Charlie knew it. Charlie's eyes lit up when he saw Noah's visible shock.

"I mean, he was always depraved. I had the misfortune of having an office that looked directly into his, and trust me, I saw how frequently he was visited by certain students. He was not…discerning in his tastes. I was waiting for something like this to happen." Charlie ran his ringer around the rim of his mug, then looked up at Noah. "You, on the other hand…"

Noah licked his lips, then said, "I am not involved in any situation that…"

"Don't patronize me," Charlie snapped. All the polite goodwill left his tone and it matched the coldness of his gaze. "You've been leading me on for years, Noah. Friendly, flirting, keeping me on the hook like there would be a time you were finally ready to get over your slut ex."

Noah bristled. "I have never, *ever* led you to believe we would date."

"You never told me no," Charlie said through clenched teeth. "It was always some excuse. Recovering from your break-up, recovering from your accident. Did you ever once make it clear you weren't into me?"

"Being friendly does not mean I was interested. I turned you down and regardless of the reason," Noah stopped himself when he felt his tongue starting to stick. "Regardless of the r-reason, *no* should have b-been enough."

Charlie looked murderous, then reached down to the side of his chair and came back up with a folder. "You made a fool out of me. And you did it with a relationship that is against university policy. Fucking some student will get you fired and him thrown out. We just watched it happen."

He's not some student, and we're not just fucking, sat on the tip of his tongue. But Ryan had coached him very carefully not to confirm nor deny a word. Charlie seemed to understand Noah wouldn't be defending himself or offering any explanation, so he flipped open his folder to reveal a stack of papers.

The first was a series of texts—screenshots and Noah immediately recognized them as his own.

"Where...?"

Charlie shrugged. "I know people too. I'm pretty sure sexting a student falls under the fraternization category. So, before you run your mouth about how I don't have proof, let me assure you, I do."

Noah felt panic creep up his spine, irrationally wanting to rip the papers away and light them on fire. The more logical side said that Charlie had nothing, that there was no way he could turn these in without revealing he had used illegal means to obtain them. His brain frantically searched for a time in the last few weeks where his phone had been out of his possession, but he came up blank.

"Not even going to ask me where I got them?" Charlie murmured.

Noah blinked at him. "Why don't you tell me what you want first? Clearly you have these and clearly you want to use them for something."

Charlie's grin widened, making him look twisted and ugly. Noah had thought he was attractive once, but he couldn't imagine finding him so now. "I'm taking your classes. You can keep Greek, obviously we don't have anyone who can fill that in. But you're taking a step down, you're removing your name for consideration for tenure. You'll be telling Lowe that he was right, that your disability has made you unfit for fulltime work and you'd like to pass your lecture classes on to me."

Noah blinked at him, and a stress-induced laugh ripped from his chest. "The *hell* I will. There's no way those texts are admissible evidence anywhere. Hacking is also illegal, you asshole."

Charlie shrugged, then flipped the pages of text over to reveal something that looked like an email. "You're not wrong, I didn't get those on the up-and-up, but I still have friends. And I know you care about Mr. Flores."

Noah's eye scanned the page and he wasn't entirely sure what he was reading. "Is that…"

"Proof of plagiarism?" Charlie asked with a shrug, then shut the folder. "It is. Like I said, I have friends too. And you might have me by the balls with the texts, but I have him by his entire future with this. I'm not sure he's going to feel very friendly toward you if you get him expelled and banned from any university worth a salt. Especially if it makes viral news that a former Marine cheated his way through college. Then the text messages might not be admissible in a hearing, but the public is a pretty decent jury in itself."

Noah felt his throat tighten, his stomach threatening to unleash what little he'd been able to stomach that morning. "And if I comply?" he said, his jaw aching from clenching his teeth. "I'm not an idiot,

Charlie. I know it doesn't end there. What the fuck do you even get out of this besides classes you don't even want to teach."

"Satisfaction," he said with a shrug. "I get satisfaction after being humiliated by some one-eyed gimp who can't even string together a full lecture without stuttering that I was right, that he *isn't* competent enough to hold down this job. That maybe it wasn't *you* who rejected *me*, after all."

Noah's entire face was burning with rage, shame, humiliation, and fear. He'd faced a lot of strange looks, a lot of pity, even discrimination from the higher ups when it came to his brain injury. But he'd never faced cruelty like this before. "And if I do this, you leave Adrian alone? You'll retract whatever the hell you did to his paper?"

Charlie sighed, circling the rim of his mug with his finger once more before finishing off the dredges. "You have to stop seeing him."

Noah let out a barking laugh. "You think I'm *seeing* him? He's a *student*, Charlie. Even if we had once entertained the idea of something more than friendship, the moment I learned the truth, it was over." It wasn't entirely a lie. What they had before all this was over. Now it was new, and secret, and dangerous. Now it became something wholly terrifying because Charlie was revealing the truth about who he was, and it was not good.

"I don't believe you," Charlie said after a beat.

Noah laughed again. "I don't care what you believe, Barnes."

Charlie reached for him suddenly, and Noah flinched back, making him laugh. "You're actually scared of me."

"I'm horrified and disgusted," Noah spat, pushing his chair back slightly. "Never in my life have I ever met someone as fragile and p-pathetic as you. So your ego was b-bruised because a bunch of assholes who don't see disabled people as people might think it's s-sad I rejected you? I thought about it, once, you know? I thought about s-saying yes, because you were n-nice, and you didn't seem to care that things were different after my accident. I have n-never really been much of a believer, but I think I might be one now, because God sure as shit saved me from something truly evil."

Charlie stared at him, eyes narrowed, cheeks pink. Then he tucked the folder away and shrugged. "You have forty-eight hours to submit your request to Lowe. Once that's done, your friend can finish his last semester here in peace."

Noah swallowed, then started to stand, but Charlie caught his wrist, fingers digging into his skin so hard his bones creaked.

"If you breathe a word to this to your little lawyer friend, if I find out you've been talking to anyone..."

Noah wrenched his hand away. "Someday, you'll regret this. It probably won't even be at my hand, either. You think you have power now, but you'll eventually fuck with the wrong person and you'll come to regret the person you are. I just hope I'm around to see it." With that, he turned and stormed out of the café.

CHAPTER FIFTEEN

Adrian paced a circle around the heavy bag, his fingers itching to do some damage to something other than an inanimate object. He wanted to go rounds with someone who could fight back, who matched him, who could take a hit. Or maybe he wanted to go rounds with the pompous piece of shit who decided to act out some rejection revenge fantasy on Adrian's boyfriend and make him cry—and bleed. A lot.

He couldn't do any of that. Anna and Wes had been trying for a second child and Anna wasn't fighting until she was sure she wasn't pregnant, Wes' legs were giving him a hard time that day, and Cole just wasn't ready. Adrian hadn't bothered getting to know anyone else at the gym enough, and he was far too worked up to trust himself.

He gripped the bag with a small groan, pressing his forehead against it, and tried to breathe. He could hear the faint jingle of Lemon's leash nearby, letting him know he could call her at any time, but he didn't want to be soothed. He wanted to work out his aggression.

Taking a step back, he held his fists up and gripped them tight enough to hurt, then loosened his fingers. His fist made contact just once before the door opened and he let out a growl of frustration. "This room is private use only."

"I know."

The voice wasn't exactly familiar, but for whatever reason, Adrian knew it anyway. He turned and saw a tall, broad man with a sweep of styled hair, sharp features, and soft eyes walking toward him. He was wearing a Baum's tank top and a pair of sweats, and he had tattered wraps curled around his hands and wrists.

"We haven't met properly," the guy said as he boldly approached the furious ex-Marine, "but I thought now was a good time."

Adrian took a step back toward the bag and used his left hand to keep himself steady as he sized the guy up. "Is that so?"

"I'm Ryan," he said, and held out his hand.

Adrian crushed his urge to take the guy's hand and tug him right into a punch, because frankly this guy hadn't done anything except make it easier for him to be with Noah. He swallowed back his unease and extended his own hand to shake. "No offense, but what the fuck are you doing here?"

"I work out here sometimes. Wes was a witness in one of my cases a few years back and we ended up hitting it off. I hooked him up with a lawyer that helped him out of that logo copyright suit, and he hooked me up with free passes for life."

Adrian licked his lips, a little frustrated with himself that he hadn't know about it, and a little frustrated that Noah's ex was so tightly knit with his own family and he hadn't been aware of it. "It's nice to meet you. Noah talks about you a lot."

Ryan's lips spread into a soft grin and Adrian hated how he could see why Noah had once been attracted to this guy. "I'm sure that's irritating, but there's nothing between us. There hasn't been for a long time."

"Since you fucked someone in your bed, right?" Adrian said a little meanly.

Ryan had the decency to wince. "Hitting below the belt, I see."

"Am I? It's the truth, right?" he pressed, panicking for a moment that maybe Noah had lied to him.

Ryan just shrugged. "Fair enough. But yeah, since I fucked up a relationship with one of the best people I have ever known, there hasn't been anything but friendship between us. But I do love him, and I wanted to come over here and tell you that I don't know exactly what happened this morning, but it isn't good, and he won't let me in."

Adrian let out a rush of air, leaning on the bag a little more as his head hung forward. "Fuck."

"That's about the sum of it," Ryan said. "I dropped him off at the café and he called an uber instead of letting me take him home. He won't answer his phone, and I know he said the two of you weren't risking calling each other so..."

Adrian swore again, curling his hands into fists and wondering if maybe he should break that rule right now. "That man had better pray to every god he's ever heard of that he never encounters me alone in an alley."

Ryan stared, then threw his head back and laughed. "I knew I liked you. Shit, I wanted to hate you, but your sister and brother-in-law talk so highly of you - and Noah was a goner from the moment he saw you going a round with Anna." He swiped the back of his hand across his brow. "So...what about me?"

Adrian frowned at him. "What about you?"

"I came here for a distraction. Actually," he corrected, shaking his head, "I came here in hopes that Noah had given up on whatever self-sacrificing bullshit hero's journey he decided to undertake and had come to see you, but that's obviously not the case. He won't answer my calls, and you can't call him, so why don't we go a few rounds?"

Adrian stared at him incredulously. "No."

"Why?" Ryan demanded, crossing his arms. "I know you're good, you can't possibly be afraid of me."

At that, a laugh burst from Adrian's chest in spite of how he was feeling inside. "I'm afraid I'm going to hurt you, and that Noah won't forgive me for it. I need someone who can keep up with me right now. I'm wound up beyond words and if I go head to head with someone, it's going to end ugly. With blood."

"I can take it," Ryan insisted. "If I can't, I'll tap out. But it's not like you have people lining up to relieve you of your stress, and we're both going to be going out of our minds until Noah calls." At that, he reached into his pocket and pulled out his phone. "Noah's number rings through no matter what. So, let's go for it until he ends this torture."

Adrian licked his lips. It was the worst idea in the world. He'd flatten this guy in two seconds and then he'd have to answer to Noah for all this bullshit and for maiming his friend. But there was also determination and fire in Ryan's eyes. There was fear, too, that Adrian felt keenly. Not of him, but of what Noah was getting himself involved in. His stomach twisted with it, wanting to be sick, and there was a creeping, ugly sensation at the base of his spine that told him tonight would not be kind when the lights were out and the place was silent.

But Ryan was offering him something, and he knew he couldn't turn him down.

"You signed a waiver, right? I'm going to be pissed if any sort of legal document shows up here after I kick your ass."

Ryan chuckled and nodded his head. "I've faced off with Anna. It only lasted like eighteen seconds, but trust me, I know what I'm getting into. And I have a feeling you know how to make it last. Probably why Noah likes you so much."

Adrian wanted to be offended, wanted to be annoyed, but instead he found himself actually liking this guy. He had always thought of Ryan as the asshole who had broken Noah's trust, but Ryan was making him think there was more to the guy. The situation seemed like a total shit-show, but at least he had something to distract him. Bending down, he picked up his gloves, then headed to the ring where his mouth guard was lying on the top of his bag. "Get ready," he ordered.

Ryan grinned wolfishly and slipped through the ropes. "Baby, I was born ready."

NOAH WAS SHAKING, his tongue refusing to move from behind his teeth. Everything in him had seized up the moment the meeting was over and he let himself out of Lowe's office. He would never forget the gleeful glow in the old fucker's eyes. The way he lit up like a fucking eighth-night Chanukkiah at the words, "You were right, I'm not fit to take on all these classes."

It was a miracle in itself that Noah managed to get the words out without stuttering, though honestly it wouldn't have hurt his case any if he hadn't managed to get a full sentence out. Lowe had been waiting for him to fall apart, and Noah had been determined to prove him wrong.

Now, Charlie had him by the balls. And worse, he had him by Adrian's future. There was no coming back from a plagiarism scandal. Maybe most of the public wouldn't care. Hell, he couldn't imagine people looking to have their bikes worked on and customized would give two shits if the owner had cheated on some paper, but maybe they would. Maybe it would destroy his future and his reputation before he even got started, and it would be Noah's fault.

Noah could do this, he could shoulder being demoted, going back to part time, giving up tenure. He wouldn't have to stay here forever. This wasn't the only university in the world. He could start over, he could find something. And he would do it with a clean conscience and a clean slate knowing he had protected the man he was falling in love with.

And Charlie…

He had to believe Charlie would get his. He was only grateful he had never given him a chance. Noah could only imagine what the man might have been capable of if Noah had been any closer to him.

Taking a few deep breaths, he felt his head give a little lurch and the threat of vertigo at the base of his skull. He just wanted to leave, to get the fuck out of there and finish his weekend before finals week was upon him. He'd finish that off, he'd send his students into their spring semester, and he'd find a way to explain what he'd done.

Noah: It's done.

He didn't think Charlie would reply, and he got a little satisfaction knowing there was at least some digital trail to prove that he had a tie to Charlie in case this went pear shaped. Or well, more pear shaped than it already was. He slipped his phone into his pocket, knowing full well that Ryan was probably going out of his mind with worry, and knowing Adrian was probably ready to murder Charlie for what he'd done. There was no way Adrian hadn't connected the dots when he got the alert that his paper was being investigated, and hopefully he wouldn't question it when he was relieved of suspicion.

His phone buzzed and he had a sinking feeling it was no one he wanted to talk to.

> Charlie: Good boy.

Noah wanted to put his fist through the wall. Instead, he turned his phone on silent and made his way back to his apartment. He had a mound of research waiting for him, and several research papers to mark before the term was over, and his final to finish writing. But all he really wanted more than anything in the world was to drink himself into oblivion.

ADRIAN'S HANDS STILLED, sticky from the salve he was rubbing into his knuckles, and then he reached for his phone which had just pinged him with an email alert. The last email he'd gotten was letting him know he was under investigation, so it was no surprise his anxiety shot up.

Lemon seemed to notice it too, pressing herself against his legs as he swiped the screen on and pulled up the notification.

Flores, Adrian
  Student ID: A289482

145

This email is in regard to case 0786. Turnit would like to issue an apology for a technical error in your paper's submission. Your account suspension has been lifted and your paper has been successfully submitted to your professor. We appreciate your patience regarding this matter, and hope you have an excellent end to your school term.

Adrian felt a wash of relief so intense he was almost sick from it. A mistake. It had been a mistake. It hadn't been...

His eyes lifted to see Ryan who was icing a bruise on his jaw, and he realized that no, it hadn't been a mistake. "He did something," Adrian said quietly. "I don't know what, but he did something." Licking his lips out of nerves, he dug one of his hands into Lemon's coat, then met Ryan's gaze as he explained the events of the morning. "The case was closed, labeled as a technical mistake, but it isn't, is it? This has something to do with Charlie, and something Noah gave him."

Ryan stood up without a word and walked to where his phone was sitting, face-down so neither of them would keep searching for messages. By the slump in his shoulders, Adrian could tell it was still devoid of any word from Noah. "I'm going to go over there in a bit if he doesn't get back to me. Anything that asshole wants from him can't be good. And Noah seems to think he can solve this for the both of you. He doesn't get that dudes like this will keep going until they've got everyone backed in a corner."

"Charlie doesn't know who he's fucking with," Adrian said in a low voice.

Ryan gave him a careful look. "I should tell you right now I'm a prosecutor with the State Attorney's office, so...I can't officially condone any course of action in retaliation."

Adrian chuckled. "Trust me, there won't be a trail. He thinks he's got the upper hand because he knows an undergrad with basic hacking skills. This will not end well for him."

"I should talk to Noah first," Ryan said. "And seriously, don't tell me anything, okay?"

"I just...how can you let this happen?" Adrian asked, and frustration welled in him. "Blackmail is *illegal*." His free hand curled into a fist, his other holding Lemon tight against his legs.

Ryan hung his head. "Noah thinks if I use any of my contacts or influence, the both of you will be exposed. And whether or not Charlie goes down, he'll take you both with him."

"It'll be worth it. For me, it'll be worth it," Adrian said. "I can tell them it was my fault, that I lied and said I was a teacher."

Ryan shook his head gently. "If Noah went this far—if Noah gave him anything at all—it was because that bastard had something that could hurt you. It's the only way he would give in. He wouldn't do it to protect himself, but you..."

Adrian's heart twisted, and he felt a rush of so many emotions at once he was dizzy with them. He wanted to run, he wanted to pummel Barnes until he barely resembled a human. He wanted to take Noah into his arms and hold him until this was over. Instead he passed a hand down his face and sighed out a heavy breath. "So, what do we do?"

"I don't know," Ryan admitted. "I'm going to talk to him, but I don't know how much I'll be able to get out of him. For now, just... just get through it. Finals, right? Go take those, do your best, don't make a scene. Trust me, men like Charles Barnes don't get away with shit like this for long. He'll make a misstep and when he does..."

"*I'll* be there to make him pay for it," Adrian said darkly, and he meant every word of that.

NOAH WAS JUST drunk enough to forget he wasn't supposed to answer his phone or answer his door. So, when there was a soft knock and familiar voice calling out his name, he sauntered over with his whiskey in his hand and swung it open.

Ryan was there, looking all kinds of hot and pissed off, and Noah couldn't help his grin. "Well, well, *well*. Look what the dog-walker dragged in."

Ryan leaned in, sniffed the air, then pulled back with a sigh. "It is three in the afternoon. What the fuck are you doing?"

"Celebrating," he said, waving his drink. He stumbled a little, his shin catching the coffee table because the edge was on his blind side. He tripped forward, turning at the last second to land on the cushions and he kicked his injured leg up. "Did you know that not being able to see out of this fucking eye *sucks*?"

Ryan turned to him after shutting the door, his face drawn and worried. Noah knew why. Of course he knew why. He was supposed to just take care of the Charlie thing and move on and tell Ryan it was all fine. Instead he'd given up most of his job, would have to be living on his savings for the rest of forever, and he was probably going to lose his boyfriend along with everything else. That was sad. Ryan should feel *sad* about it.

"I want to take my eye out," Noah said suddenly, the pressure of the prosthetic making itself known. He reached for his face, but Ryan caught his wrist and pulled his hand down.

"God knows where the fuck you've been today," he chastised, setting Noah's hand flat on his thigh. "You'll get an infection and that's the last thing you want."

Noah pulled a face, feeling a fantastic pout coming on. "You know you want to see it, Ry." It wasn't a lie. Ryan always wanted to see it. The grotesque left-overs of the accident, of having his entire world changed by one stupid fucking driver who ran a stop-sign. Everyone wanted to see it. "You're always trying to sneak a peek."

Ryan flushed and shook his head. "Noah. What happened today?"

"I'm not supposed to tell," he said, giving an indignant sniff. "I can't tell *you*, anyway."

"Yes, you can," Ryan said.

Noah reached out, grabbing Ryan's wrist, squeezing as though somehow the pressure of his fingers would make him understand. "I…" He narrowed his gaze at a blooming bruise on Ryan's jaw. "What the hell happened to you?"

Ryan frowned, then reached up and touched his face. "Your boyfriend has a pretty amazing right hook."

148

Noah sat up straight, abandoning his glass to the floor and paid no mind to the spread of amber liquid soaking into the carpet. "You saw Adrian? God, did he look hot? He is so *hot*."

Ryan chuckled and pushed Noah back to the cushions. "Yes, I saw him. We were worried and waiting for you to call, so we went a few rounds in the ring. He kicked my ass, just like he warned me he was going to do. Also, he's fucking head over heels for you, Noah, so you need to tell me what's going on."

Noah dragged both hands down his face with a groan, then rubbed hard at his blind socket. "Charlie happened. That fucking scum of the earth *shai-getz*." He rubbed his face again, then let his head fall back. "I had to quit three classes."

"What?" Ryan asked, loud enough to draw Noah's gaze. "You *what?*"

Noah shrugged. "He...fucked up. He fucked it all up. Hurt Adrian, fucked up his paper, tried to..."

"He told me about the plagiarism investigation."

Noah curled his hands into fists, and he felt some of his anger take the edge off his inebriation. That was the last thing he wanted right then. "He said I had to quit. He had screen caps of our texts, Ryan." He closed his eyes. "M'so drunk. So drunk. I'm not stuttering. I should be drunk all the time. Look ma, no stutter!" He threw up his hands without opening his eyes, and he felt Ryan take his wrists again.

"No one who cares about you minds the stutter," Ryan said softly. "Tell me what else."

Noah sighed, feeling exhausted all of a sudden, and he turned his head to look at Ryan properly. "He told me he'd go public with everything, ruin Adrian's chances at starting a business if I didn't give him my classes. I'm keeping Greek, but that's it. He made me tell Dr. Lowe that he was right, that I was unfit to be a fulltime teacher. Made me humiliate myself to make up for him feeling humiliated because the *disabled* guy rejected him."

Ryan made a growling noise in the back of his throat and released Noah's wrists. "Noah..."

"Don't," Noah said, waving his hand. "It's done. It's just...done. So,

I'll just…teach my Greek and Adrian will graduate and that's…it." His eyes started to close. He didn't like the dark. Sometimes he was terrified he'd wake up from sleep and suddenly the rest of his vision would be gone. But he was so, so tired.

He felt a hand on his face, then Ryan eased him down to the pillows and put his feet up. "This isn't over. He's not going to stop with just this, Noah."

Noah rolled onto his side and groped until Ryan's hand found his. "I think I'm in love with Adrian and I just…I can't lose him. I can do this for him. I don't care about the fucking university. I don't care if I had to prove Lowe right. He was never going to believe in me anyway."

Ryan pushed Noah's hair back from his forehead. "I'm not going to let him do this to you, Noah."

Noah shrugged. "S'long as Adrian's okay…" He felt sleep tugging at him, and he couldn't find a good reason to resist it.

CHAPTER SIXTEEN

drian felt like he was about to lose it completely. He hadn't slept more than a couple of hours a night in eleven days, hadn't heard a word from Noah or Ryan, hadn't seen a glimpse of them, and neither Wes nor his sister seemed to know anything. He'd spent more days in the last week and a half taking his emergency Xanax and sitting in the corner of his closet with Lemon than he had in years.

He managed to scrape by on his finals, his professors posting his final grades of low Bs and high Cs for the last exam. It wasn't the best semester, but he felt it was a little bit of a triumph considering how it ended. His proposal still went ignored, but his papers had all been accepted without incident. He'd seen Charlie Barnes only once, and it had taken every ounce of his self-restraint not to cross the courtyard and lay the guy out. He hadn't seen Adrian then, but he walked with the same arrogance, the same smirk, saying hi to students he'd clearly fooled into thinking he was a good guy.

Adrian wanted to make him suffer, make him feel every moment of pain he'd felt since all this had fallen on his shoulders. He didn't know what was happening now, and he had no idea what the future held for him and Noah. Maybe this was it. Maybe the silence was

Noah's way of saying he was willing to pay the price for Adrian's career as a student, but that was all he was willing to give.

His heart was aching, and he wanted to curl up in his bed and just not get out again.

Still, he couldn't let himself do it. He was better than that, braver than that. He'd survived his body being shredded and burned, survived months in the hot desert, on little food, little water, and the threat of capture. He could survive a little heartbreak.

He reminded himself of that while he was waiting for Anna to drop off Maggie. Anna was officially pregnant now, only a few weeks, but she was over the moon about it and wanted to celebrate with Wes. Adrian agreed to take his niece for the day, heading up north to the aquarium, then to a movie, then to grab food before heading back down. He honestly needed the day more than anything. Sitting still and thinking about Noah was doing him no good.

"Tiyooooo!"

Adrian laughed as he opened his door and the small whirlwind breezed past him. Her dark hair was tied down her back in two plaits, and she was wearing space-themed leggings and a thick, furry sweater that made her look like half a marshmallow. She grinned at him, then launched herself at Lemon who hadn't been strapped into her vest and put to work just yet.

Anna came up a moment later, looking a little green around the edges. "Sorry," she said, leaning in to kiss Adrian's cheek. "It's a little early for morning sickness but my body decided to ignore that memo."

Adrian's brows furrowed. "Shit. Do you need anything?"

She waved her hand at him. "No. Trust me, it's fine. Wes is getting me a frozen lemonade while I'm dropping off the monster, then we're going to have a chill day. Just don't stuff her full of sugar before you get back. I cannot handle that right now."

Normally Adrian would have tormented her with the possibility of dropping off a slightly sugar-manic toddler, but he could see how exhausted she was, and he really wasn't in the mood for joking. "Don't worry, she'll eat at least three green things today that are not made out of corn syrup."

"Thank you. Maggie, *mahal*, come give me a hug!"

Maggie jumped up and threw herself into her mother's arms. "Bye mama."

"Be good for your uncle, you hear me?" she ordered. "No misbehaving."

"Kay!" She rushed back to the dog and Adrian gave her a smile before showing his sister to the door.

"And you," Anna said, taking his arm, "cheer up."

Adrian sighed. "I'm getting there. I promise. I just wish…"

"I know," she said softly. "And I promise if he shows up, if he calls, anything, I will let you know." She gave him a kiss on the cheek, then headed out.

When he closed the door, he affected an expression far happier than he felt, clapped his hands, then turned to his niece. "Ready to go pet some stingrays?"

Maggie shot to her feet with a squeal. "Yes!"

TWO HOURS and twenty minutes later, one irritated toddler, one dog anxious to relieve himself, and one ex-Marine on the cusp of hangry arrived at the aquarium parking lot. Adrian pulled up to the disabled parking spot near the front, then fetched his manual chair out of the back so he'd be able to keep up with Maggie's pace. He was oddly grateful for Wes' own disability, which had taught Maggie early on the essentials of wheelchair etiquette and how not to run off from her guardian.

She didn't think twice about it, either, just grabbed Lemon's leash to keep the dog near where Adrian was wheeling himself. It wasn't his choice method, but the stress of the last two weeks had taken a toll on his body as well as his emotions and his mind, and today was gearing up to be just as long as the others.

"Okay, I'm going to buy tickets, so you take Lemon right there," he pointed five feet away to a tree sitting in a patch of half-grown grass, "and let her go potty." He kept one eye on her as he wheeled up to the lower window and presented his card.

The woman gave him *The Look*, the one full of pity and confusion, and when her eyes flickered over to Lemon, he thought she was about to protest the dog's entry. Then she seemed to notice the vest, and the bold black letters reading **Service Animal**, and she sighed, swiping his card and presenting the tickets.

"Do we pay here for the stingray feeding?" he asked as Maggie skipped over with Lemon close at her heels.

"They have a booth inside," the woman said. "Do you need an escort?"

Adrian scowled. "No, thanks. We've got this." He held the door for Maggie, then gave the woman a look before pushing himself through. His irritation melted away the moment they entered the lobby. It was vast, a domed ceiling, each wall covered in aquarium glass with schools of brightly colored fish swimming. Maggie was just as entranced, her mouth hanging half-open, stepping close to Adrian's leg.

"I wanna...I wanna swim wiff the fish," she told him.

He laughed and tugged on the end of her braid. "I don't think so. We're going to look, and maybe even pet some of the creatures, but there is absolutely no climbing into any water. Am I clear?"

She pouted. "But..."

"Magdalena," he scolded.

She sighed and flopped her arms down, head lolling back on her shoulders. "Fine," she groaned. "You never...let me haff some fun!"

"Yes, I'm an absolute tyrant. Now, let's go see the sharks first, and then we can check the stingray feeding schedule, okay?"

That immediately tore her out of her mood, and it was all he could do to keep up with her fast pace.

THE AQUARIUM HAD A LOW TURN-OUT, being the middle of the morning on a Wednesday, which was a blessing in itself. There were small children running around, but the volume was quiet, and Maggie was more interested in looking and making up stories about fish families to tell Lemon than she was trying to run off.

Still, looking after a four-year-old was exhausting, and when they made it into the children's play room with crafts and toys, Adrian sagged back in the chair, grateful for the reprieve. He set Lemon down near his left wheel and waved Maggie on to go run through some of the interactive ceiling lights that made it look like she was chasing off schools of fish. He took a few pictures for Anna and Wes, and as he was putting his phone away, he heard a soft voice speak behind him.

"*Adrian.*" It was a near whisper, but he would have known it anywhere. His heart was hammering against his ribs as he took his wheel and shifted to see Noah standing there.

He looked almost terrified, thinner if that was at all possible, and pale. He had his arms hugging his middle, his tight jeans looking delicious, a sweater so large it hung off one shoulder. His hair was brushed but unstyled, and he looked like he hadn't slept in days.

"What are you doing here?" Adrian asked, his voice far more gruff than he intended.

Noah flinched. "My brother is in town. He wanted to go, but he fucked off with his girlfriend." He let out a sigh, letting his arms flop to the sides, then he curled his hands into fists. "You uh…you've got Maggie."

Adrian gestured toward the middle of the floor where Maggie was lining up stuffed fish in a row. "Yeah. Anna's pregnant, she needed a day off, so I volunteered." His head was spinning, having Noah close enough to touch but without any idea if he was allowed to reach out for him. His hands burned, his body aching to feel Noah pressed up against him.

Clearing his throat, Noah shuffled a few steps closer. "Are you okay?"

Adrian frowned. "Considering the circumstances," he started, but then realized what Noah was talking about. He gave the wheel a pat. "I had no idea how big this place was going to be, and I can't run after her fast enough on my crutches."

"I get it," Noah said softly. "Fuck. It's so g-good to see you." His voice cracked at the end, his stammer making a quick appearance.

"You haven't called," Adrian said.

Noah's gaze flickered away for a second. "We agreed it was better if I…I wasn't sure if I should…" He cleared his throat. "I haven't seen Ryan much, and I was afraid Charlie was watching the gym."

Adrian felt that burning hot anger in his chest again, furious that this pompous, piece of shit man could come between them like this. "I miss you," he admitted. He decided his pride could take the hit, even if Noah decided now was a good time to end it for good. "I fucking miss you, and I've been worried out of my mind."

Noah bit his lip, both eyes going bright with tears, and he had to look away. "I…me too. So much. This has been one of the worst weeks of my life and that's saying something."

Adrian couldn't help his laugh. "Yeah, I know exactly what you mean. I wasn't sure if you were just done, if you couldn't take the pressure or…"

"No," Noah interrupted, closing the distance between them. He dropped to his knees beside the chair and finally, finally, took Adrian's hand. "I just got him off my back, but Ryan pointed out that guys like him never stop at the first thing. There's always more, and I didn't want to give him another reason to target you."

Adrian turned his hand so their palms pressed together, and he tugged Noah as close as he could get with the metal wheel between them. "You promised me time away. I need that. If I'm going to survive barely seeing you over the next sixteen weeks, you have to give me something."

Noah's eyes looked bright again, but this time it wasn't with pain. "You still want that?"

"Fuck yes I do," Adrian said. "Talk to Ryan. We can figure it out through him. Wes' family has some private property up north—it's gated, right on the edge of a lake. No one can get to it without a code. I don't care who the fuck that asshole thinks he knows, he can't get in there. I'll talk to Wes when I drop off Mags and see what we can do."

"That would be," Noah said, but fell quiet when a small figure popped up on Adrian's other side. "Hi there," he told her.

Maggie cocked her head to the side. "You haff pretty eyes."

Noah looked startled. "Oh. Thank you."

Right then, Lemon lifted from her place on the floor and walked into Noah's side, putting her head against his thigh. He laughed and scrubbed her ears. "She likes you," Maggie pointed out.

Noah gave the dog a small, one-armed hug. "I like her too."

She nodded, satisfied by his answer. "I wanna feed the fishies, tiyo. Can we? Can weeeee?"

Adrian laughed and pulled his hand from Noah's. "I promised a stingray feeding."

Noah smiled softly. "Would you mind some company? I think my brother and his girlfriend are making out in some corner somewhere. I have no doubt they're going to be arrested for indecent exposure and I'll be on my own for a ride home."

Adrian chuckled. "I have room in my car." They both sobered quickly when they realized that would be playing with fire, but Adrian refused to retract the statement. They were two and a half hours away, in another city. They could have this. They were allowed this time together. "Come on, smelly shrimp is all on me."

NOAH WAS STILL REELING from seeing Adrian at the aquarium, sitting there in his wheelchair watching his niece dancing around to motion lights. He wasn't sure if the universe hated him or loved him at that moment, but he'd gotten to brush his lips along Adrian's, to feel Adrian's fingers brush along his cheeks before moving to the next room, and Noah considered that a small token of reprieve.

Part of him wanted to run away. Charlie had instilled a paranoia so intense, so powerful, he felt compelled to look over his shoulder at every turn like maybe he was being followed. He had refused Charlie's demand that he never see Adrian again, but only under the pretense that he wasn't seeing him in the first place. There was no telling what Charlie could get him to do if he was found out.

But, he reminded himself, they were two hours and a full city away from home. If Charlie was having him followed, Noah would take drastic action because he might be willing to give up work and give him his freedom under the bastard's watchful eye on campus, but not here. He would take sanctuary wherever he could get it.

A touch at his wrist startled him, and he saw Adrian looking up at him with a small smile. "The stingray feeding isn't for another hour. Want to hit up the café? I think Mags is getting restless."

Noah glanced over at the four-year-old who was pressing her face right up against where an octopus was stuck to its tank and he smiled. "Yeah. Before she decides to make her own sushi."

Adrian led the way to the little Coral Reef Café and Noah was pleased to note it was nearly empty. Adrian gestured to a collection of tables near the play area, then gave Maggie a pat on her back. "Go on and Mr. Avidan and I will get lunch."

"I want peanut butter!" she cried, then ran off to the little plastic slide shaped like a whale's back.

Adrian rolled his eyes and wheeled to the counter where a bored teen was tapping away on her phone. When Adrian cleared his throat, she looked up, then down, and blushed. "Sorry, sir," she said.

Adrian shook his head and gestured for Noah to come up. "Whatever you want, it's on me."

Noah wanted to protest, but he didn't want to make a scene, so he ordered the first salad he could find and went to snag a couple of water bottles from the cooler. Adrian paid for everything, then they moved to a table where he parked his wheelchair and moved to sit next to Noah in the hard plastic chairs, settling Lemon at his feet.

After some hesitation, their hands rested on the table top and linked together. "I'm still in shock you're here," Noah confessed. He rubbed his thumb along a callous on the side of Adrian's finger. "I was trying to figure out a way to get in touch with you, but I just…it was so…"

"What did he do?" Adrian asked quietly.

Noah felt his cheeks heat up and prickle with a little panic. He recalled Charlie's threat clearly which was exactly why he'd kept his mouth shut after his drunken rambling the afternoon Ryan had found him halfway into a bottle of Jack. Once he'd sobered up, he'd begged Ryan to say nothing, and, though it seemed to kill his friend to do it, he agreed.

"Nothing big," Noah said eventually.

Adrian scoffed, shaking his head. "Bullshit, Noah. He was trying to have me thrown out of school for plagiarism. There's no way he would have backed off unless you gave him something he really wanted."

Noah bowed his head and clenched his teeth together. "He wanted me to…" Licking his lips, he looked up and met Adrian's gaze. "Promise me you won't try to do anything about this, okay? Because trust me, what he was asking for, I was happy to give him if it meant getting you off the hook. And it's already done."

Adrian's hand tightened on his, and after an agonizing moment of silence, he nodded. "Fine."

Noah swallowed and glanced over to where Maggie was playing. "He wanted my pride."

Adrian's fingers twitched against his, then he tugged on Noah until the other man glanced over. "What the hell does that mean?"

Dragging his free hand down his face, Noah let out a ragged sigh. "He wanted me to tell my boss that he was right, that I wasn't competent enough to teach all those classes, and I had to relinquish everything but my Greek classes to him. He agreed to back off if I made a production out of telling him my injury made me unfit to work full time."

"Noah," Adrian said, the word coming out in an angry hiss. He pulled his hand away and made like he was going to stand, so Noah grabbed him by the front of his shirt and hauled him down.

"You promised," Noah reminded him. "And like I said, it wasn't a price I couldn't afford."

"He just took your job," Adrian spat.

Noah shrugged. "Lowe has been gunning for my job since my accident. Charlie knew that and he just decided that my humiliation was enough for him. It's done, okay? I resigned the classes, Lowe was happy, Charlie backed off and we…"

Adrian gave him a flat look. "And we still can't be together because I'm still a student and you're still a professor. And we still can't be together because if that asshole even *suspects* something is going on, he'll ask for more."

Noah squeezed his eyelids tight and tried to breathe through the tension in his shoulders. "Sixteen weeks, Adrian."

"I'm not the kind of man who lets someone else control my life. Not like that," Adrian told him, his voice low and dangerous. "I have no problem backing off because it's a university policy and I understand it. It protects people from being taken advantage of, and I won't spit in the face of that. But you're asking me to let this guy hold me by the balls, Noah. You're asking me to stay silent and let him do whatever the fuck he wants to you or me simply because he can. He's a sick fuck and I can't just do nothing."

Noah licked his lips. "If you think this is easy for me…"

Adrian opened his mouth, but right then the café worker dropped off their food, giving them a look, which told Noah they hadn't been as quiet as they meant to be. Adrian snatched the cut up PB&J from the tray, spilled a few carrot sticks off to the side, and set it in front of an empty chair.

"I don't think this is easy for you," he said gruffly. "And I'm not asking you to put yourself in further danger. But I am asking you to let me try and work another way around this. I'm more capable than you think."

Noah laughed quietly. "If you think I don't know exactly what you could do to him, you don't know me very well at all." He pulled the plastic dome off his salad, then stopped and reached out to cup Adrian's cheek. "Let's talk about it. When we get away together, let's talk about it. I don't want to live the next sixteen weeks in fear of what Charlie might do, and I refuse to let you live that way either."

Adrian shook his head, but his expression softened at Noah's touch. "You got me all wrong if you think I'll *ever* be scared of that bastard. I just need to find a way to make him understand that." Then he turned his head and called to Maggie. "Come eat, baby girl. Then we can go feed the stingrays."

ADRIAN SET his chair in the corner of the stingray pool room and ordered Lemon to lay down next to it, then helped prop Maggie on the side of the pool so he could help her feed them with the little tray of shrimp. He enjoyed watching her laugh and yank her hand away every time one of their soft bellies swam up against her hand, but more than that, he enjoyed the way Noah was pressed against his side, gently easing Maggie's hand down into the water to help her with the task. It felt...domestic. It felt nice, and warm, and everything it should have felt. It let him, only for a moment, forget how fucked it all was.

By the time the little tray was empty, Maggie was starting to lag a little and Adrian could tell it was time to make the journey back home. He hadn't anticipated a day like this, one he'd intended to have several weeks ago before plans were cancelled, and they were never able to get back on their feet again.

What he wanted more than anything was a promise that there was normalcy, that this would eventually end, and they'd all be okay.

What he wanted more than anything was to get Charlie Barnes on his knees, a little battered, a little bloody, begging for forgiveness.

Adrian never claimed to be a particularly nice man, he just loved fiercely. And maybe it wasn't love with Noah yet, but he could feel the stirrings of something big, something gorgeous, if only the universe would allow it. He was tired, he was frustrated, he was often overcome with the belief he didn't deserve nice things. But he was also bound and fucking determined to see this through. Noah wasn't giving up, and Adrian wouldn't let him fight alone.

"So, is your brother still here?" Adrian asked as they headed for the exit.

Noah flushed, rubbing the back of his neck the way he did when he was nervous. "N-no," he started, then licked his lips to calm his stammer. "No. I told him I could catch a ride back with a...*friend*."

Adrian sank his teeth into his lower lip, glancing over to where Maggie was holding one of Noah's hands in hers, and the leash in his other. Lemon trotted between them, and Adrian couldn't help his smile. "A *friend* is more than happy to give you a ride."

"You can drop me at Ryan's," Noah said after helping Maggie climb inside the back seat. He strapped her into her booster chair as Adrian disassembled his wheels and stowed the chair in the back. "I haven't heard from Charlie, but my apartment..."

"I get it," Adrian said, and though it irritated him a little, he actually liked Ryan and trusted there was no actual competition there. He motioned for Noah to get in the car, then started it up and pulled out onto the road. Days like this, he wished he could be on his trike. His anxiety was like a slow, quiet burn in his gut, a promise of a rough night, and an open-road journey would have done wonders.

But at the same time, he wouldn't have wanted to be anywhere else but in that car with two people he adored and the dog who, more often than not, saved him from himself. He tapped his fingers on the wheel, then looked into the mirror to find Maggie had immediately fallen asleep.

Noah turned his head to look back, then laughed quietly. "God, I wish I could do that."

"Me too," Adrian agreed. "Even when shit isn't going off the rails, I could never sleep like that." He sighed, pulling onto the freeway, staring at the mostly empty stretch of road that would lead them back to the chaos that was their life. "I got to know Ryan a little bit," he said after some time.

Instead of looking surprised, Noah just smiled. "Yeah. He showed up at my place looking more relaxed than I'd seen him in a long time, sporting a pretty nice bruise on his cheek."

Adrian flushed a little, shrugging. "He asked for it."

"I have no doubt. It was a rough day. He caught me drunk off my ass and babbling like a moron. I think I puked on his shoes, too, but he hasn't given me shit about it so it must have been awful." Noah ran a hand down his face, then raked his fingers through his hair. "He likes you too, for what it's worth."

"You care about his opinion, so it's worth a decent amount," Adrian answered simply, because it was the truth. "I figured I'd hate the guy who cheated on you and fucked you over, but I couldn't. I tried."

Noah laughed softly and laid his head against the seat, turning his head so he could see Adrian properly. "He kind of does that to you. I've wondered for a long time why he hasn't been able to settle down, but I think he's been punishing himself for the idiot he was in law school. We kind of went back and forth about it the other day and I'm hoping he can forgive himself because I'm over it."

"Yeah?" Adrian asked. He'd had a handful of relationships here and there, none of them ended particularly well, but they didn't end in cheating, either. He wasn't entirely sure he would be capable of forgiveness the way Noah was.

For his part, Noah just shrugged. "It's not worth it to hold on to a grudge. I got a good friend out of it, and thanks to him being a dipshit, I was able to eventually meet you. Things aren't great right now, but you're worth the fight."

Adrian felt affection and warmth blossoming in his gut. It didn't erase the anxiety, but for a moment, it eclipsed it and he was grateful for that reprieve. "So are you, babe," he managed.

Noah reached over and stroked his hand along the back of Adrian's malformed ear. He felt more than heard when Noah jostled his hearing aid, then shivered when he felt blunt nails drag along his scalp. His hair was long enough to cover the bald patches from the scar tissue, but when Noah's fingers brushed along them, he felt the sensitive tingles right down to his toes.

"I'd like a week. I know you have the garage so if you can't get away that long, I'll understand. But what I want is a full week of just you."

Adrian glanced over at him and couldn't hide his smile. "I will do everything in my power to make that happen."

CHAPTER SEVENTEEN

"**Y**our boy just texted."

Noah looked up from his laptop as Ryan walked into the room, holding his phone out like an offering. Noah sighed and made a grab for it, but Ryan yanked it away at the last second and collapsed on the couch a space away from him, grinning. "Asshole," Noah muttered.

Ryan shrugged, unrepentant. "He says you're good to go on Saturday, but you have to be out by Thursday because Wes' parents are using the place that weekend. He wants to leave at two am which frankly I think is a crime against humanity and you should just let me go beat Charlie unconscious so you can get out of town that way."

Noah sighed, leaning back with his arms crossed. "I haven't seen or heard from Charlie since I put in the class resignation. I don't think he's watching right now, but Adrian wants to be safe and I don't blame him." Noah rubbed at his blind eye, fixing his other on Ryan's face. "I'm worried he's going to think you and I are together."

Ryan frowned. "Why does that worry you? Shit, you'd think that would be a good thing considering he can't come after me for anything."

Noah shrugged. "Because I'm afraid if he thinks I'm with anyone he's going to do…try something else. Something new. I think he wants me alone and miserable."

Ryan set his phone down and grabbed Noah's wrist, pulling him over until Noah was plastered against his side. "I have never known you to run scared from anything. Ever. And this guy is a bastard and he might have balls the size of the Liberty Bell, but he can't control you forever. What more can he do?"

Noah shrugged. "I don't know. That's what scares me."

"We're going to end this, you know. I've been hanging out at the gym lately…"

Noah's head snapped up and he fixed his gaze hard on Ryan. "I fucking told you to leave Wes and Anna alone."

Ryan rolled his eyes. "Honestly, they've more than hinted they're open to a third person getting involved. But they want commitment and that's more than I can give right now. Plus, there's this cute as shit boxer girl—like barely five foot, I want to put her in my pocket and carry her around, she's so adorable—and I think there's something going on there with her and them. So no, Noah, I'm not getting involved, thank you very much."

Noah's eyebrows rose, feeling a little hurt and frustrated that he wasn't in on this stuff. He'd been too afraid to show his face at the gym since the Charlie thing started, and he was missing out. "Fine. So what, you've been trying to scam on my boyfriend?"

Ryan looked hurt and Noah realized how sensitive this topic might actually be. Before he could open his mouth, Ryan put a finger against it. "It's fine. I mean, it stung, but I know you know I'm not going to do anything to hurt you. And as it happens, I've been helping that gorgeous boyfriend of yours train one of his guys. I think you might have met him once. Cole?"

"The blind guy?" Noah asked, startled by that revelation.

Ryan nodded. "He's been working toward taking on sighted opponents and since I'm basically the worst still, he's starting with me. He hasn't seriously kicked my ass…yet. But," he said, and hesitated for a moment, "he's also got some serious computer skills. He was in some sort of technological espionage training or something in the British military and he's got scary skills. Like so good that once he's cleared to go back to work, he'll be listed as an active-duty member."

Noah blinked. "So, does that mean he's going back to England?"

Ryan looked momentarily hurt by the thought, and Noah was slammed with the realization that it was more than just boxing training, even if Ryan wasn't ready to admit it. "He didn't say, but he made it sound like he was here for a while. Maybe even for good. Anyway, I haven't told him anything about our situation, but he knows something is going on and he offered to help. We might want to consider it."

Noah sighed, pulling himself up and rubbing at his face. "I don't know. There's not a lot we can accomplish with illegal hacking. And Charlie can still get me fired and Adrian kicked out for what we did."

"Are doing," Ryan pointed out.

Noah rolled his eyes. "Thank you."

Ryan shrugged. "It's my job to be frank about it. And yes, that's true, he can. But if he's determined to take you down, take him with you. This ends somewhere and I bet my left nut Cole can find some deeply dark shit on him."

Noah pulled his bottom lip between his teeth, then finally nodded. He really had little else to lose. "Okay. I mean...not okay. Let me think about it and talk to Adrian first. If we can come to some sort of agreement, I'll let you know."

Ryan gave him a look, then smirked. "I don't think you'll have any trouble there."

HE WAS PACKED. He was packed, and ready to go, and all he needed to do was sleep one more night, then settle in at Ryan's until Adrian picked him up. Yes, it was absurd they were stealing away in the middle of the night just for a week alone without a risk of Noah's damn blackmailer finding out, but he would take it.

Mostly because there was some promise on the horizon that this might end, that they might get something on Charlie bad enough it would even the playing field. Noah needed to sit and contemplate what he might do with his freedom after that, though he knew getting his job back would be next to impossible. He'd given Lowe all he needed to bar him from becoming full-time again and from getting tenure at this university. Short of coming in with evidence to prove that Charlie had blackmailed and coerced him into resigning those classes, there was nothing he could say to the head of the department that would make the old bigot change his mind.

And in all honesty, Noah wasn't sure he wanted to go back to working for them. There was another major University an hour and a half south of them and though it would be a commute, it was one he'd willingly take on if it meant freedom from this mess. Maybe their department would be stable, maybe tenure was achievable, maybe the prejudice wouldn't follow him there.

He didn't know how likely any of that was, but he could hope. He had to think beyond his immediate life. He'd never ask Adrian to pack up and move, but he still had options that didn't tie him to one place forever.

With a sigh, Noah decided to run out and grab a quick bite to eat. He didn't think sleep would come easy, so at the very least he could grab some comfort food to get him through the long night. It was a Friday night and since the campus was mostly deserted, it would be easy for him to pop in and out and get back home in time to put his feet up and chill.

At the door, he grabbed his cane and shoved it into his pocket, then headed out for the curry shop a few blocks away from him. He was happy to see the lobby empty and was greeted immediately by a tired looking server at the counter. "What can I get you?"

"Spicy shrimp Malabar," he said, eyeing the dairy-free options on the menu. "Extra rice, and some roti, no butter." He handed over his card, then moved to the window seat to wait. It was always a little eerie over winter break. Only a handful of students bothered with the short winter term, and since it was all online classes, most of them went home to do it. The dorm buildings were dark, half the bars and shops had closed early, and most of the people around were locals walking their dogs or hoping to grab a drink while the streets were calm.

The food was ready quickly, so Noah slipped a few bills into the tip jar, grabbed his bag, and headed out. He was a few feet away, standing at the mouth of the building's alley when his phone began to buzz in his pocket. Thinking it might be Ryan with a message from Adrian, he turned his back to the street and peered down at the screen.

UNKNOWN.

SOMETHING about the word made his skin breakout in bumps, and he swiped his thumb to answer it. "This is Dr. Avidan."

"Enough is enough," a raspy voice spoke. As it did, he swore for a second he heard an echo, the words coming seconds before the ones in the speaker.

Noah lifted his head to look around, and that's when something painful and heavy connected with his sighted eye. All the breath left him, his knees buckling, and as he scrambled for purchase, two massive hands had him. One curled into the back of his jeans, the other wrapping around his neck. He struggled to turn his head, but his eye was shining with stars. He could feel the skin swelling, and he started to panic.

"Help!" he started to cry, but his words were silenced when the hand around his throat tightened. His mouth opened, gasping for breath, and his front was slammed into the bricks. The fist caught him in the eye again, twice, then his forehead was pressed to the bricks as the fist hit him in the ribs hard enough for him to feel a dull crack.

Noah tried to pull his head back, but the hand around him slammed his face into the wall. He felt his prosthetic dislodge and with the second collision, it tumbled down his cheek. Desperate, terrified, he tried to open his sighted eye, but it wouldn't obey. His mouth felt puffy and he tasted copper on his tongue.

"What," he managed.

Hot breath ghosted over the back of his neck, a set of lips brushing over his ear as a raspy, unfamiliar voice spoke on his blind side. "You think this is bad, just wait. Be seen with the gimp again and this will feel like a fucking massage compared to what I'll do next."

Noah was released, collapsing to the ground. His body felt almost nothing at that point, though he knew he was shaking, and knew he had gone into shock. When it wore off, he'd be in a world of hurt, but for now he had to collect himself. He could hear the person's footsteps retreating, and when he was certain he was alone, he pulled himself up so his back pressed to the brick.

He licked at his lip, feeling the cut there, then he reached up and tried to pull his eyelids apart. He felt a moment of instant relief when light stabbed through, but he realized he couldn't actually see anything. It was a thin strip of blurred colors and nothing more. When he dropped his hand, his eye closed again, and he was left in nothingness. His stomach started to churn, and he had never felt so lost.

Cocking his head to the side, he heard nothing. No footsteps, no people, no cars. He had no idea if he was facing toward the street or toward the alley, but he knew he had to try and move. His hands swept out in front of him, and he almost sobbed in relief when his fingers came into contact with the smooth, rectangle that was his phone.

He cursed the touch screen, then pushed the home button down. "Hey Siri."

"*What can I help you with?*"

"C-call..." He hesitated for a moment, but somewhere in his shaken brain he realized that it might not have been Charlie who attacked him physically, but he was behind it. And he was done being cowed by that man. "Call Adrian."

"*Calling Adrian Flores.*"

The electronic voice died off in favor of the phone ringing, and it went on so long Noah was terrified Adrian wouldn't pick up. Then, by the grace of god, Adrian's voice sounded on the other line. "Noah?"

"I...I," the events of the night suddenly hit him. His head gave a violent spin and his tongue glued itself to the roof of his mouth. "M-m..."

"Noah," Adrian said, his voice soft, determined, but grounding all the same. "Are you okay?"

"Mm mm," he said, making a negative noise.

"Are you at home?" he asked.

Noah heard voices in the background, and a noise like keys. He made the same negative noise.

"Are you close to home?"

"Mmhm." Noah took a breath and tried to force himself to speak. "C-c-cuh..."

"Breathe, baby. I'm on my way, just give me something. Anything."

"Cuh...curry," he said.

"Curry Pot," Adrian said, sounding full of relief. "Fuck, baby, that's so close. Stay right there, okay? Don't hang up, just stay with me. Are you alone?"

"Mmhm," he said, though he wasn't entirely sure. He was certain he looked like a fucking mess, and now that the shock had subsided, things were starting to hurt. Badly. His face was swollen, his mouth aching, his ribs burning. He could breathe okay which probably meant if anything they were just cracked, but he still couldn't see, couldn't pick himself up and move.

He let his head fall back against the brick and realized Adrian was still talking to him.

"...going to be there shortly. I'm at the light on First and it's red, but I'm gonna run it. There's no one out here and nothing can keep me from getting there. Got that? I'm two minutes away. Just give me something baby. You still with me?"

"Mm," he said. His head started to feel a little floaty, like he wanted to drift off, though something in the back of his mind told him to wait. Wait until Adrian was there, wait until he knew he was safe.

He flexed his fingers and they ached, but they moved. He was hurt, he wasn't broken.

It felt like an eternity passed as Adrian dictated his every move, then he heard him curse softly. "I see you. Fuck... *what?* I'm pulling over I..." The call went dead.

ADRIAN WAS ANTSY, knowing that in a matter of hours he and Noah would be on the road, heading to a little sanctuary where the two of them could just be and not worry about anything for a while. It wasn't permanent, and he was still feeling a little lost as to what they were going to do about it for the next four months, but he was taking this reprieve as the gift it was.

He was also letting himself enjoy the evening. Ryan showed up after the last class to go a few rounds with Cole, and Adrian was enjoying watching the dance the two men were engaged in. Not just in the ring, though Adrian could feel the sexual tension pouring off them with every dodge and every jab, but in their quiet flirtation and sarcastic shit-talking Adrian knew all-too well.

Ryan was a typical lawyer most of the time. Worried about work, too busy, too stressed, too literal. But there was something else about him he noticed that Cole could drag to the surface with his dry wit and his inability to let anything slide. Adrian could tell Ryan liked it, and he only hoped Cole would let the other man in.

They would be good for each other that much was obvious.

Adrian had stopped to grab some water when he noticed his phone was going off, and his heart almost stopped when he saw Noah's name on the screen. Noah would only call if it was an emergency, and it took him a moment for his fingers to work properly enough to answer.

He had expected something, but not the stuttering, pained noises Noah was making. He had no idea what happened, but he knew he was in trouble.

"I'm on my way," he told him. That got Ryan and Cole's attention who rushed to his side and Adrian put his hand up, covering the speaker. "Go to Wes', he has a key—he's in his office, tell him I said I'll be bringing Noah. Take Lemon there and wait for me. I don't know what the fuck happened, but Noah is in trouble and I'm going to pick him up."

"I'm coming with," Ryan said decidedly. "If he needs help…"

"Then you can be at Wes' place waiting for us," Adrian all-but barked at him. "Bring Cole, I was his ride home. You don't mind waiting around, do you?"

Cole immediately shook his head. "Of course not." He reached for Ryan, grabbing his arm. "Honestly, it's fine. Adrian knows what he's doing, and you and I can be there in case Noah needs us."

That seemed to snap Ryan out of himself and he gave a curt nod. "Then go."

Adrian wasted no time rushing to his car, moving faster than his legs wanted him to, but he didn't care. He tore out onto the street, talking to Noah softly, waiting for those quiet noises to let him know he was still there, he was awake, he was alive. Adrian was shaking from head to toe by the time he pulled up to the Curry Pot and he almost lost it when he saw the state of his boyfriend.

Noah was pressed up against the brick wall at the mouth of the alley, his face a bashed-up mess, lip bleeding, eye swollen shut, the other half open showing the white of his implant. Noah's hands were shaking, and his head was lolled to the side like he was holding on to consciousness by a bare thread. Adrian grabbed his cane, forcing his legs to get him over to Noah's side.

When he touched Noah's ribs, his boyfriend hissed and pulled back. "Broken?" he asked.

Noah shook his head. "N-n…"

"Come on. Brace yourself on my arm and let's get to the car. It's only a few feet away, alright?" Adrian was seeing red, and only the fact that Noah needed him calm and present kept him from dropping everything and hunting that bastard down. Because this was Charlie's work. Somehow, Charlie was sending a message, and Adrian was going to kill him.

He managed to get Noah into the seat without his legs giving up on him, and he threw his cane in the back before sliding behind the wheel. Looking over, Noah's head was resting against the window and his breathing was rapid. "I should get you to the hospital."

"N-n," Noah said. He licked his lips and winced. "P-please, n-no."

"You could be seriously hurt. Your face is a fucking mess, Noah. I can't just…"

"P-please," Noah asked again.

Adrian couldn't deny him again. It was foolish, but Noah was at least coherent enough to speak—even if it was only a handful of stammered words. Adrian knew the signs of concussion very well, so he promised himself he'd allow this only as long as Noah didn't show any. He put the car into drive and pulled out.

When Noah's hand sought his, Adrian took it, pressing a fierce kiss to his knuckles before letting him go to steer. "Was it Charlie?"

Noah took a moment before answering. "N-no. No, it w-wasn't. B-but he duh-d-did this. It was a m-message."

Adrian clutched the wheel, wishing he could reach over and hold Noah. "Just…just try and rest. I'm taking you to Wes and Anna's. Ryan and Cole are already there, and I've got something you can take for pain."

Noah made a small noise, then reached for Adrian, grasping at the back of his neck like he needed the touch to ground him. Adrian shifted close and was grateful when his sister's place came into view. He pulled up to the curb a little more recklessly than he intended, but he was grateful when he saw Ryan throw the door open and all-but rush out to greet them.

"What the fuck?" he said in a low whisper when Adrian got Noah's door open. His face immediately drained of color and he turned dark eyes on Adrian. "What happened?"

"He's too worked up to tell me much right now. My legs are fucked, I need you to help get him inside."

Ryan looked like he wanted to say more, but he quickly snapped into action, easing Noah to his feet. Noah's head lifted and Adrian could see his swollen lids working to try and open. "W-w…"

"Hey," Ryan said, gently putting his hand around Noah's lower waist, "come on, babe, I've got you."

"Adrian," Noah managed, and Adrian's heart began to thud against his ribs.

"I'm here," Adrian said gruffly. "Let's get to the living room couch, okay? Are they home?"

"Wes is out walking Lemon and Anna's asleep. Cole's in there, though, and he said he has some first aid training."

"Wes was a medic," Adrian told him, though he was more than grateful for the offer. "He can fix him up. I tried to get him to agree to the hospital, but he refused."

"This fucker," Ryan growled as they passed through the door.

Adrian held up his free hand and shook his head. "We'll deal with that after we get a good look at the damage." He was surprised at his own pragmatism, how he was staying calm and not rushing off to show Charlie exactly what he learned in his long years of both military and being a fighter. There would be time enough for that later. Noah's quiet whimpers of pain kept him focused on the task at hand.

Cole was in the living room, seated in the arm chair with his dog at his feet. He looked tense, his head cocked with his ear toward them as they entered the room. "How bad is it?"

Ryan sighed. "Bad. He's beat to shit and he's not really able to talk much right now."

"I'm f-fine," Noah ground out as he eased down on the cushions. He sat like everything hurt, but there was color coming back to his cheeks which eased a sliver of Adrian's anxiety. "I'm h-here too s-so you f-fuckers can st-stop talking ab-abuh-bout me."

Ryan chuckled and shifted aside when Adrian walked up and knelt down on the floor near Noah's side. "I guess I was wrong. Like usual."

Adrian reached out, gently dragging his fingertips along the bruising and cuts on Noah's face. There was a decent mark on his forehead, right above his eye socket he would bet everything had come from being bashed against the wall. The damage to his sighted eye looked like a bare fist, and same with his mouth.

"Can you tell us what happened?" Adrian asked, pulling Noah's hand to his mouth. He pressed his lips against Noah's knuckles, just resting there, just needing to feel him. Noah let out a small noise of pain, but he didn't pull away.

"He grabbed me from behind," he said, his words deliberately slow as though he was trying to control his stammer. "F-fucker," he spat. "Someone called my phone, I d-didn't recognize the voice. It was him. I could hear the echo. Then he t-took me by my shirt and hit me in the f-face. Then I hit the wall. T-told me if I k-kept s-seeing Adrian this would feel like a m-massage next time."

Adrian curled his other hand into a fist so tight he felt his nails bite into his palm, and it was all he could do not to stand up and just go. He was ready to kill, but Ryan's gaze pinned him there, reminding him there were better ways of going about this.

"I think he knows about our t-trip," Noah finished on a sigh.

Adrian closed his eyes and forced himself to take several breaths. "We can't let him get away with this."

"You're right," Noah said, startling Adrian. Adrian had fully expected Noah to heed this warning, to give in to Charlie and agree that it was over. He hadn't expected the vicious determination in his tone as he pushed himself up to sit in spite of his pain. "I'm d-done. Cole? Adrian said y-you were here."

"Right here, mate," Cole said softly. Adrian looked behind him as Cole sat forward in his chair. "I've been filled in a bit with the situation, but not everything. I'm going to go out on a limb and say someone's after you?"

"He's being blackmailed," Ryan filled in. He stood up and walked over to Cole's side, dropping a hand on his shoulder, holding his hand gently over the compression sleeve. "Noah's a professor at the university, and he didn't realize Adrian was a student there until after they started dating. One of his colleagues found out and used some third-rate student hacker to get a transcript of Noah's texts to prove it, then forced him to give up most of his classes. We thought it might be over then, but apparently not."

"He wanted m-me humiliated," Noah spat, gently prodding at his eye until Adrian grabbed his wrist to pull his hand away. "I thought it was enough."

"It's never enough for people like that," Cole said quietly.

Ryan scoffed. "I told him as much."

"Can we save the I-told-you-so for when Noah isn't bleeding all over the sofa?" Adrian spat, feeling protective and ready to fight anyone who came at the other man.

Ryan held up his hands in surrender. "I didn't mean it like that. I just mean this isn't unexpected and I'm glad Noah's ready to fight back."

"We need something on him," Adrian said. He turned to sit down, keeping Noah's hand firmly in his, pressing it against the back of his cheek as he spoke to Cole. For his part, Cole sat in the chair, head tipped forward with his hands clasped between his knees. "There's no way this guy doesn't have shit that we can find and use against him. For people like him, this won't have been the first time he's done it."

Cole licked his lips, then lifted his head up and put one hand over Ryan's which was still resting on his shoulder. "I have people I can contact, but it might take me some time. If you want a hope of taking this bloke down..."

Cole broke off when the front door opened, and Adrian heard Lemon's nails clicking on the floors before she came around the corner and made a bee-line for him. She could clearly sense the high anxiety in the room, and Adrian motioned her up on the sofa which she immediately obeyed. She shuffled close to Noah who curled into her, his free hand digging straight into her coat and he made a quiet noise.

Adrian looked back up at his brother-in-law who was staring at Noah with an expression of surprise and horror. "Someone needs to fill me in - like yesterday," he demanded.

Ryan let go of Cole's shoulder. "I will. Let's go talk in the kitchen. We need to get Noah some food so he can take something for the pain."

Adrian thought for a moment maybe he should go too, but the idea of leaving Noah's side was like asking him to hack off a limb. Noah was still trembling a little, but with Lemon against him, he was starting to calm. With a huff, Adrian finally pushed up to his feet and took a seat next to his boyfriend.

"How bad is the pain? And don't lie to me," he warned.

Noah let out a tiny laugh and shook his head. When he spoke, his voice was more measured, the stammer calm for the moment. "The pain sucks, but it's not as bad as it was when we were in the car. I just ache all over."

"Wes is going to bring you something and we're staying here for the night. I still think you should get looked at…"

"No," Noah interrupted, but softened the blow by bringing Adrian's hand to his lips for a soft kiss. "If we're going to do something against Charlie, I don't want this on the record. Nothing's broken and I'm not concussed. At worst I have a fractured cheek, and maybe a few cracked ribs. I've had a lot worse and I can get through this." He swallowed, then said, "Charlie had someone do this to me. I want to know who, and I think we can find out if we can get access to his phone, maybe his laptop, bank records. There has to be a trail somewhere."

After a beat, Cole rose and made a clicking noise, his guide rising to her feet to stand next to him. "I'm going to go make a couple calls, okay? I'm going to need some info on this guy though."

Noah frowned. "What kind of info?"

"As much as you can get your hands on," Cole told him. "All the important shit, address, date of birth, employee ID, all that."

Noah squeezed at Adrian's fingers, then said, "I can call a friend in. She works in admin and she'll probably be able to get me some of what I need."

"It'll be asking a lot of her," Cole warned. "It'll put her at risk—not just for getting sacked, but maybe even charges."

"You're talking about Esther, right?" Adrian asked. He hadn't met Noah's friends yet, but he knew Esther and her wife cared about Noah like family. "She'll do it. She won't care. When she finds out what Charlie did," he began.

"We can't tell her everything," Noah said in a rush. "She and Sabrina are trying to get pregnant, I can't put them at risk like that. But she can get us something."

"Something will work," Cole said, offering a smile. "Don't you fret, okay? I've taken down powerful men. This little professor is nothing to me."

Adrian felt some of the tension bleed out of Noah's shoulders, and he tucked him in closer, mindful of his sore ribs. "Thank you," he said softly.

Cole nodded, then took up his guide's harness and left the room.

When they were finally alone, Adrian took Noah's face by the chin and turned it. He brushed along the swelling of his eye with ginger fingers, prodding but not too firmly. Noah sucked in breath through his teeth and let it out in a shaking sigh.

"I can see out of it. Sort of. I pried it open when I was on the street and there was light and color, but I couldn't...there w-wasn't..." he stopped.

Adrian cupped his cheek. "I've had a shiner like this before, and it fucks you up for a bit, but your eye is one of the fastest healing organs in your body. I know why this is terrifying for you, babe, but it's not permanent. I'll have Wes take a look when he comes back with food, okay?"

Noah licked his lips, wincing at the cut, but he nodded. "Okay."

Adrian held him tight until Wes returned with some soft bread, a mug of something warm, and a small medkit hanging from his wrist. Adrian motioned Lemon to get down and Wes took her placed, putting a careful hand on Noah's knee.

"Can I take a look at you?" he asked.

Noah shifted and turned his face toward Wes. "I'm...I'm mostly worried about my eye."

"Your prosthetic?" he asked.

Noah shook his head. "That's long-gone. I heard that f-fucker step on it. I have spares but m-my socket is too swollen to p-put anything in tonight."

Wes hummed to acknowledge Noah's words, and he opened his kit. "The swelling should go down in a day or two. I'm guessing by tomorrow you'll be able to open your sighted eye again, and any blurry vision should be gone within the week."

"So, I'm b-blind until then," Noah said. "I'm glad I've been working to prepare for this m-moment."

Adrian heard the attempt to be lighthearted and cover up his fear, but with the stammer, it missed the mark. Instead of a jesting tone, there was abject terror and Adrian wanted to wrap Noah up in his arms and hold him until his wounds were healed.

"Is Ryan here?" Noah asked after a moment.

Wes pulled out a packet of alcohol wipes and ripped them open. "He went to drive Cole back home, said he had a couple calls to make and he'd be by in the morning. I think he's up to something he doesn't want us in on."

Noah scoffed, then winced when Wes began to dab his cuts and scrapes with the disinfectant. "Just like him. It's probably better that way, though. He's a good guy, but he can be…dark."

"I think in this case," Wes said, patting Noah's face dry with a bit of gauze, "that's a good thing. This fucker is walking on thin ice and it's just a matter of time before it breaks."

Adrian heard the promise in his brother-in-law's voice, the tone that said anyone who fucked with the people he cared about would pay. Adrian was right there with him, but he didn't think those were words Noah needed to hear right then.

"I think you two should still go," Wes said after he spread a layer of anti-biotic ointment over Noah's cheeks.

Adrian frowned. "Where? To the vacation house?"

"I'm going to call my mom and tell her to cancel the weekend. You two head up there to recover while we handle shit down here."

"No," Noah said, pulling away from Wes' hands. "Look, this isn't your problem."

"It is when someone is threatening people I care about. Friends, family, it doesn't fucking matter. And like it or not, you're one of them. He fucked with Adrian, and now this?" Wes took in a breath, unclenching his hands. "He underestimated us because we're not what he considers normal, or capable. That was his mistake, but I'm grateful for his bigotry because that's what's going to take him down."

Adrian felt a wave of appreciation and love for this man—a friend since childhood, a former brother-in-arms, and a brother by law. He'd never been more profoundly grateful Anna had chosen this man to be her husband. "He's right," he finally said, pulling Noah's hand to his lips again. He spoke against the cool skin of Noah's knuckles. "We should go. You need time to recoup and we need to trust that the people who love you are going to help you."

Noah's jaw tensed like he wanted to argue, then he deflated and leaned back against the cushions. "Okay. I guess at this point there's not much else Charlie can do to me. He's taken my job, my dignity, and now he's had me beaten to a pulp to prove that I can't even defend myself there."

Adrian felt white-hot anger course through him. "He attacked you from behind, in a dark alley like a fucking *coward*. I have years and years of training, but that doesn't mean a person couldn't get the jump on me too."

"Right," Noah said with a scoff.

Wes reached out, squeezing the top of Noah's thigh. "He's not wrong. I was mugged. Before my injury," he clarified. "I was on leave and we decided to take a little trip to Rome—me and a couple of the guys. We'd just finished this huge meal and they were wasted so they decided to go clubbing. I was tired and sober and really not in the mood for their shit, so I decided to walk back to the hostel. I was about two blocks away when this guy came out of fucking nowhere, right up behind me and got me in the back of the head. I went down, he got several good punches in, grabbed my wallet, phone, keys, everything. I had years of training, I'd been boxing since I was thirteen, I had championships, medals, titles, not to mention years of military training, and this asshole in a dark alley brought me to my knees and made me feel weak and terrified."

Noah licked his lips, his brows furrowed. "I..."

Wes quieted him with another touch. "I never really told anyone about this, but for years after that, I was terrified of walking around the streets at night. I was hyper vigilant and stronger than before, but when I was alone having to cross through a dark alley, I was like a scared kid because I knew that no matter what, there's always a chance someone could get the jump on me. So no, that piece of shit attacking you like that does *not* make you weak and does *not* mean you can't defend yourself. It only proved he's a coward because the only way he feels strong is if he's oppressing someone else and that shit does not fly with me."

Adrian looked up at Wes and made sure his face showed his absolute gratitude. "Wes isn't the only one whose been taken down, babe. I have too. But when you're better, you can start coming to the gym more. I'll train you—Wes will train you. It doesn't guarantee no one can ever touch you again, but it helps."

"It'll allow you the chance to take some of the power back," Wes told him.

Noah swallowed and when he spoke, his voice was thick. "Thank you."

Wes chuckled, then pressed a small, white pill into the center of Noah's palm. "Take this, then get your ass in bed. You need to sleep this shit off as long as you can because you are going to be hurting in the morning."

Noah sighed but didn't argue as he put the pill on his tongue and accepted the mug from Wes. Swallowing it all down, he handed it off then accepted the bread, chewing mechanically as he leaned into Adrian's side. When he was finished, Adrian rose to his feet and carefully helped Noah up.

"Come on, we're in my room," he said.

Noah shuffled along, his hand gripping Adrian's arm like a vice. Adrian was mindful of his uneven gait, of every potential obstacle between the living room and the room he occupied at Anna's. They got there without incident, and Adrian carefully guided Noah's hand to the edge of the bed.

"Here. Now, strip down and get under the covers. I'm going to be here if you need the bathroom or anything, okay?" he said, and tugged at the hem of his own shirt.

Noah started to undress, then froze and turned his face up. "Wait, Adrian, you can't stay here with me."

Adrian frowned, his arms frozen in the aborted motion to undress. "Why not?"

"Because this night was fucking stressful," Noah said. He turned and sat down hard, wincing at the pain of it. "There's no fucking way you'll be able to sleep with another person like that. It's...it's fine, really. I'll be fine."

Adrian shook his head, walking over to kneel down next to his boyfriend. He put both palms flat over the dirty jeans covering Noah's thighs and squeezed. "I'm not going to sleep tonight, trust me. But I *am* going to rest, with you in my arms, knowing that for now, no one can touch you. Trust me, I've stayed up a lot damn longer than a single night and was just fine. I need this, I need to be with you tonight, so please, let me have this."

Noah's mouth softened and he made a soft noise in his throat as his hands reached up for Adrian's face. They found his cheeks, cupping them softly, and they pulled Adrian into a careful, chaste kiss. "I don't deserve you," he murmured.

Adrian felt his heart wrench. "You deserve way better than me, babe. I'm difficult and messy, but I'm going to do my damn best to do right by you. I'm starting tonight with holding you, and tomorrow by making sure that piece of shit can't get near you ever again."

Noah swallowed, tensed his jaw, then nodded. "Okay."

Adrian wasn't sure he believed in Noah's easy acquiescence, but the night had been too damn long to push it. Instead, he stripped down, then helped Noah get out of his clothes and up against the pillows. He tried not to let the anger at seeing the sunset of bruises send him flying into a rage, and instead focused on the way Noah melted into him, and breathed steady and even, and slipped into a gentle slumber.

CHAPTER EIGHTEEN

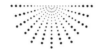

A drian got Noah to take a second dose of pain killers around three in the morning, and by five, he was still out but Adrian was feeling restless. Lemon was cuddled up at the end of the bed, so he motioned for her to scoot up next to Noah and take his place.

Strapping on his braces, he tugged on a pair of basketball shorts and a t-shirt, then wandered into the kitchen to find Wes fiddling with the coffee maker. He turned to see Adrian and offered him an exhausted smile.

"Did you get any sleep?"

Adrian sighed and lowered onto one of the barstools. "I think I dropped off a few times, but I wasn't expecting much. You?"

Wes shook his head. "Ryan called around two and let me know that he's got a friend who can take care of Charlie today, long enough for you two to skip town."

Adrian's eyebrows shot up toward his hairline. "What the hell does that mean?"

"He's a state prosecutor," Wes reminded him. "I think you know what the fuck that means. Either way, the house is protected and if you leave late like you were planning to…"

"Yeah," Adrian said, accepting a mug of coffee with a grateful smile. He took a sip, the bitterness of it waking him more than the caffeine or the heat. "Shit, I can't...Wes," he said, his voice breaking a little as he looked up at his brother-in-law, "when I saw him lying there on the street like that..."

Wes reached out and squeezed his wrist. "You don't have to tell me. If that had been Anna, I would have lost my damn mind."

Adrian dragged a hand through his hair, then down his face as he let out a frustrated sigh. "Tell me we're going to get this fucker. Noah was onto something with Cole. He's having him try and find the trail between Barnes and the guy he hired to fuck Noah up. If we can do that, we might have something to use."

"Ryan's pretty sure we won't be able to do this legally," Wes warned him.

Adrian let out a dark laugh. "That's the last fucking thing I want. I want to feel bones crack under my fists. This man does not know who he fucked with."

"He doesn't," Wes agreed. "He will, though."

Adrian felt satisfaction in that. "Just don't take any action until we get back. I want this guy scared, and I want him to see my face when he's pissing his pants."

Wes grinned at him, and maybe it made Adrian a bad person for the joy he took in it, but he didn't care. Not after this. He shouldn't have let it get this far and he would be beating himself up for years at his dumbass hesitation. "It'll be fine. You two go get some rest, do some good fucking when he's up for it, and when you come back, we should be ready to make a move. Cole's a terrifyingly smart guy, I don't think it'll take him long to come up with something."

"You know," Adrian said, a little guilt welling up in his gut, "I feel like such an ass. I didn't want to take Cole on when he first started. I didn't want someone else's hang-ups fucking with my progress. But he's proved me wrong at every turn."

"He's been asking to compete," Wes told him, and that was no surprise to Adrian. He hadn't directly mentioned it, but there had been hints. "He knows there's no place in the professional world for him. Regulations won't allow it, but I could set something up for him. It'll be nice to make him feel at home."

Adrian lifted a brow. "You're not thinking about..."

Wes laughed, shaking his head. "Nah, man. I don't think he's into women and that's a deal-breaker for Anna. Besides, she's massively crushing on someone right now and we have a date this weekend."

Adrian blinked, then smiled and shook his head. "You're out of your fucking minds, the both of you. One kid, baby on the way, and a boyfriend?"

"Girlfriend," Wes corrected.

Adrian froze, then his eyes widened with realization. "You don't mean Connie?" They'd been taking care of the woman for a while now—she'd been coming to the gym for over a year, trying to get over her abusive ex and take some of her control back. The guy wouldn't leave her alone, and they'd been chasing Mike off for months. Adrian also couldn't pretend like he hadn't seen the way his sister was taken with the little spitfire, and he couldn't blame her. If Adrian had swung her way, he wouldn't have been able to resist. "How do you feel about that?"

Wes dragged a hand down his face. "I love that girl to death," he said, and that was true. He'd doted on her since she started working for him. "But she's got a lot of issues and baggage, and I'm not sure she's ready for what it means to be with two people."

"But it's not just a hook-up?" Adrian pressed.

"No. Anna's not into it, and it gets a little exhausting. We want something stable," he said with a shrug. "I've been busier lately, and with a new baby on the way, Anna needs that. She'll be fine without, but we're too old for hooking up like that anymore."

Adrian nodded his understanding. "I get it. And there's no sweeter girl," he said, meaning every word. The Baum Boxing family had taken her into their protection without hesitation, and thinking of Connie in a relationship with Anna and Wes felt strangely right. "If it works out, I'm happy for you."

"Thanks," Wes said. Then he grinned at Adrian. "And you, man."

Adrian held up his hand. "Look, we all know you want to give me

185

shit over this, but let's wait until we deal with everything else. Then you can fucking throw an I-told-you-so party in my honor."

"Deal," Wes said with a shit-eating grin. "Now, I'm going to head downstairs to hop on the treadmill, then I'm off to the store. Send me a list of shit you guys will need for the trip and I'll pick it up. I promise we'll get you out of this mess, okay? We just need to be patient."

Patient was the last thing Adrian wanted to be, but Noah deserved no less.

Noah came to in fits and bursts, aware of the pain first before anything else. When he didn't see the usual wash of light from the morning through his eyelid, that's when the panic set in. His head was fuzzy, everything hurt, and he *couldn't see*. Noah sat up with a gasp, his fingers pushing at his face until a warm hand closed around his wrist and pulled it down.

"Stop," said a familiar voice. *Adrian*. "You'll just make the swelling worse."

"Swelling," Noah repeated, his voice hoarse and cracking. His throat felt like he was speaking through razor blades, and he swallowed against the harsh ache. Swelling.

The memory of the night before came back in a rush. Leaving the curry shop, the hands on him, his throat squeezed, his face bashed into the wall. He couldn't see because his sighted eye was swollen shut from a vicious right hook, and his throat hurt from when the stranger had squeezed it until he'd gone silent.

Noah reached out, finding Adrian immediately, and he sagged against his warm cotton t-shirt. After calming himself, he very carefully attempted to open his eye. He was startled when his lids obeyed him, only a fraction, but there was still light and color. His tear ducts both watered up and he felt his blind socket fill with the salty drops and spill over his lower lid. He prodded at it, feeling the slightly more pliant eyelid there and sighed at the loss of his expensive prosthetic.

"How's your pain?" Adrian asked, his hands brushing through Noah's hair.

"Not great, but not as bad as I thought it would be," he told him. That much was true. He'd expected to be completely stiff and immobile not only from the beating, but from the tension. And he did feel a little like he'd run a twenty-mile marathon, but it was a dull ache instead of a vicious burn. Even his ribs seemed to have appreciated the night of rest and the pills Adrian had fed him when he'd woken up.

Adrian's fingers touched his chin, and Noah sat back as he let his boyfriend examine him. He felt Adrian's fingers push at his shiner, and he let his eye open as best he could to show him. "Can you see anything?"

"Light, blobs of color," he said with a shrug. "How's it look?"

"Blood-shot," Adrian told him honestly. "That will last longer than the swelling, but I've had one that bad before."

"How long till you could see again?" Noah asked softly, trying not to let his anxiety get the better of him.

"A few days. By the time we head back to the city, you should be fine," Adrian promised, though Noah didn't know if he was simply trying to placate him. Noah had experienced what it was like to wake up shattered and broken after his body had been ravaged. He had a nasty black-eye, broken nose, several cracked bones, and one of his eyes had been permanently blinded. This was a lot like that, only where the accident had felt senseless, Noah knew exactly why this happened to him.

"Any news?" he pressed after some time. His bladder started to make itself known, but he wasn't ready to get up yet.

Adrian sighed and brought Noah's hand up to his mouth to kiss his palm. He'd done that a lot since the night before, and Noah was curious, but he didn't want to draw attention to it. He liked it too much to make Adrian self-conscious about the gesture. "Ryan called around two this morning, talked to Wes and said he's going to have Charlie taken care of for the next twenty-four hours. I don't know exactly what that means, but we'll be able to skip town without being noticed. Or at least, we should be able to."

Noah bit his lip against a smile. "He had a pretty intense friends with benefits thing going on with ah…a guy."

"A cop?" Adrian pressed.

"Yeah, I'm not gonna confirm or deny that," Noah said with a half-laugh. In truth, it had been the police chief, but it had been incredibly hush-hush. Ryan had over-shared on the details—bondage ropes, blindfolds, the works. In the end, Ryan had decided that lifestyle wasn't for him, but they'd stayed friends and Ryan was allowed to call in favors from time to time. "Either way, that makes sense."

"Can I ask you something?" Adrian said after a beat, letting his thumb rub small circles over the pulse in Noah's wrist.

"Anything," Noah said.

"Why didn't you have Ryan use that contact before? If he knows a guy who can get Charlie detained for twenty-four hours, I'm sure the guy can do more."

Noah shook his head. "Ryan does not like to call on that guy for favors, and it's not without some cost. We don't really talk about it, but this isn't like getting out of a parking ticket. And even if the guy had picked up Charlie back then, he wouldn't have had anything to hold him on. Which means you would have been charged with plagiarism and I would have been fired."

Adrian's hand stilled, then he leaned in and kissed Noah at the curve between neck and shoulder. "Okay. What do you need now?"

Noah was surprised Adrian was dropping it just like that, but he appreciated it. "Uh, I need to piss, which is probably going to be embarrassing so maybe you can just point me in the right direction and then I'll figure it out?"

Adrian chuckled, then rose and helped Noah to his feet. And yeah, he was definitely more sore than he thought. Every step was a trembling ache from his toes to his hips, and not being able to see anything other than a sliver of light on one side was terrifying. But he trusted Adrian to get him where he needed to go.

"Here," Adrian said once they crossed the threshold into the bathroom. He pressed Noah's hand to the toilet tank. "It might be better if you sit for now. Sink is directly to your right, you'll be able to touch it from the toilet. The hand towels are on the wall by the door, and I'm going to wait out here."

Noah bit his lip, nodding. "I hate this," he admitted in a quiet whisper.

Adrian cupped his cheek, pushing in close so their noses rubbed alongside each other. "I know, but it's not forever. Every day it'll get better. You'll heal, and that asshole will be taken down before your last bruise is gone."

Noah wanted to believe him. Desperately. But Charlie had taken his confidence and bashed it until it was unrecognizable. The only reason he was feeling as steady as he did was the fact that everyone had rallied around him and was not letting it go. Noah wished he hadn't stayed silent when Charlie first made his move. Maybe it wouldn't have ended that way. But hindsight and all that—20/20, even if he was currently blind.

He managed to take a piss and not make a huge mess on his own, and even got his hands washed and dried without too much fumbling. He could feel his head spinning a little, the vertigo not easing up even when he couldn't see the room moving. Adrian was true to his word, though, and was waiting directly outside the door for him.

They made it to the living room where Wes had bagels and coffee, along with another pill to ease Noah's pain. He curled up with his feet tucked under Adrian's thigh, nibbling at the burnt edges of the toasted bread and listened to the news Wes had switched on. Nothing new there—the world was still a dumpster fire, the country's leader was still a useless hack, and people were trash. Same old, same old.

He made himself focus though, because not being able to see left him with his thoughts, and if he considered everything Charlie had put him through, he was liable to fall apart completely. He snuggled into Adrian's side, and a few minutes later he heard the jingle of Lemon's collar, then the soft coat pressed up against him as she settled into his side.

E.M. LINDSEY

He couldn't help but laugh as he reached out to pat her. "Isn't she supposed to be your support dog?"

"Yes," Adrian said quietly, and Noah marveled at how he could actually hear the smile in his voice. "But apart from that, she's also a *good* one. It's why we work so well together. She senses when things are bad more often than not, and she knows what to do. There's nothing I want more than to see her helping you right now."

Noah sighed. "But if you need her…"

"She'll know when to come to me," Adrian told him, then pressed warm, dry lips to Noah's temple. "Her comforting you is also for me, Noah. Because you are important to me."

Noah felt that deep in his chest, settling behind his ribs to live there and give him warmth when everything else felt so sharp and so cold. He let himself get lost in the gentle swirls Adrian drew along his thigh, and the way Adrian's chest rose and fell in his rhythmic breathing, and the knowledge that whatever else happened, they were in this together.

———

ADRIAN WAS HAULING one of their bags to the living room when Wes stormed through the door and held up his hand. "You can't go."

Adrian blinked at him, his hand frozen in midair with the bag hanging from his wrist. "Why's that now?"

"We've got him," Wes said. He dug into his pocket for his phone and swiped his screen open, showing the message to Adrian.

Cole: This guy is an idiot, which is brilliant for us because it took me all of nine seconds to track his finances. He paid the guy off with a cheque written from his personal account. I'm actually a bit worried this is some sort of ploy to throw us off, but my gut is telling me he's nothing more than an arrogant wanker who doesn't think anyone can get to him. I've got emails as well. Apparently, he's got a friend who turned him into the idea of blackmail. I've got a long history of him talking about the months he's spent following Noah without him realising it. Ryan says he can work with his police friend on probable cause to have him detained if Noah agrees to report him for the attack. Ryan thinks it's a good idea, and to sweeten the deal, let Noah know that I've got into his records and managed to cause a glitch which erased the text messaging transcripts from his mobile service website. It shouldn't be traceable—I'm good at what I do. It's a lot, but we can get this guy locked away for what he's done.

Adrian read the message three, then four times before handing the phone back and looking up at Wes. "I don't know what to say."

"Cole is offering us the opportunity to take this into our own hands if we want to. We can keep the evidence on the downlow, fuck him up, then tell him if he opens his mouth again, we have everything we need to destroy him."

Adrian licked his lips, then said, "It's not really my decision. I need to talk to Noah and see what he wants to do. More than anything I want to beat this guy until he's unrecognizable, but another part of me wants to see him suffer for a lot longer than healing after a beating."

Wes nodded. "Then you best go talk to your boy and see what he wants out of all this."

Adrian turned on his heel, slowly making his way back to the room where Noah was packing. The swelling in his eye had gone down a significant amount from the meds and the ice he'd been using. He didn't have much usable vision just yet, but his sight was slowly coming back hour by hour which was enough to ease some of his anxiety.

When Adrian walked through the door, Noah lifted his head and smiled. "Ready?"

"We need to talk," Adrian said.

Noah dropped the sweater he was holding and braced himself on the edge of the suitcase. "Okay, that doesn't sound great."

"It isn't bad," Adrian told him, sitting down next to the open case. He fiddled with the zipper to give his hands something to do. "Cole came through a lot faster than we expected."

Noah blinked rapidly. "Oh. I…oh. I-is…" he groped behind himself. "Is there a chair or something? I need to sit."

"Three feet behind you," Adrian told him, and watched as Noah reached for it, found it, then plonked down hard enough that his jaw clacked together. "He found the trail. Apparently, Charlie was stupid enough to pay the guy who attacked you with a personal check. There's a trail, which can probably lead to the phone number of the man who called you. He also found," Adrian said, then stopped because telling his boyfriend that the man who attacked him had also been stalking him for who the hell know how long was almost too much. But Noah deserved the truth. "He also found evidence that Charlie's been stalking you for a while."

As predicted, all the color drained from Noah's face. "What?" he whispered.

"I don't know the details," Adrian told him, wanting desperately to reach for him, to comfort him through all this. "Cole sent a text to Wes letting him know what he found. He said he managed to wipe your phone records so whatever Charlie had on us from texts no longer exists in the system. It means we're safe. Charlie can't prove anything."

"Right," Noah said flatly.

Adrian squeezed his eyes shut. "I'm sorry. Maybe I shouldn't have told you or…"

"No," Noah said fiercely, rising halfway from the chair. "Jesus, Adrian, no. Of course you should have told me. It's just…fuck. I knew the guy was a creep, but I had no idea. All of this," he waved his hand at his face, "it wasn't about me dating you, it wasn't about him being humiliated because I turned him down. He's well and truly…"

"Evil," Adrian supplied.

Noah swallowed thickly, sitting back down slowly and nodding. "Evil is about right." He dragged both trembling hands down his face, then leaned forward over his knees. "What do I do?"

Adrian rose, taking careful steps over until he was in front of Noah, then knelt down and placed both hands around Noah's calves to keep himself steady. "I can't tell you that. If you go to the police, you'll have to report the attack and it's going to be emotionally draining after everything you've gone through. It means you're going to have to tell them why you didn't report the blackmail when it first happened, and if Charlie takes it to trial, his lawyers will turn this around on you. But it also means he'll be paying for his crimes for a long damn time. I know there's no guarantees, but with Ryan on your side, there's a real chance he's not going to walk away with just a slap on the wrist."

"And if I don't?" Noah asked.

"I can't promise that we won't make Charlie pay for what he did," Adrian answered honestly. He reached up, cupping Noah's cheek and let his thumb rub over the puffy, swollen skin just under his eye. "He hurt you and I won't let him get away with it. But how we move forward is up to you."

Noah licked his lips, nodding, and Adrian could tell he'd already made up his mind, he just needed the courage to say it. He pulled one hand up, curling it around Adrian's wrist, and held his palm tight to the side of his face. "I should…I should call Ryan. If anyone comes with me to report it, it should be him."

"I agree," Adrian said, hating that Noah was right because he wanted to be with him, but the best way to have this done without complication was letting Ryan take over. He had the connections, and he loved Noah. Although he wasn't the only one, and Adrian was coming to realize that. "There's something you need to know," he said, and went on a desperate search for his bravery. Pushing all the way up on his knees, praying his legs would hold him up for just this moment, he cupped both sides of Noah's face. "I'm falling in love with you."

Noah sucked in a startled breath and breathed out his name. "*Adrian.*"

"I know it's soon and we've been through a lot. And I don't need you to say it back, but I do need you to hear it because it's true and it's something you can take with you. Okay?"

Noah seemed incapable of speech, though he wasn't incapable of pulling Adrian down and into a fierce, hot kiss. It felt like an eternity since they'd been together, the last time Adrian was really allowed to touch like this was the night before it all went to hell, and it felt like coming home, it felt like he could breathe again. He gave everything he had into that kiss, every ounce of love and promise he could give, and Noah drank it all in with gentle, probing swipes of his tongue.

They broke apart in biting, searching pecks, Noah still holding Adrian's hands to his face in a vice-like grip, and he was breathing a little shallow. "Thank you," he murmured. There was more than gratitude in those words. There was a reciprocation Noah might not have been ready to say yet, but Adrian heard it all the same and accepted it for what it was.

"Let me get your phone and you can make the call. The sooner the better, yeah?"

Noah nodded and reluctantly let him go. With some struggle, Adrian rose to his feet and used the desk to steady him as he went for Noah's phone which was charging. He pulled up Ryan's number, then tapped his name and pushed the phone into Noah's hand.

"It should be ringing," Adrian told him. When Noah put the phone up to his ear, Adrian took that as his cue and left Noah to it.

CHAPTER NINETEEN

The rest of the events happened in a whirlwind. Ryan picked Noah up from Wes and Anna's and whisked him off to the hospital. When he reported the attack, the police were called in, and he gave a statement amidst scans, blood tests, and the doctor poking at his injuries. His socket was examined and pronounced healthy enough for his prosthetic, and the doctor informed him that he had every reason to expect his vision to return to normal within the week.

Ryan threw his status and connections around, and before they left the hospital, the officer assured Noah that Charles Barnes was being picked up for questioning.

"They'll get his phone as evidence and see if there's any proof which will allow them to book him," Ryan said as he helped Noah get into the car. "According to Cole, there is plenty so I wouldn't worry too much. Chances are they'll also be able to pick up the asshole who attacked you."

Noah felt his stomach twist, both pleasant and unpleasant. "Then what?"

"Then you might be asked to come in and do a vocal ID on your attacker. They'll set bail, and Charlie will get a lawyer and start preparing his defense."

"And me?" Noah asked.

"I have someone you can call," Ryan told him, reaching for his hand. Noah startled when warm fingers grabbed his, and he peered through his hazy vision at the blob he knew was his best friend. "It's going to be okay."

Noah licked his lips, then nodded. "Yeah. Yeah, I...it finally feels like it. There's just one more thing I need to do, and I'd like you to take me there soon." Ryan didn't say anything apart from an affirmative noise, and Noah had a feeling Ryan knew what his next step was. Which wasn't a surprise. Ryan knew Noah better than he knew himself sometimes, and it was a testament to their friendship that he didn't try to stop it.

Adrian wasn't the most pleased at Noah getting up at the crack of dawn to run another errand a few days later, but Noah stopped him with a hand to his chest and a soft kiss pressed to his lips where Adrian had fallen asleep on the sofa the night before.

"Trust me. I'll be back, and when this is all over, we'll get to take that trip up to the fancy house by the lake and have our week away from everything. I just have to tie up all these loose ends first."

Adrian grumbled, but he pulled Noah into a hot, sensual kiss which left him tingling even as he made his way out the door and to Ryan's car. He was navigating better with both his cane and his returning sight, and though he hated to show up like this—a hot mess who couldn't see beyond his nose—he knew it was time. Noah had readily given into Charlie's demands that he relinquish his classes, and there was a reason why. It was the blackmail, yes. It was to protect Adrian, yes.

But it was more than that.

"Dr. Lowe?"

There was a grunting noise, then a gruff, "Come in."

Noah pushed the door open and made a rather large display of using his cane to find his way to Lowe's desk. He felt for the chair, then sat down and fixed his gaze to the big, heather-grey blob sitting in front of him. "Sorry to drop in on you like this," Noah said.

"Good god, man. What the hell happened to you?" Lowe demanded.

Noah sighed. "It seems one of our trusted colleagues had a bit of an obsession problem. I was attacked over the weekend and Dr. Barnes was arrested for orchestrating it."

The silence was so thick, Noah would have been able to hear a pin drop. "You're not serious," Lowe said after a moment.

Noah let out a humorless laugh. "I'm afraid I am. I assume you'll be notified of it shortly, as there are several charges pending and I don't believe he'll be able to fill those classes he took over when he black-mailed me into relinquishing them."

"Well, I..." Lowe sputtered.

Noah didn't give him the chance to go on. "Unfortunately, I won't be available to take them back, either. You've never believed that I was capable of recuperating enough to take on the burden of a full-time professor. You stood in my way when I wanted to apply for tenure, and you were more than ready to believe me when I was coerced into saying I was unfit for the position in spite of my long history of proving to you that was anything but the case." Noah gripped his cane tight enough his knuckles ached. "Because I'm not contracted, I'm under no obligation to continue on into the next term, so consider this my full resignation from this institution." He started to rise and walk off but froze when he heard Lowe make a choking sound.

"You can't just *leave*. We don't have any member of the staff capable of teaching your next level of Greek."

Noah let himself smile just a bit. "I'm sure you can find someone."

"This will destroy your reputation. You'll never find work at a reputable university again," Lowe protested. "If you think I'm going to give you a recommendation..."

"Never dreamed of it," Noah said. "But I have faith that my TCEs over the years, as well as my online ratings from loyal students will be taken into consideration for my future. I do hope you're able to recover the loss of two professors, Dr. Lowe. I wish I could say it was a pleasure, but we both know that's not true."

With that, it was done. The final piece of the puzzle that was turning into his future had fallen into place. He had a boyfriend who loved him—who was willing to walk through fire for him—and he was willing to do the same. He was building a community with Wes and Anna, he was finally able to recognize his friendship with Ryan as something beautiful and important than the toxic romance they'd once shared when they were too young.

And he had hope. That was the most important part.

He'd been dealt several blows over the last few years, all of them cruel and below the belt, but he'd recovered. He'd managed to walk taller each time and recover stronger with each one. It was all coming together, and he only had one final thing to do before he felt complete.

"You want to get breakfast?" Ryan asked as he pulled out onto the road. "Cole was thinking we could meet up at Harvest for brunch if you're interested."

"No," Noah replied with a small grin, shaking his head. "I'll leave that to you. I have something very important to do this morning."

"You mean besides quitting your damn job?" Ryan asked.

Noah grinned. "Yeah. Besides that."

ADRIAN SWIPED his hand across his mouth, tasting copper, grinning around it. His mouth guard bit into his gums, but the discomfort was a welcome distraction. He glanced to the right where Cole was icing his jaw, then back at Wes who was circling him with slow, easy steps.

"It's been a while since we've done this," he said, his voice muffled through the plastic guarding his teeth.

Adrian took two shuffling steps, as quick as he could make them, and went for Wes' face with two sharp jabs of his right fist. Wes dodged the first but took the second hit to the padding on his temple.

His eyes blinked to focus, and he laughed before his counter throw which Adrian easily dodged.

They weren't out for blood today. In the last seventy-two hours, Charles Barnes had been arrested on three felony counts of stalking, harassment, and orchestrating an assault against Noah. His bail was set—Adrian didn't remember the amount, and there was every chance he would post it. But the ball was rolling, and Noah was taking charge of his future with a determination Adrian had been waiting to see.

He was out with Ryan to finish up some business at his office, and though they wouldn't be able to take their vacation until well after the spring semester, they no longer had to walk around in fear. Adrian had a ride planned after this, and as soon as Noah arrived with lunch they could transport on the trike, he planned to spend the entire afternoon doing everything in his power to make Noah forget—even for just a short while—about the chaos their life had been recently.

It was those distracting thoughts which let Wes get in a couple of good shots, and Adrian tapped out before his head could be knocked around too much and he wasn't able to steer his bike. Wes laughed and they touched gloves before breaking off, Adrian leaning against the ropes to regain the balance in his legs. He glanced down to the chair where Cole was sitting, still icing his jaw but showered and ready for Ryan to pick him up.

Sliding down to the floor of the ring, Adrian shuffled to the edge and let his leg bump into Cole's shoulder. "Wes says you two are planning a couple of competitions in the next few months."

Cole turned and grinned. His eyes were starting to look better, still a little deflated and red from the infections and the chemical burns, but he was healing up nicely. Adrian could see what it was Ryan was attracted to in the guy—not just the way he looked, though there was no denying Cole was an attractive man. But his determination and his ability to accept when things became too much was a rare gift. Most people who came back with their lives irrevocably changed the way Cole's had been were angry. They wanted to achieve their old normal, to get back to a life they'd known instead of a new one. Cole wasn't that guy. He didn't shy away from his fears or frustrations, either, but he allowed them to exist as part of him and Adrian found himself jealous from time to time at the strength it took to live like that.

"Why, you want to sign up?" Cole asked, reaching down to pet his dog.

Adrian snorted. "You know, I'm actually thinking about it. I haven't done any prize fighting in a long time, and it might be good to get back in the game. You got any other contenders?"

"Ryan's thinking about it, but I'm not sure that's a good idea. He's a fit guy, but he'll get his ass handed to him." Cole smiled fondly and Adrian didn't need to look that deep to see where their relationship was heading.

"I don't know about that. He did alright up against me the other day." It wasn't entirely true. Adrian could have flattened him in minutes if he'd been putting in a real effort. But all the same, Ryan was skilled for an amateur. "We could have a white-collar day."

Cole threw his head back and laughed. "That would be…interesting. I'll run it by him and see what he thinks. I bet he's got an office full of uptight lawyers with their knickers all twisted up against their bollocks. Could do with a round or two before a nice shag."

Adrian felt the corner of his mouth lift higher, but before he could come up with his own witty response, the door to the boxing area swung open and the aforementioned stuffy lawyer came in with Noah right behind. Noah's vision was even better now, though he was still using his cane to combat the blurring he suffered from the injury. If Adrian let himself think too much about it, his anger threatened to take over, so he focused on everything else that had happened since.

Mainly that he could hop off the ring, take Noah into his arms, and kiss him without fear. Which was exactly what he did.

"Mm, you're all sweaty," Noah murmured, licking a little just under Adrian's ear.

"Keep it up and we won't be leaving the gym. I have the key to the back office, and I know for a fact the sofa in there is plenty comfortable." He punctuated his sentence with a biting kiss at Noah's lips, and when he pulled back, he laughed when he saw Ryan and Cole had escaped.

Noah sighed, nuzzling up against Adrian's jaw a moment, then pulled away. "Go get washed up. There's food waiting and I want to get out for a bit."

Adrian sighed, but kissed him once more before making his way to the locker room to clean up. He didn't linger, a quick soap up and rinse off, and he threw a handful of gel in his hair before sitting down to tie up his boots and throwing on his jacket.

He walked out to the main lobby where Anna was behind the desk, Lemon's head in her lap, and she was explaining the monthly rates to a client on the phone. She held up her finger for him to wait, and he nodded, spotting Noah outside by the trike waiting for him. He drummed his fingers on the desk loud enough to be annoying, and eventually she sped up her conversation and ended the call.

"That is my monthly revenue, you asshole," she said.

Adrian grinned and shrugged. "Yeah, well, I have a hot as hell man waiting outside for me to take him for a ride. Both literally and metaphorically so…"

"First of all, gross," she said, ticking off her fingers, "second of all, I'm not going to keep you. I just want to say Wes and I are having a get-together this weekend and we want you and Noah there."

Adrian rolled his eyes. "When have I ever turned down Wes' barbeque?"

She shrugged. "I just know you've been making private plans lately to have all your sex which I do not want to hear about, thank you, and I want you to carve out some time for us. Connie's going to be there."

Adrian raised his brows and waited to see if she planned to add to that, but when she remained silent, he sighed. "Fine. Who else is coming?"

"Cole and Ryan, of course," she said, and he wasn't surprised. In the short time all this had happened, both men had become a fixture in their lives, and each other's even if they weren't official yet. "Also, a couple of Wes' buddies from his Core classes. Nothing special, we just wanted to take some time to finally relax without some fucked up situation breathing down our necks."

Adrian narrowed his eye at her. "You're going to jinx it."

"Your superstitions have never intimidated me. Anyway, go before your boy paces a hole in the pavement and I have to get out there and repave it."

He pulled a face at her, then leaned in and kissed her forehead before making his way out. Noah turned when he heard the doors open, reaching for Adrian who went willingly into a soft kiss. "You ready?"

"More than," Noah said. "I heard back from HU and they want me to come in for an interview Monday. They have several spots in the department and apparently I was recommended from a couple of my old professors at Duke."

Adrian grinned, spinning Noah a little as he kissed him. "That's fucking amazing, babe. I'm so proud of you."

"I just…it feels good, finally. To be free of that shithole department, to never have to pander to that crusty old man again. To know that no one is holding anything over me." He reached up and touched Adrian's cheek. "I can almost totally see you now when you're this close and I love that too."

Adrian felt his throat tighten a little. Since saying the words right before Noah reported the attack, he hadn't said them again, and Noah hadn't reciprocated, though he showed just how deeply he felt with his actions every day, and Adrian wasn't about to squander that. Still, hearing that four-letter word in any capacity from Noah's lips set his heart beating.

"Let's get going and I can show you something else you're going to like." He thrust his groin against Noah's leg, making his boyfriend groan.

"Pain in the ass."

"You love it," Adrian countered.

Noah smiled softly and said with devastating tenderness, "Yeah. I really do."

The drive wasn't too long. They picked their favorite spot, a little grassy area off the side of the main road which overlooked the city. Noah still couldn't see all of it, but the sun was out and bright, and the air was crisp and oddly warm for the dead of winter. They were still bundled in their winter clothes, Noah's scarf up his neck so high it nearly covered his mouth, and Adrian wanted to pin him to the ground and take him right there.

Instead, he linked their hands together as they dug into the sandwiches Noah brought along from the deli. It was a damn-near perfect day, even if they had months of waiting, then a trial, and everything that came after. Adrian brought Noah's hand to his mouth, kissing his knuckles first, then his palm, then the inside of his wrist.

When he tried to pull away, Noah turned his hand to capture Adrian's, tugging him close so they were nearly nose-to-nose, and Adrian felt the hot puff of Noah's breath across his cheeks. "I know that a lot of how we feel is probably because of what we've been through," he started softly, bringing one hand to Adrian's face. He caressed the skin there, the unblemished and the scarred, and his eyes fluttered closed. "But I also know my own heart and I know it's telling me that this isn't something I ever want to let go. I don't think I've ever felt this way about anyone before, and I need you to know that when you told me you loved me, I knew then I loved you too."

Adrian let his own eyes slip closed and he felt the words burrow under his skin. *"Babe…"*

"I should have said it then, but I was afraid it would feel cheap. I had so much to sort out, and I know we still have so much ahead of us, but I wouldn't be able to do this without you. So, I love you, okay? So much."

Adrian felt his lips tug into a smile, and he pressed one finger under Noah's chin, lifting his face to capture his mouth in a slow, deep kiss. He shivered at the feel of Noah's hot, velvet tongue sliding against his own, and he groaned into the other man's mouth as his hands moved lower to wander, to tug Noah as close as he could get him. They couldn't take risks here in the open like this, but he was almost willing to.

"I love you too, but you already knew that," he finally said when he could find the words.

Noah chuckled. "I do, but I won't ever get tired of hearing it." He took Adrian's hand and pressed it to the rapid thumping of his heart. He didn't need more words after that. All of this? It was exactly enough.

EPILOGUE

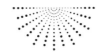

Pressing his hand to the glass, Noah let the cold seep in to his palm, watching a ring of fog surround his digits. Beyond lay banks of snow, cascading in gentle, rolling hills toward the dock, and the lake with sheets of ice and floating snow drifts. It was like no other place he'd ever been, and he let himself think back to a time he wasn't sure he'd actually be able to have this.

A warm body pressed itself to his back, and Noah let his head fall against Adrian's shoulder as warm lips descended against his temple, making a slow, wet, searing path along his jaw, to the crook of his neck.

"I've been waiting for this all day. You have five seconds to decide if I'm going to fuck you right up against the glass, or if you want to find a bedroom."

Licking his lips, Noah reacted almost viscerally to the sound of his lover's deep-chested murmur, but all coherent thought left him as Adrian's hand pressed a firm path down the center of his chest, cupping him where he wanted to be touched the most. His dick swelled, twitching like it was trying to get itself up against Adrian's naked palm.

"Bed," Noah managed as he unstuck his tongue. "Fuck, how f-far…"

Adrian chuckled against his ear. "Just down the hall." He rubbed the heel of his hand along Noah's hard length. "I love when I get you worked up into a stammer."

"I bet," Noah groaned, pushing his hips once, twice, thrusting against Adrian's hand before he forced himself to step out of the circle of his arms. "Come on, I've been waiting on this all fucking day."

It was an anniversary of sorts, the trip to the gated home at the edge of a lake, just over a year after the two of them had met. It was also exactly eight months since Noah began his new job teaching at a university two hours away from his apartment, and lastly six months since Charles Barnes had been sentenced to twelve years in prison after being officially charged with stalking, blackmail, and hiring someone to assault Noah in the alley near his apartment.

It had been a nightmare for a while. Noah had sat through interview after interview, listened to the way Charlie's lawyers had tried to paint him as the reason Charlie had lost all sense, the reason he felt forced to act in such a manner. They tried to destroy his character by bringing Adrian into it, but unfortunately the defense had come up against a wall—the lack of evidence thanks to Cole's work.

In the end, Charlie accepted a plea agreement. He turn-coated on the man he'd hired and agreed to a deal. Twelve years, serving five before he was eligible for parole. He'd be given therapy and a chance to work through whatever it was that made him the type of man capable of all those things.

Noah still had nightmares. Nightmares of being attacked, of waking up to find Charlie standing over him. Sometimes he relieved the attack, and he didn't walk through the streets alone at night anymore. But he was getting better, and he still had four years of peace before he had to worry about Charlie's presence in the world again.

A lot could happen in that time.

One thing, he hoped, was the answer to a question he planned to ask later in the night, with a small, black box in the middle of his palm. He was fairly sure Adrian knew it was coming—if not now, then around the new year when they were finally back at their home.

But he wanted it to be special—just not public, or a big to-do that both of them would have hated. He wanted an audience of one—wanted Adrian's dark eyes fixed on him, wanted no one in the world to hear those words but the man he was desperate to marry.

For now though, that could wait. For now, he was being methodically stripped, every inch of him nibbled, and licked, and kissed as Adrian went after every sensitive place on his body. Noah simply spread himself back on the mattress, arms and legs out, pushing into every caress, every graze of teeth or swipe of tongue.

When lubed fingers pressed between his cheeks, he crooked his legs up, arching his hips so Adrian could push deep inside him. Noah nearly lost it, his eyes slamming closed as Adrian's warm mouth closed around his dick and sucked him into the back of his throat. His hand thrust hard, a finger-fucking to be remembered, and it was by sheer force of will he didn't come right there.

"Wait," he gasped. "W-wait. Want you in m-me," he begged.

Adrian pulled off with a firm suck, letting Noah's dick dribble precome across his bottom lip as it slipped from his mouth. Noah's body gave a violent shudder as he watched Adrian's tongue dart out, licking up the sticky trail of clear fluid, and then he lost all sense when he felt the fat, lubed head of Adrian's cock pressing against his hole.

"D-do it," he begged.

Adrian took one of Noah's legs, pushing it up, and wide, then with a firm slide, moved all the way in. Noah gave an animal growl as he lifted his head to meet Adrian thrust for thrust. He felt wild with arousal, with want, like they couldn't be close enough, like they never would. He wrapped his hands around the back of Adrian's neck, pulling him in for a biting kiss as he pushed back against the cock battering against his prostate, and he felt his balls pull in tight, his orgasm cresting.

"I'm g-g-g," he tried, but it was useless.

Adrian understood him—always had, always would. He increased his pace, gripping at Noah's hips, and without being touched, Noah's dick swelled and then spilled, dribbling right onto his stomach.

Adrian, who was looking down with hooded eyes, was on the brink. That was all it took to send him crashing over the edge, and he buried his face in the crook of Noah's neck, letting out a long groan as his dick pumped over and over, spilling inside him.

They came down slowly, Noah petting Adrian's hair as he slumped over Noah's sticky chest, and eventually he pulled out and rolled to the side. They were a mess, but it was a perfect mess, something Noah would carry with him for weeks to come, if not forever, depending on the answer that came next.

He tried to sit up, but Adrian pinned him to the sheets, nuzzling along Noah's shoulder with the tip of his nose. "No, don't."

Noah brushed his blunt nails along Adrian's scalp, then down his defined biceps which were still strained from how hard he'd been fucking Noah. He moved his hand around his back, where the scarring was the worst, and he felt over the hills and valleys like a braille map of his lover. "I'll just be a second. I need to grab something from my bag."

Adrian let out a groan of dissatisfaction, but he eventually released his hold and Noah slipped off the edge of the bed. The floors were chilly against his bare feet, but he didn't have to go far. The ring was in the front pocket of his zip-up travel bag and he pulled it out, holding the box in his palm as he climbed back under the sheets.

Adrian was ready to take him into his arms again, but Noah stayed carefully out of reach as his fingers traced around the edges of the box's opening.

He cleared his throat, willed his tongue to obey him for this. He knew Adrian didn't care about his stutter—loved every piece of him no matter how it looked or sounded or performed. But he wanted the words to come alive, without his brain getting in his way, and he made sure he was as calm as possible before presenting the box to his love.

"I've wanted to do this for a while, but I realized there's no better place than here. It's where we might have gotten our real start, if everything hadn't gone to shit. Instead it's become our second chance, it's the last p-piece," he stopped to calm himself again. "It's the last piece to this puzzle, and I'm hoping you might want to start a new one with me as one." He didn't dare look at Adrian's eyes. Not yet. He couldn't deny it made him a little bit of a coward, but this was the biggest risk he'd ever taken. Flipping the top, he displayed the simple deep black silicon ring which Adrian could wear at all times—even while boxing. It was untraditional and maybe even a little ugly, but the moment Noah had seen it, he knew it had to be the one. "Will you marry me?"

The silence went on so long, Noah couldn't help but lift his gaze. He wasn't sure what to expect, but he found Adrian's watery eyes staring at him. Hard. When their gazes connected, Adrian smiled. "I wasn't about to say yes without you looking at me."

Noah's heart started beating again, though he hadn't realized it had stopped until just then. His breath came out in a whoosh. "Is that a…"

"Yes," Adrian said quietly. He reached out and ran a reverent finger down the center of the band. "It's a yes."

Noah used trembling fingers to pluck the ring from the soft velvet, sliding it over Adrian's knuckle and watched it settle into place. It looked so right, it stole all the air from his lungs and his head grew dizzy with it. "I love you," he managed, because it was the only thing to say.

There was still an entire world out there, an entire universe that had plans, and schemes, and wouldn't always make things easy. But this—loving Adrian, being loved back—well that he could do. He closed his eyes against the warm palm that cupped his cheek, and he leaned into the kiss, pouring every ounce of adoration he had for this man into that gesture. When he felt it given back, he clutched at Adrian's hair and smiled into the embrace.

ALSO BY E.M. LINDSEY

ABOUT THE AUTHOR

E.M. Lindsey is a non-binary writer who lives in the southeast United States, close to the water where their heart lies.

Join EM Lindsey at their <u>newsletter</u> or join their <u>Patreon</u> and get access to ARCs, teasers, free short stories, and more.